GROWING PAINS

Cass Lennox

RIPTIDE
PUBLISHING

Riptide Publishing
PO Box 1537
Burnsville, NC 28714
www.riptidepublishing.com

Growing Pains

Cover art: L.C. Chase, lcchase.com/design.htm
Editor: Chris Muldoon
Layout: L.C. Chase, lcchase.com/design.htm

ISBN: 978-1-62649-490-9

First edition
March, 2017

Also available in ebook:
ISBN: 978-1-62649-489-3

GROWING PAINS

Cass Lennox

RIPTIDE
PUBLISHING

For anyone who's ever had a really *crappy weekend.*

TABLE OF CONTENTS

CHAPTER ONE

Gigi Rosenberg sat in the driver's seat of his rented car and glared through the windshield at his boyfriend. Brock stood in the driveway, hands in pockets, his face set to that miserable expression Gigi was starting to despise, not least because it always tugged at his heart, and *definitely* not least because Brock had been using it a lot lately.

And why the fuck was that again? *Oh, let's think.*

Ire fully loaded, he lowered the driver's-side window and leaned out. "Last chance, boyfriend!"

Brock seemed to curl in on himself. It would have been pathetic if he were any less built, those big shoulders rounding by his ears and his chiselled face dipping into his chest.

No, actually, even with the muscles it was still pathetic.

"I can't," Brock said.

Typical. Fucking *typical.*

A red haze clouded Gigi's peripheral vision, and he slammed the car horn multiple times as he bellowed, "Fuck you!" Then he pulled his head back in, released the car from park, and began reversing down the driveway.

Unbelievable. Unbe*lievable.* This had to be a sign right? *Yeah. This is totally a sign that I'm meant to be wild and free and* not *attached to some overbuilt*—he turned into the road—*oversensitive*—shifted into drive—*overworked*—stomped on the accelerator—asshole *of a dude who would rather stay home than support his beloved boyfriend.*

Gigi looked in the rearview mirror as Brock's house fell farther behind him. In the backseat, he could see his duffel bag, suit bag, coat,

Toronto gift hamper, wedding present, and snacks for the journey. Too many snacks, of course, because his supposed boyfriend wasn't coming anymore.

He paused at the corner, then made a right. Brock's street was behind him now, out of sight in the rearview mirror. At the next red light, he punched at the GPS and glared as it began chirruping directions to Highway 400.

Highway 400, which then turned into the Trans-Canada Highway. North on that for almost four hours of forest, then a turn off after Sudbury for another hour of more fucking *forest*. God, Gigi thought he'd never have to deal with nature again after leaving home, or if he did, it would be a nice distance away. Like Niagara Falls, all safe behind a viewing platform and some cliffs. Being in a car would help, sure, but he'd have to drive through kilometres and kilometres of goddamn trees and leaves and moose and shit, and all he'd get for his trouble was his hick hometown in the middle of Nowhere, Ontario. *Alone.*

After all, it wasn't, like, *important* they go or anything. So what if his big sister, Sophie, was getting hitched to love-of-her-life and all-around-decent-heterosexual Alan, and Gigi was so excited and happy for her he could barely express it? Sure, no big. No big at *all*.

Seriously, didn't Brock get what a big deal that was to him? To his family? Sophie deserved all the happiness he could imagine.

Even though happiness apparently meant holding the wedding in their hometown because Maney in the autumn was *lovely* and *beautiful* and she wanted her poor fiancé to see *where she came from*.

Please. She wanted to rub her yummy fiancé and big, fancy wedding in the faces of all those hometown hosers, the ones who'd told her she'd be lucky to get a boyfriend, let alone a husband, especially with a brother like hers. Part of him was ecstatic at the idea of helping her, and another part was scared shitless.

Brock might have been grumpy as shit most of the way there, but his grumpy company was always better than no company at all. And no company was what the journey now promised.

Ugh.

No, wait. That's good. *Fuck him.*

His fingers tightened on the steering wheel.

Thing was, he'd had *such* hopes for rest stops. "Rest" stops where they rested their mouths on each other's dick and maybe swapped drivers. But no, he wasn't even going to get pit stop blowjobs now.

It almost made him pull into the nearest parking lot to turn around.

What the hell was Brock's problem? Okay, he hated their putrefied waste of an ex-hometown as much as Gigi did, but he'd definitely had an easier time of it there as a teenager, *and* he wouldn't be the only openly gay guy there this time around. Gigi remembered their teen years like they were yesterday, and he knew Brock did too, but those years were gone. Past. Freaking Sean Penn to Guy Ritchie to Independent Madonna. All Brock had said was that he didn't want to go back there *ever*, and not even Gigi's sister's wedding was enough incentive, apparently.

Did other divas ever have to put up with shit like this? Probably. He could see Guy Ritchie being all whiny and clingy and Madonna having to bitch-slap his English ass into behaving. But they were divorced now, so obviously she hadn't put up with whatever bullshit he'd dished. Beyoncé and Jay Z had been tight . . . but then *Lemonade* had happened. Nah, Kylie did things right: all gorgeous boy toys and nothing long-term. Smart girl.

Actually, he was seeing a pattern there that he wasn't entirely sure he liked.

The passenger seat was empty and it seemed wrong, but Gigi elected to ignore that and focus on the drive, on getting the car through Toronto's Friday traffic. It was just before lunchtime but somehow still bad. The red haze faded from the edges of his vision the closer he got to Highway 400.

He hadn't even left Toronto, yet the 400 still felt too close to home.

If he were being honest—and Gigi prided himself on knowing exactly when to be honest and when bullshittery was needed—he couldn't blame Brock. Going back to their hometown, The Place Where Death Went to Be Bored, was in their top-five Things They Never Wanted to Do. It was also in their top-three things of Stuff I'll Only Do With You.

For him it was a no-brainer: he'd left the relentless homophobia of his adolescence behind and was so uninterested in visiting it, he might as well wrap it in grey and stripes and call it a police cell.

Brock, though, was being totally closemouthed about whatever *his* exact problem was. Who knew what it could be? From what little he'd mentioned over the year and three months they'd been dating, and the fact that Gigi had never heard him speak to or mention his parents, Gigi guessed that it had something to do with Brock's family. But he'd never said anything, so Gigi didn't actually *know*.

And when that lousy, traitorous wimp had dropped that *I can't* this morning, shut down and pulled out—and *not* in a sexy way—it had really hurt. Gigi was furious and fucked—also not in the good way. There wasn't even an excuse this time. Just *I can't*. If Gigi could make himself go—not like he had a choice or anything—Brock could put on his big-boy pants and come with.

Gigi's fingers were all tight on the wheel again, knuckles showing white. Oooh, that couldn't be good for his skin. Age showed in the hands. He took a few deep breaths, forcing his hands to relax.

All right. So. He was going all toned, sexy, fabulous, and *alone*.

Well, if Kylie and Gaga could do it, so could he.

He flipped his hair—not that there was much to flip, but that wasn't the point—and at another red light, dug around for his iPod. If he was going to be driving for the next five-ish hours without any prospects of blowjobs or bitching about this stupid hometown wedding, he needed the next best thing: spiritual sisterly support. He found the iPod and stuck the cable into the car's USB port.

The synthetic opening of Lady Gaga's "Applause" beat into his car and Gigi grinned. *Yes.*

He emphatically did *not* think about Brock, or Brock's expression as Gigi had yelled at him, or how tense and monosyllabic Brock had been in the last two weeks. Nope. And, okay, his phone chimed and lit up repeatedly beside him on the passenger seat, but like hell he was going to check it. He was *driving* and he was *going to Maney* and nothing was going to stop him.

He reached the junction that fed onto the 401 Expressway, the road that would then feed onto Highway 400. *Fuck. Here we go.*

Something ticked over in his brain, and before he'd realized it, he pulled off the road, into the parking lot of the Yorkdale mall, and stopped in the first bay he saw.

Deep breaths. Centre yourself. Think about this.

What was he doing? Was he really going to go back to Maney alone? Okay, Sophie and his parents would be there, and it was only for four days, but they wouldn't be with him all day. They'd be focused on the wedding, not on dealing with any shit from the neighbours or from people he'd known at school.

Gigi could handle himself. He'd been handling himself since he was twelve and Turk Rogers had caught him reading men's health magazines in the only bookstore in town. He was twenty-five now and a queen. If he wanted to, he could go full Priscilla on their asses, stroll down Main in a frock and ten-inch stilettos, and use those stilettos to punch holes in anyone who so much as looked at him wrong. Maney was going to get Gigi LaMore, because his queen was who he channelled these days, who he really was, not shy, scared, chubby Toby Rosenberg. Toby was long gone.

The problem was, no one else would see him as Gigi. They'd still call him Toby, still know him as the gay kid who ate his feelings and did theatre and sang too much. He didn't mind his family calling him that, because they loved him, but having no one else there who knew and appreciated Gigi as his full and complete self was going to be hard.

Brock knew him. Brock loved him.

Or so he said.

Gigi felt tears threatening, and leaned forward to rest his forehead against the wheel. Fuck. He did need Brock. He really did. Why the hell couldn't Brock *be* there for him? What was four days of crazy and a wedding? *Four days.*

Maybe Gigi could have tried to persuade him instead of throwing down a Mariah and driving away. Brock's expression was starting to seem less selfish and weak, and more scared stupid. Still *stupid*, because they'd had a year to discuss this. A *year*. And all Brock had said was yes to going, right up until he'd said no.

Maybe Gigi should reconsider that *last chance* thing.

His phone buzzed again, and he picked it up. Fifteen missed calls from Brock. Three messages. Gigi didn't even read them, he just called Brock.

"Thank God," Brock answered. "Babe, I'm sorry."

The anger was back, but it was caught up in a bucketload of relief. "Sorry isn't good enough, but I'm glad you called."

"I know." Brock hesitated. "I have never seen you that angry. Not when we had to cancel Montreal. Not even when Woody's dropped your show during makeup."

And that really *had* been some bullshit. But it was liveable bullshit. And Brock didn't get to use Montreal like that. "Hey, we cancelled Montreal because *you* had to work. *Again.*"

"Babe—"

"Fuck you for bringing that back up again, by the way. This is not Montreal. This is my sister's wedding. This is not a weekend trip or a fancy restaurant or one of my shows. And by the way, I'm over you cancelling that shit too. If you tell me right now that you couldn't go to my sister's wedding because of work, I will fucking end you when I get back."

Brock took a deep breath. "It's not work. It's not."

"Then *what*?"

His voice quivered slightly. "I promised myself I wouldn't go back there. Not for anything."

"So did I, but life's a bitch, honey." Gigi paused. "Not for anything? Not even for me? What about what we talked about? You and me, together. Remember that?"

Brock was silent.

"So, not even for me. Thanks a lot, boyfriend." Tears were close again. Gigi sat back against his seat, staring out at the parking lot. He hated this. He really, really hated these kinds of conversations. "What are we doing?"

"What do you mean?"

"What is this? I'm sitting in fucking Yorkdale, staring at cars—by myself—because you can't man up and visit the shithole that is our hometown. I hate it too, but I'm doing it, and I'm the one who got more shit for being gay there than you ever did."

"I—"

"I'm not done yet. What I can't do is explain to my sister why my boyfriend isn't going to be there, because all I got is *his principles are more important than my family*, and that's too crappy a reason to give her, by the way. Because I'm wondering if it's not something more like *he doesn't want to be seen with his femmy queen boyfriend in public there.* Because why else would my boyfriend of over a year keep cancelling on me? Why *do* you keep doing that?"

"I don't mean to. I want to do well at my job. You know that." Brock sighed. "I'm sorry. I'll try harder, and I won't drop plans again. I promise, it's nothing to do with you. I love you exactly the way you are."

Gigi had heard that before. He'd heard that the first night they'd gotten together, one year and a summer ago, and he'd heard it since, and somehow it no longer meant anything. "Yeah? Prove it."

A note of anger appeared in Brock's voice now. "What do you mean, 'prove it'? Haven't I already done that?"

Crap. That hadn't come out right. *Deep breaths. Collect and try again.* "Look. Babe. What I mean is that this is important. You don't cancel a wedding unless it's an emergency, and this isn't. People in relationships don't do that to each other. So this thing that's happening right now? It doesn't feel like a relationship." As soon as he'd said it, Gigi realized with a shudder how true it was. "You've been a grumpy asshole for how long now? Since you graduated? And you won't tell me why. You don't tell me *anything.* You just work and let me come over to suck your dick and cook food. You're not happy. And I'm not happy. And now you're letting me down big time, and I'm *tired* of all of it. Is this how we are now?"

Brock was quiet for what felt like a long time before he said, "Are you . . . are you breaking up with me?"

Oh *please.* "Like hell I'm showing up unattached at my sister's wedding. I'm going to Maney and telling them all about my hot boyfriend and sweet job so they see how awesome my life is, *then* I'm going to come back and dump your ass."

Which he was angry enough to do right now. When Sophie'd announced the engagement last year—and once Gigi had stopped flipping his shit at the location of the wedding—he'd slowly concluded that maybe this wasn't an entirely bad thing. He'd pictured returning home, all toned and sexy and fabulous, with his gorgeous boyfriend on his arm, showing off just how wrong everyone there was about him and his sister *and* Brock. He wanted to fuck his boyfriend in the room he'd had as a bullied, outcast teenager. He wanted the dumb hicks who'd tortured him to see him happy and out and attached. He wanted to dance with Brock at his sister's reception. It would totally bring things full circle.

And if he couldn't do those things, he was going to do the next best thing and lie through his winningest smile with a pic of his boyfriend at the ready on his phone.

But, damn it, he really wanted to do those things.

He also wanted to take everything back. Brock had a quaver in his voice that Gigi hadn't heard in a long time, which had him checking himself. Had it really come to this? Was he really going to dump Brock over this? What was he doing?

Gigi cast back over the last year. The last three months or so had fucking sucked, like seriously sucked, but it'd started out so well. How had they reached this point?

Regardless of good beginnings, they couldn't keep going. Not like this. So now was as good a time as ever to—

"No." Brock's voice *growled* through the phone. Goose bumps rose on Gigi's skin. Oooh, he knew that voice. He *liked* that voice.

"No what?"

"No to everything you just said. I don't know if you're trying to threaten me or manipulate me, but there is absolutely no way I want to break up with you, babe." His voice lost the edginess. "Are you really that unhappy with me?"

A lump lodged in Gigi's throat. "I don't want to go to Maney. If I have to go, I want to go with you. You keep saying that you have my back, but you're not here and I don't understand why. I feel like you haven't been with me for months now."

A long silence followed his words.

Brock couldn't believe he'd fucked up this badly.

He'd been trying. Ever since he'd convinced Gigi he was serious about him at the start of last summer, Brock had made sure he was the perfect boyfriend. They'd met each other's friends. Taken weekend breaks in Niagara, Syracuse, and Buffalo. He'd gone to as many of Gigi's shows as he could—the dance performances, the small stage roles, the drag shows when Gigi LaMore came out to play. None of them had been left out. He'd been nothing but supportive of Gigi's drag and creative pursuits. He even called him Gigi instead of Toby at his request, even though Brock's memories of Gigi were irreparably tangled with seventeen-year-old Toby Rosenberg. Guilt alone over their history would have ensured his game was up and on point, but he did love Gigi. When Brock thought about it, he wasn't sure there had ever been a point since he was a teen when he hadn't loved him.

And he'd assumed he was doing okay there. Making ads was earning Brock the most money he'd ever made, and even though he sometimes had to cancel stuff lately, he'd helped Gigi out with money for other things. And he was building some savings so they could do something together for their future, like buy an apartment or go on some crazy overseas trip. He knew he wasn't around as much now, but Gigi's jobs had led to cancelled plans too, so it wasn't as though he was the only one who prioritized work.

He'd *tried*.

Only, somehow he was standing in his living room, on the phone with a very upset Gigi and feeling like everything was falling down around his ears. Gigi sounded so far away, and not just physically. He sounded like he was poised to go and, apparently, to never come back to him. To Toronto, yes, but not to *him*.

How had he let things get this way?

Brock flopped down on his sofa, a tattered and ripped thing he and his housemates had dragged off the street when they'd moved in. The cell felt hot in his hand, as though Gigi's anger had infused the metal and plastic. His stomach roiled.

He didn't have a choice. Not really.

"I hear you," he said. "I'll go."

A slow exhalation. "You saying that because you think it's what I want to hear?"

"No. I'm saying it because I don't want to have this conversation on the phone. And I don't want . . ." *you to stop loving me. You to leave me.* ". . . to let this go. I'll go to Maney with you."

He heard some muffled movement from Gigi's end. "I'm still angry at you, asshole." Gigi's tone had lightened slightly, which gave

Brock a sliver of hope. "But I know it sucks. I promise, it'll be better if we're together, okay? I'll try too. You have an hour to get to Yorkdale. I'm going to walk around and resist buying the entirety of Zara, but I'm not waiting forever for you, got it?"

"Got it."

"Bye."

Gigi hung up, and Brock rose heavily to his feet.

So, he was doing this after all. Going back.

Shit.

Returning to their shitty hometown for Gigi's sister's wedding had seemed . . . well, not fine, but kind of doable when Gigi had first mentioned it a year ago. There were awkward things about that which he'd meant to discuss with Gigi before they went. But life had been too perfect to screw up with an argument, and there *would* be an argument if Gigi knew just how not-out Brock was to his parents, and how he wanted to remain that way. Three months into this relationship at the time felt like too soon to have that kind of argument. He'd wanted Gigi too long to wreck it.

So there was no choice now. Stay and lose him, go and maybe try not to lose him. A total no-brainer.

He called a taxi, then quickly packed a bag. He'd started packing the night before, but midway the thought of going back had paralyzed him to the point that he'd crawled into bed instead, mind playing through how he could tell Gigi in the morning.

All the scenarios he'd thought of paled in comparison to reality. Gigi had been absolutely livid. Of course he'd been—and honestly, Brock was kind of dumb for expecting anything different. He knew Gi. The man was a queen who saw life as a permanent stage and any hiccups as attempts to upstage him. He'd flipped his shit in a display worthy of Mariah Carey and barely paused before sweeping out and screeching away. No questions, no concern for Brock at all, no attempt to try to understand that Brock *could not* and *did not* want to do this. Nothing except some scathing one-liners and insults Brock couldn't bear to respond to.

The thing was, Brock got it. He totally did. But, and not for the first time, he wondered if it would kill Gigi to calm the fuck down for once.

Also not for the first time, he wondered if it would kill *him* to actually fight back and stand his ground instead of folding like this. Seriously, it wasn't like it was the worst thing in the world, right? He could have explained himself a year ago, six months ago, six weeks ago. He could have sat Gigi down and explained just how fucked up his family was, and why his gap year had turned into two gap years, and why he never spoke to his parents, and why he never ever wanted to be in the vicinity of his parents ever again. But he hadn't, and now it was too late. Now any excuses would just show how much of a coward he was.

And he *was* a coward. Big time. Because despite refusing to go back and hiding that he was still in the closet where his parents and Maney were concerned, there was one thing he was especially scared of: killing this relationship. That was enough to make him backtrack on everything else.

Problem was, he'd trapped himself. Too scared to go back, too scared to stay. And while it was so tempting to sit here and pretend his promises to himself mattered more than his boyfriend, Brock knew Gigi wouldn't forgive him if he stayed here this weekend.

So. He was going. Because if there was a sliver of a chance he could mitigate that whole coming-out thing better while being there, he might be able to keep his relationship. Hopefully.

As he tossed in boxers and a clean sleep shirt, he paused at the sight of lube and tissues on the dresser. A new bottle, unopened, ready for action. Would it be too presumptuous to take it with him? Maybe. Maybe not. He tossed it in the bag.

One suit, shoes, phone charger, some spare socks, and a shirt, and he was good to go.

His stomach tied itself in knots as he put on a jacket and got into the taxi, twisting further the closer he got to Yorkdale. By the time he paid the driver and went into the mall, his stomach was a lead weight. He was well within time, but the centre was huge and his boyfriend wasn't patient.

He texted that he was at Starbucks, bought some coffee, and waited.

Oh *God*, he was really doing this. He was going back. With his *boyfriend*. They'd be open as boyfriends in front of the homophobic assholes who'd made Gigi's high school years a genuine misery and Brock's a closeted wreck. He'd be out in front of everyone who'd once known him. The idea of being out in front of Mrs. Sable from down the road and his English teacher who'd hated him and anyone from school who was still there and his *parents* was horrifying. Being boyfriends in Toronto wasn't a problem, just as being out in Toronto wasn't a problem. But in Maney?

And having to deal with all that in front of Gigi as well as dealing *with* Gigi . . .

The coffee was a mistake. The lead in his stomach had turned into heavy roiling acid, ready to be ejected all over the shiny mall floor.

He saw Gigi before Gigi saw him. Not difficult—the man stood out in a crowd. He was practically walking art: lean and muscular from dancing, spangled with jewellery from earlobe to glittery shoes, and hair dyed to a deep red like fallen leaves. There was a now-familiar surge of blood as Brock watched him, and his stomach somersaulted before settling back down again—a little lighter and steadier this time.

Under the red hair and sparkles, Gigi's face was wan and frowning as he walked towards the store. *"I'm not happy"* replayed in Brock's head, and he fought to keep from laughing hysterically. If Gigi wasn't happy with him now, despite everything Brock had done to be the boyfriend Gigi deserved, he was going to be miserable by the time they came back to Toronto. Guaranteed.

This weekend is going to be a fucking disaster. Maybe I should just stay here and save us all a lot of trouble.

Yeah, no. Going back was happening.

Brock took a few steps to meet Gigi, coffee in one hand and weekend bag in the other. Gigi glanced him over, unimpressed. "That's all you're bringing?"

"I didn't want to be late."

"Please tell me there's at least a suit in there."

"Yes! Not everyone needs five outfits a day."

That took Brock back to their Syracuse trip, when he'd taken two shirts and a mountain of lube and condoms, and Gigi had brought a massive suitcase stuffed with clothes. They'd teased each other in between kissing and fucking and eating and taking in the sights of Upstate New York. It had been Gigi's first time out of Canada. Granted, it hadn't been exactly *far* out of Canada, but it still counted.

That had been an amazing trip.

Gigi stiffened, his eyes narrowing. "You're meeting my *family*."

"I'm pretty sure I can buy anything else I need in Maney."

Gigi crossed his arms and looked aside. That set jaw meant he was either angry or nervous. Maybe both. If he was nervous too, that was something. Brock gripped the handle of his bag tighter and watched Gigi refuse to react—he could tell, he knew how Gigi's mind worked. The sounds of the mall filled the silence between them. His coffee warmed his fingers through the thin cardboard cup.

So stupid. And weird. Why all this over a trip? Over *clothes*? How could someone he understood this well also be someone whose reactions sometimes completely confused him?

"You done here?" Brock gestured to the mall.

Gigi nodded, the movement jerky. "Let's do this."

Brock followed him out into the parking lot. The day was bright and sunny, a pleasant autumn day, which was a perfect contrast to the black mood between him and Gigi. Brock trailed behind him, sipping his coffee and watching Gigi's ass flex as he walked.

One year and three months ago, he'd watched that ass walk up to a dance audition stand and he'd been unable to look away. Not that he'd been expecting to know the owner of the ass at the time—Brock was only there to do a documentary with his friend and project partner, Katie. As far as he'd been concerned, Gigi was just another dancer in the dance competition they'd be filming.

Brock had been setting up the camera, gauging light and focus and watching the dancers congregate next to the stands. Strong, lean, tough bodies flexed and stood and sipped coffee, completely unaware of their beauty or the looks they were getting from passersby. Brock lifted weights and jogged, so he knew he was built, but the athleticism here was something else.

And so was the last dancer to show up: tight jeans and a T-shirt that gave everything away, iced coffee in hand and wide grins for his fellow dancers. His hair was dyed an electric purple, earrings sparkled from both lobes, and his ass looked tight enough to spank back. Beautiful and crazy sexy.

So obviously when he and Katie approached the dancers to introduce themselves, he'd approached the hot guy with a grin.

Sexy Ass smiled widely back at him, a thrilling, cheeky smile that seemed familiar and made Brock's blood surge. One dextrous, elegant hand was held out—not for Brock to shake, but to kiss.

Brock took it gently. "I feel like we've met before."

Sexy Ass frowned and cocked his head. "Hmm. Possibly. You . . . Wait, maybe you know me as Gigi LaMore." His expression turned sultry. "I've had some *very* fun shows."

"How would he recognize you out of drag?" his fellow dancer, Tyler, asked.

"Hush you." Gigi batted his eyes at Brock. "Enchanted."

A drag queen. That explained a lot. Smiling, Brock bowed over Gigi's hand, almost but not quite kissing it. Queens could be temperamental about that. "Pleased to meet you, Gigi." He straightened. "I'm Brock Stubbs."

Gigi stiffened and went pure white, grey eyes wide. He whipped his hand out of Brock's. "Y-you don't say."

Just like that, the flirty vibe was gone. Looking back, Brock could see this was when Gi had recognized him, but at the time, he'd just been taken aback by the one-eighty.

Katie had stepped in, given them some spiel about looking forward to working with them, then hustled Brock back to their equipment. Throughout the auditions, Brock had kept eyeing Gigi, a feeling that he knew him niggling away in his gut. No particular thing stood out, but the guy just seemed so very familiar. Had he slept with him and forgotten? Brock doubted it. Gigi looked like he'd be a memorable lay.

Gigi kept glancing at him too.

A few long hours later and Gigi was finally assigned to a sporty guy named Mark, who had a very supportive girlfriend in the audience. Katie groaned when Mark and Gigi met, Mark shaking his hand enthusiastically and Gigi looking like he'd touched something gross.

"Christ, this is going to be a mess," Katie murmured to Brock.

"What? Why?"

"Look at them. Hetero überjock with gay sex kitten." She popped her gum. "Guy's practically allergic to Mark. It'll either be hilarious or mortifying on film."

Brock let his eyes linger on Gigi. "What's Gigi's deal?"

"Deal? He's a dancer. He's . . ." Katie looked between Brock and Gigi, the penny obviously dropping. "*Him*? Really? I thought you went for the serious, conscientious type, not—" she waved towards the dancers "—that."

"Hey, what do you mean by 'that'?"

She gave him a hard look. "You remember telling me about Toby?"

A bolt of guilt went through Brock. Toby. He'd never get over Toby. Wait, how did she know about him? "No," he said honestly.

"Thought not. You were wasted. End of semester party at my house, remember? I got you to the bathroom okay, and after throwing up, you mumbled something about trying to find Toby because he was the love of your life and you wanted to make things up to him." She shrugged. "I figured you wanted to find your high school boyfriend and play house, not chase tail."

"But look at the tail."

Her jaw moved as she frowned at him. "Brock, you're the kind of guy who wants to settle down with a nice man, adopt a few babies, and grow old together. Do you even do flings and one-night stands?"

"Uh, yeah?" Was that how he came across? He knew he wasn't sex on legs like Gigi over there, but he didn't do badly in the gay scene. Especially once he'd dropped his hang-ups about his sexuality, which had happened during his extended gap year. After doing charity work in Indonesia for a year, then working and fucking his way through Europe for another year, he'd definitely sorted through the mental scars his upbringing had left about sex and same-sex relationships. No more closet for him. That meant having fun in Toronto's Village and gay bars while also keeping a lookout for Toby's face. Because yeah, he had to find him and at least apologize for what he'd done.

"It's just that the way you were about this Toby guy made it seem like that's who you're holding out for. You were *so* into him." Katie snapped her gum again. "Gigi, on the other hand, is a high-maintenance queen; even I can see that."

Brock grinned. "Maybe so, but he's fucking hot."

"Ugh. Just don't do anything that jeopardizes this project." She pointed at the dance machine where two girls were waiting. "Film them. I think one of them knows Tyler. She might get through based on friendship."

After the auditions were over, Brock had packed up the camera and headed to lunch with Katie. Thoughts of Gigi warred with memories of Toby throughout lunch and well into the afternoon.

Toby Rosenberg. Brock had moved to Toronto specifically to find the guy and make amends with him, and to finally attend university, but he'd been here for three years and hadn't seen so much as a hair. He wasn't on Facebook, none of Brock's gay friends knew of him, Brock hadn't spotted him out in any of the gay clubs and bars, and Brock was starting to wonder if Toby had given him the wrong information about his university plans back in school.

The Toby in his memories had been tall and overweight, with big grey eyes, floppy dirty-blond hair, and a filthy mouth. Adorable. A drama club member who could sing and dance, Toby had haltingly told him about his dream to move to Toronto, leave Maney behind for good, and take the stage. The Maney gossip mill backed that up; he'd gone to Toronto, been in a few plays. But Brock hadn't seen him, so was he still here? Or had he moved on to somewhere more exciting for actors, like New York?

It had been seven years since he'd last seen him, and, sure, Brock had figured Toby would have grown up a lot, but he'd been counting on recognizing him by the eyes and hair. Maybe a secretive part of him had hoped he'd recognize him no matter what, that their connection had been deep enough to keep them attuned despite the years.

Yeah, no such luck.

Then Gigi had introduced himself to Evie the next day, in front of Brock and Katie, as Gigi Rosenberg, and that had been it.

Seriously, it was like electricity shivering through him, lighting up every nerve and cell, and afterwards Brock had been overwhelmed by absolute and complete certainty. Gigi was *it*. Brock had never been more sure about anything in his life, and it felt *so good*. He wasn't religious, but this moment came damn close. It was like the clouds had parted and a freaking ray of sunlight had beamed onto Toby/Gigi's head and revealed all the features Brock had once known like the back of his hand. The wicked eyes, the wide mouth, the long nose, all of those were still there and so obviously Toby's that Brock had wondered how he hadn't recognized them before. Okay, he'd gained a ton of definition and muscle, and sure that changed his outer shape, but the core of him was still there.

So, he'd finally found Toby Rosenberg. The search was over. Brock had decided then and there that he wasn't letting him go ever again.

Now, in this parking lot, that decision was laughable in its optimism.

They reached the car. Brock dropped his bag into the back, then settled into the passenger seat. Gigi fussed with his seat and belt, avoiding Brock's gaze.

What was the phrase? Cut the tension with a knife? This felt more like a suffocating cloud of bad energy.

He could try to clear the air? Or give Gigi an opportunity to speak his mind? Things tended to go better if they spoke (ranted) openly about problems.

Brock took a deep breath. "It's a mistake that I'm coming."

Gigi turned to him, eyes flashing. "You trying to convince me, sweetie?"

"No. But you'll see once we're there."

Gigi rolled his eyes. "*I'm* supposed to be the dramatic one. It's not a mistake. It's a wedding. And it's four days." He stared at Brock. "We can handle four days."

"It's not the time, it's the people."

Gigi blinked, then his expression softened. "I know. I'm scared too. But we can handle them. We're adults now, you know?"

Brock wasn't so sure about that. "I . . ." *I don't want to go back there. I don't want my parents to know I'm in town. I don't want you to be exposed to them. I don't want to come out to them.*

He couldn't say that. Not with their history. Not when Gigi had no sympathy for closet cases. Saying he was scared to be out in Maney and could they maybe please not be all over each other would get him dumped and out of the car quicker than it took Gigi to rip a heckler to shreds.

Such a coward.

His throat closed up, and he looked out the window.

"What? You *what*?" Gone was any softness or understanding from Gigi's voice. "Finish the fucking sentence."

"It's nothing."

Gigi made a noise of frustration and started the car. "See, this thing you're doing? Right now? This is driving me fucking nuts."

Oh, like *he* could talk? "And you getting on my case because I decided to *not finish a sentence* is getting real fucking old."

Gigi shifted into drive with unnecessary force. "To think I was vaguely missing you before you came here. Clearly absence *does* make the heart grow fonder."

Brock's own heart panged. "What is this? You were the one saying you wanted to break up."

"I do *not* want to break up!" Gigi glared at him. "But this isn't working, *babe*. This fucking sucks."

"I'm here. That's what you wanted."

"I didn't want to *make* you come to Maney with me! Not like this!"

"Then like how? I don't want to do this. I don't want to be here. I can't suddenly want to go just because it's important to you. I want to be at home, with you, queuing up some shitty movie on Netflix, and settling into the weekend."

Gigi's eyes took on a glistening sheen, but he scowled and blinked it away. "Then how about you queue up some shitty movie on your phone so that at least you're doing something important to *you*?" He took his foot off the brake, and the car began rolling forwards. "And don't talk to me. I want to drive, not crash into a tree for some freaking relief from bullshit."

Fine. Fucking *fine*.

Brock pulled out his cell and headphones and turned to stare out the window, wishing this weekend was over already.

CHAPTER TWO

Last autumn

Gigi curled up in his chair, hands over his eyes so he could block out the screen in front of them. Oh God. It was unbearable. Too horrific to watch. So *gross*.

Brock nudged him. "You can look now."

Gigi uncovered his eyes to see Carmen and Claude stumbling around on the screen instead of him and Mark. He breathed a deep sigh of relief.

Katie and Brock's documentary about the summer's dance competition, *Fierce*, was being shown in a U of T screening room, and Gigi and Brock were watching along with the other participants and most of Katie and Brock's film class. So far it was kind of amazing to see each couple progress through their routines, to watch them become friends and discuss LGBTQIA issues on screen. Seeing the progress condensed into twenty minutes alone was awesome.

Or it *would* be if the camera hadn't added like twenty pounds to Gigi. Why? *Why?* He looked like the Stay Puft Marshmallow Man galumphing around with Mark. You'd never know the guy behind the camera was dating him. *Jeeesus.*

He jerked up straight, struck by a horrifying thought: what if the camera wasn't lying? What if that was actually how he looked? *Omigod what do I do?*

Brock took his hand as the film went from Carmen and Claude to Tyler and Evie. Gigi watched them dancing, totally oblivious to the camera. It really was very sweet the way they looked into each other's eyes and kept blushing and laughing. It was less cute when they were doing it now, in the seats next to him. Practically vomitous. That was a word, right?

"Oh fuck," Brock gasped, dropping Gigi's hand.

Hey. What's that about? Gigi looked over at him, then heard the questions start on screen. Katie was asking Evie and Tyler about the routine, then *Brock* interrupted with some kind of freaking monologue about how great they were.

Gigi watched in disbelief as Brock sat in a circle with Evie and Tyler, getting *love advice* from them. The audience around them chuckled as Brock blatantly broke documentary fourth wall logic or whatever the film rules were, but Gigi barely heard them. Brock's face on screen was totally desperate. He was begging for help with Gigi. With *him*.

Brock had done this? Why hadn't he said anything? Didn't he realize how totally . . . how unbelievably . . .

Gigi didn't even have words for this.

He glanced over at his boyfriend. Brock's hands covered his face as he slumped in his seat. *So cute.* He turned back to the documentary and watched Evie hatch a plan to get Brock together with him. A plan that had worked *very* well, incidentally. Three months later, they were totally dating and *serious* about it.

Like, Gigi had daydreamed about being boyfriends with someone and doing all the cutesy shit couples seemed to do, but it turned out getting to that reality was difficult. Not that he had problems meeting guys and hooking up or whatever, but sometimes he'd thought it would be impossible to meet someone and actually *be* with them.

But Brock was easy to be with. And right now, Gigi wanted nothing more than to fuck his adorable, devoted, completely amazing boyfriend until they both passed out.

Unfortunately, they were in public, so Gigi reached over, pried one of Brock's hands off his face, and held it tightly instead. Brock made a whimpering noise, then sunk farther back in his chair, only relaxing once the scene was over. They didn't let go until the film was over, then the lights came on and the audience began buzzing around them.

"I begged Katie to edit it out but she wouldn't," Brock said immediately.

Gigi leaned over and kissed his cheek, then whispered in his ear, "We need to go home so I can fuck you."

Brock went bright red. "Uh. Okay. So that wasn't as embarrassing for you as it was for me? Good to know."

"I wondered how you'd react to that," Evie said behind Gigi.

He turned around. Both Evie and Tyler were grinning knowingly at him. Gigi channelled some LaMore and arched an eyebrow. "I am *amazed* that you two could watch yourselves up there. Practically screwing on screen. Filth, darlings."

Evie scoffed. "Not *quite* sure how you pulled screwing out of stepping on each other, but all right."

"Gigi is just uncomfortable with portrayals of honest intimacy," Tyler said teasingly. Gigi knew he was joking, but that was totally unfair. He could do intimacy!

"Just so you know," Gigi said, "the only reason I'm even discussing this with you right now is because you're blocking the way out of the row."

"I'm stoked you all liked it. Katie and I really wanted to capture the three different kinds of relationships that evolved over the competition," Brock started behind them. "So, Evie and Tyler falling in love"—they blushed—"Claude and Carmen doing this student-teacher thing while exploring alternative ways of expressing female desire, and you and Mark becoming friends even though you're very different people. It was *all* really honest and open, and I think it's one of the best pieces in my portfolio."

His baby was so smart. *So* smart. He was going to do great things when he graduated next spring. Gigi turned and kissed him. "You made a movie, sugarplum, and it's wonderful. Even if you made my ass look big."

Brock cocked his head. "It's a documentary, and I don't know what you mean? The camera lens we used was the standard—"

"But it's okay. I forgive you." Gigi turned back to Tyler and Evie, who weren't even trying to hide their laughter. "You still here?"

Tyler rolled his eyes. "Come on, Evie, I think we're delaying something." He began shuffling along the row of seats. They left en masse and joined the audience filtering through to the bar next door, where a bunch of people descended on Brock and began asking him questions.

Hmph. Well, Gigi *guessed* fucking until they passed out could wait. People were coming up to *him* to ask questions too, given his lardy butt had been captured teaching Mark proper hold for twenty minutes, and that apparently merited attention from complete strangers.

Okay, being asked questions because he'd been in a movie was kind of awesome too.

In fact, he was sort of enjoying it all until he noticed two guys talking to Evie and Tyler. One of them was tall and looked like an artist, if that artist had five hundred dollars to spare on a jacket. The other was compact and a little shorter, with sandy hair, and an ass to kill for. He was also cruising Brock from across the room like it was open season on beef.

Oh.

Hell.

No.

Luckily Brock didn't seem aware of him. And he wasn't going to be. Gigi excused himself and went over to his boyfriend, winding his arm around his waist and kissing his cheek. "You almost done, lover?"

The people in front of Brock smiled, and Brock went red. "Almost. Everyone, my boyfriend, Gigi." Gigi nodded at them before glancing back over at Mr. Boyfriend-Thief.

Who winked at him, then turned to the artsy guy next to him and put an arm around *him.*

Unbelievable.

Some people needed to be kept on a leash.

Finally Brock was done and Gigi could hustle him outside into the brightly lit streets of downtown Toronto. He dragged him onto the TTC and off it again near his house.

"Gi, what's the rush?" Brock asked as Gigi marched them through suburbia.

"I need to get you home."

"Why?" Brock's voice was oddly strained. "Did I do something?"

Did he do something? *Did he do something?* Oh, only made the most romantic gesture Gigi had ever seen on film. And Gigi had seen a *lot* of rom coms. God, Brock's cluelessness was adorable sometimes.

Gigi spun around on him. "Why didn't you tell me about that scene in the documentary? The one where you asked my friends for help?"

Brock's shoulders rose. "Um. Yeah. That was super embarrassing, so I kind of just decided to forget about it. I, uh, didn't really think that one through."

Gigi took Brock's face in his hands. "Sweetie. No one's ever done that for me before. That was *amazing.* You totally blow my mind, you know that?"

Brock smiled, a tiny little ray of sunshine in the autumn night cupped in Gigi's palms.

Something bubbled up in Gigi, burst into a warm, searing heat, and he leaned forward and kissed Brock. "I am so fucking in love with you."

Brock's eyes widened, and his hands gripped Gigi's waist. "You are?"

He was. He really was. It wasn't even the stupid documentary or how sweet Brock had been since they hooked up or the weirdly messy tangle of feelings Gigi had always had for him (well, strictly speaking that Toby had had for him, but that was ancient history now). It was that Brock was completely, absolutely into him, and had been since the beginning.

That just screwed with Gigi's head in all the right ways. That *never* happened to him. Or to guys like him. The swishy femmy ones who wore sparkly things and spoke too much.

"Yeah," Gigi said. "I am."

"Me too. I love you too."

No shit he did. It was kind of obvious by now. But hearing it still made that messy tangle of feelings loosen and settle down just a little. A warm glow in Gigi's chest matched the one in another, lower part of his body. His (thinking) head was so pleasantly screwed now that the rest of his body needed in on the action.

Gigi drew him closer. "Do you understand now why I need to get you home?"

Brock's head bobbed up and down. "Hell yeah. Let's go."

Once at Gigi's house, Gigi barely paused to lock the door, he was so focused on getting Brock to his bedroom and pulling all his clothes off. They stopped to kiss in the hallway, Brock slamming Gigi against the wall between pictures of Gigi as the drag queen Gigi LaMore, all bedecked in glitter and feathers and eyelashes. Gigi had put them there deliberately to test the people who visited him and his roommate; the first time Brock had seen them, he'd touched one and told Gigi she looked beautiful.

Such a keeper.

Gigi pressed himself against Brock, needing to feel that solid body along his. Hands dug behind him to cup his ass, Brock's tongue flickered along his lips, and Gigi groaned as Brock rubbed his groin into Gigi's. So, *so* good.

"Bedroom," he muttered against Brock's mouth.

Brock lifted him with a heave, and Gigi wrapped his legs around Brock's hips, kissing him hard. Brock staggered them both into Gigi's room and clumsily kicked the door shut with one foot. Then Gigi was pushed up against the door, Brock ravaging his neck as his hands dove under Gigi's shirt.

After that, it was a frenzied mess of hands under clothes and murmured instructions that somehow resulted in them on the bed and semi-undressed, touching each other as though there wasn't enough time to spare for unnecessary problems like ties and socks.

"You feel so amazing," Brock breathed against his neck before sucking.

Gigi tugged at Brock's shirt, wanting it off. Brock leaned back enough for him to do that and pull off Gigi's, then returned to attacking Gigi's neck. *Ugh.* Gigi could barely think when he did that. His body felt like it was consumed in flames, Brock's hands were so hot, and Gigi was so desperate. He pushed his head back into his duvet and let go, finally coming into the perfect heat of Brock's mouth minutes later, stars exploding behind his eyelids.

Brock finished a moment afterwards, shuddering against Gigi's chest, eyes closed and face screwed in an expression of total abandon. Gigi drew him close with jelly arms, sleep clouding the edges of his mind. Brock still breathed fast and heavy, and when he finally opened his eyes, they held a sated, happy expression that twisted something deep in Gigi. He'd never expected to be the reason for someone to look like that. Had anyone ever gazed at him with that much emotion before? He didn't think so. He had also never thought he'd see that from Brock, not after what had happened between them at high school. If he was honest, it was bringing out some Toby in him. He wanted to pet Brock and keep him around, naked and wearing that look for, like, ever. It was too much. Too big. But somehow, also perfect.

And so not cool. He'd left all this sappy shit behind with his teens and his virginity. Hadn't he? Thankfully, sleep dragged him down before he could think too much about that.

Brock watched him sleep, mind churning over this evening.

He hadn't expected Gigi to be *impressed* by that scene. Fuck, it had been embarrassing. But embarrassing was what got him on a date with Gi in the first place, so maybe it was a pattern that more embarrassment got him a declaration of love.

Gigi Rosenberg loved him.

Him.

This was possibly the best day of his life. He relived that moment when Gigi had grabbed him and said it, then rolled onto his back and let himself have a little swoon. Oh God. What had happened to him? How could anyone deal with this much happiness?

Evidently by napping, then waking up for another round. Somehow everything was more intense tonight, more real and focused. The sweet breathy sounds Gigi made when he was turned on, the rub of their bodies and the urgency with which they moved against each other—it all melded together with Brock's feelings into something like a natural high, something he could barely express in words or in touching Gigi.

Actually, it kind of reminded him of being sixteen again. Even though back then he'd been tongue-tied every time he tried to speak to Toby in between stolen kisses, Toby had still known what he meant. The connection they'd had, the understanding and silent communication, all of that was back.

And in the morning, they woke up, looked at each other, and couldn't stop smiling. It was like a scene out of a rom com or something. Brock honestly thought this was it: they loved each other, they were together, he could finally be with Gigi Rosenberg the way he'd always dreamed of, and everything was going to be okay.

They stumbled into the kitchen, hair askew and yawning every few minutes. Brock busied himself with making eggs and toast while Gigi brewed coffee and checked his phone. Brock plated up and was trying to get Gi to put his phone down so they could talk over breakfast when Gigi gasped at something on his screen.

"What?" he asked.

Gigi grinned at him. "My sister got engaged!"

That was exciting. Brock's memories of Sophie Rosenberg were of a loud, sporty girl who'd beaten up a few of Gigi's bullies before blasting out of Maney to university. She sounded cool, and she and Gigi got along super well, which was great to see. Brock was an only child, and while he generally thought that was a good thing, he'd occasionally wished for a brother or sister to just . . . share things with. To have someone on his side, who knew him in that deep, all-encompassing way only siblings seemed to have.

"Congratulations," he said.

Gigi shrugged. "She's a lawyer who's been dating another lawyer. I kind of expected it to happen. He's a cool guy though."

"They live in Toronto, right?"

Gigi nodded. "Yeah. We can meet her and Alan soon, if you want."

Brock liked the sound of that. Meeting his boyfriend's sister. That sort of made them family, right? Kind of? "Sure."

His boyfriend (who *loved* him) looked up with his devilish grey eyes and smiled. "You wanna be my plus-one to the wedding?"

Hell yeah. Absolutely *yes*.

CHAPTER THREE

hree hours later and Gigi was sick to death of the Trans-Canada Highway. Trees and rocks and occasional water and construction and then *more fucking trees*, rinse and repeat. Yech. Okay, they were changing colours and dropping leaves and it was very pretty and nice, but Gigi was over it. Like, he could look at that in a painting or whatever.

He'd pulled over by an interesting bit of water surrounded by dead leaves—and more trees—so they could stretch their legs and swap drivers. That was how he found himself staring at autumn colours—not normally something he did—while pretending not to watch Brock pace restlessly around the edge of the pit stop area.

Brock hadn't spoken since Gigi had told him to shut up. He'd settled into the passenger seat, brow furrowed, and watched *an actual movie* (Gigi had been *kidding* about that, Jesus), then stared out the window. Gigi had been so tempted to break the silence, but he didn't know what to say.

He hadn't *meant* to snap at the guy. It had just come out of him, lightning-quick, like his reads on stage. The mental reflex helped with his dancing and performing too; he could improvise like a pro and think on his feet. But even though Gigi was right about this—and he was *so* right about this trip and Brock's shitty attitude toward it—he didn't need to be spiteful at the same time. His boyfriend wasn't a heckler or a critic.

Well, not generally.

This trip sucked balls, and they weren't even near Maney yet. Like, compare this awkward ride of nerves and sulky boyfriend with their road trip down to Syracuse last year: now *that* had been a blast. They'd talked the whole way, stopping only for food and impromptu car sex, had cozied up in a hotel and had more sex, then explored Syracuse. Repeat on the way home.

See, that was what road trips with boyfriends *should* be like. None of this passive-aggressive silent shit.

Brock walked up to him and stood quietly, his jaw tight and arms at his sides. As Gigi watched, Brock's hands twitched nervously, then his arms crossed in front of his chest.

His expansive chest. Which Gigi knew barely had a hair on it, lucky bastard. Gigi had to wax for every LaMore performance, yet there was Brock, his masculine boyfriend with a hairless wonder of a chest. Utterly wasted on the guy.

Not wasted on Gigi though.

"Keep practising that brooding pout," Gigi said. "I think you've almost got it."

Brock scowled. "Can I have the keys, please?"

Gigi handed them over. "You ready to go?"

"No."

Brock jammed hands and keys into his pockets and turned away, walking toward the rail at the edge of the pit stop. Gigi pushed away from the car and followed him. Beyond the rail were the pond and trees, and Brock came to a stop just as Gigi drew level with him. He saw the distant look on Brock's face and figured he wasn't actually admiring this mosquito-infested spot of mud.

"I was just thinking about Syracuse," Gigi said.

Brock made a noncommittal noise.

"That trip was more fun than this one."

Brock snorted. "No shit."

"But this could still be fun." Gigi bumped his shoulder. "My crazy sister is getting hitched. You're going to meet the Rosenberg clan."

For some reason Brock went pale.

"My parents are awesome, and so're my aunt and two uncles. There's another aunt, but she's super conservative and homophobic, so she wasn't invited. My cousins are *great*, and their kids are really sweet. It'll be a packed house." Gigi could picture them all now, sleeping on cots and in sleeping bags and sharing rooms in his parents' large fake

Victorian homestead-style house. It would be cramped, but for two or three days it would be fun. He'd insisted on Brock staying with him anyway, of course. Even if sex in his room didn't seem a likely prospect right now. "And it's a wedding! All the hooch you could want."

Brock eyed him, and Gigi smiled at him. Brock didn't smile back.

Aw, jeez. Time to bite the bullet. "I'm sorry I said I wanted to break up with you. Or implied it."

"Are you really that unhappy?"

Gigi glanced out at the pond. It was a greeny-brown colour and reflected the trees on the other side. Ugh. "No. Yes? I don't know. Things changed. You changed."

"I changed how?"

Gigi couldn't put his finger on it, so he just shrugged. "Dunno. You're just not there as much."

Brock scowled. "How about you figure it out *before* telling me I'm a failure?"

The hell? "I didn't say that. All I said was that this—" he gestured between them "—isn't working. We're both unhappy." The lines on Brock's face deepened. "So how about you stop putting words in my mouth and step up."

Brock winced.

Damn it. This wasn't how Gigi had envisioned this little moment happening.

"Look. *Look.*" They still had at least two hours of driving to go. He had to make things okay. Well, okay-ish. "We can figure this out when we get back to Toronto. I'm not down for fighting every time we look at each other." He put a hand on Brock's arm. "Can we get through this weekend without bitching at each other? Please?"

Brock jaw tightened. "Sure. We can do that. I like your sister, so no, I'm not going to let our drama ruin her wedding." Brock rolled his shoulders. "For the record, that would be easier if I wasn't even *going.*" He turned away. "Let's move."

Just like that, huh? Well, it was better than nothing. As Gigi followed him back to the car, he wondered if there was any way Brock could be more of a baby about all of this.

He found out when Brock refused to speak a full sentence to him all the way up to Sudbury. Just grunts and one-word responses.

Well, sooorry. Gigi ended up putting in his earbuds, turning on the *Book of Mormon* soundtrack, and thinking over that little moment in the pit stop. The entire freaking day, actually.

What *had* changed between them? Had Brock changed? Not in the basics, Gigi noted with a wistful glance at Brock's lap. Physique aside, Brock was still the sweet, intense guy he'd always been.

Only, that sweetness and intensity had been a lot more exciting at the beginning of everything. He'd literally gone down on his *knees* for Gigi. He'd embarrassed himself on camera by asking for boy advice. He'd bought flowers and showy meals out and fancy lubes—the really expensive ones that were totally worth the money.

Gigi knew him better now, and considering how quiet and moody he could be, it was kind of amazing Brock had even pulled off all that stuff in the beginning. The guy was freaking *stoic*. He was like one of the damn trees they kept passing by, silent and solid, deep roots and changing leaves. This kind of relationship stuff wasn't something people talked much about—maybe because it didn't happen to other people? Gigi wasn't sure. How did people talk about realizing that there were all these depths to a person, that they were sometimes a surprise waiting to happen? Especially when said person seemed incapable of talking about them himself? Was incapable of talking about *anything*, actually . . .

Like this weekend, for example—Brock was totally not okay, but was he saying anything? Like hell. What was a boyfriend to do with that?

He sat back and flickered another glance at Brock.

In a way, things had been easier at the beginning. Where had all that passion gone? Where were the declarations delivered on bended knee now? They hadn't even gone clubbing in the last three months, for fuck's sake. Brock hadn't let Gigi suck him off in public since Syracuse. Now they bounced between each other's home and work and the occasional bar, and it was *boring*. The sex was good, but somehow it wasn't the same. Seriously. No one mentioned this part of relationshipping.

His phone vibrated in his pocket, and Gigi pulled it out.

Mom: *Where are you guys now?*

Gigi: *Past Sudbury. Half an hour away.*

Mom: *Great! You're on time for dinner.*
Gigi: *Later than anticipated, but yeah.*
Mom: *We're looking forward to seeing you and Brock!*
At least *someone* was excited about this weekend.

Gigi's estimate turned out to be slightly off: forty-five minutes later, it was dusk, and the car headlights lit up a sign saying *WELCOME TO MANEY, ONTARIO* beside the dark exit ramp off the highway.

Oooh, wow, okay—here they were. Just like that. That was definitely the familiar rectangle of green and white, suspended in a twilight of forest and badly lit road ahead of them. Gigi's stomach roiled, and he crossed his arms over his chest, hunching over slightly to stop his stomach from actually flipping out of his mouth. Not that it seemed likely, but weirder things happened to people's bodies all the freaking time. Gigi had seen *Emergency Room* and *Trauma*.

The car was slowing down. The Maney sign loomed larger, then sped past. Gigi looked over at Brock, who stared straight ahead, absolutely stiff. Sweat glittered at his hairline, and his knuckles stood out on the steering wheel.

Oh no. Poor guy. Gigi leaned over and pressed one hand on Brock's thigh. "Breathe, baby."

Brock exhaled sharply. "Fuck." A pause. "I'm going to throw up."

"Me too."

To Gigi's surprise, Brock unclenched one hand from the steering wheel and picked up Gigi's hand from his thigh, giving it a squeeze. "I'm glad you're here."

Aw. He did care. Maybe they'd get through this.

They passed the first few houses, and Brock abruptly wrenched the car to the side, stopped it, stumbled out the driver's door onto his hands and knees, and actually threw up.

Okay then. Gigi had spoken too soon.

He got out and walked over to where Brock crouched, careful to avoid any splatter. *Yech.* "You weren't kidding."

"I hate you for bringing me here," Brock rasped.

"You were the one driving that last half of the route."

Brock heaved again.

Oh man, his baby was *not* well. "I'll drive us to my house."

"I can do it." Deep, rough breaths. "I remember the way."

Brock knew the way to Gigi's old home? That was . . . unexpected.

Ugh, no it's not. He'd been gone too long. Knowing where Gigi had lived meant nothing. Everyone knew where everyone else lived; it was a small town. Back in school, he'd known where Brock had lived—and where everyone in theatre group had lived, where nearly everyone in his year had lived, the teachers, the librarians, the freaking book club moms that his mom liked to hang out with . . .

Brock's colour was a bit better, but there was still a tinge of *ready to chuck his guts out.*

"You don't look like you can stand up, let alone drive," Gigi said.

Brock flipped him the finger. "I'll be fine in a minute."

Yeah, that was promising. Gigi glanced around them. This was the very outskirts of town, where there were large gaps between houses and the forest fell away before suburbia. Brock had chosen a nice grassy spot near some trees and between two houses that appeared abandoned. The forest, now quite dark as the sun left the sky, provided the backdrop of the gap, and Gigi realized as he stared into it that he knew this spot: he'd been dared to run around the Maney perimeter when he was eight. A stupid dare from other kids, to test their boundaries and bravery. Maney was small, but it was definitely large enough for the town border to be out of bounds to the under-tens. He'd made it here, scratched his initials into a tree, then run back with a stick to prove he'd been there, which made no sense now but had at the time. Instead of finding his friends, he'd found his pissed-off dad.

Brock sat down, breathing heavily. Gigi turned, found a spot upwind of the puke, and squatted next to Brock.

"You feeling better?" he asked.

Brock closed his eyes. "No. Now I feel angry, gross, *and* embarrassed."

Please, like anyone cared. Gigi grinned and stroked his shoulder. "Little bit of puke never hurt anyone."

Brock closed his eyes and turned into the touch, shifting towards him. Gigi kept stroking his shoulder, loving the feel of the tight muscle through his shirt. Brock's shoulders and arms were possibly Gigi's favourite part of his body, after his dick and smile. The first time they'd stumbled into Gigi's bed, he'd practically torn Brock's shirt off in order to molest those shoulders.

That first time. Brock gazing hungrily in the dark club. Clutching each other in the taxi on the way home. Fucking like there was no tomorrow. Where *was* that? Why had it gone? Now there was all this anger and confusion.

And puke.

Brock's forehead hit Gigi's chest. "I'm sorry." His words were muffled by Gigi's sweater.

Gigi moved his hand from Brock's shoulder into his hair, stroking it. "Don't apologize."

"I can't believe I actually threw up."

"I can't believe I haven't."

Brock snorted. "Right. You were the one who actually had the horrific childhood here."

"Yeah, because seeing all that homophobia didn't affect *you* either, boyfriend." Which it totally had, just not in the exact same way. Not that Gigi planned on reliving any sort of homegrown homophobia, but it seemed kind of inevitable here.

"How are you so calm?"

Gigi lightly scratched Brock's scalp, making him shudder beneath him. "I'm looking after you, dummy."

Brock snorted again but burrowed his head into the curve of Gigi's neck.

They stayed like that for a few moments more, letting the quiet and cold of the dusk seep into their bones. Brock was a warm spot against his chest. It was nice to have him lean on Gigi like this.

Gigi didn't think he'd ever seen Brock throw up before. He'd seen him in bed with the flu, but only briefly because Brock hadn't wanted him catching what he had and had ordered him away until he was better. Like, seriously wouldn't-let-Gigi-into-his-house kind of away. A week later, he was back to full health and it was like he'd never been sick.

"You ready to move?" Gigi asked him eventually.

Brock sighed. "Nope, but I'm cold."

With stiff legs, they stood up and went back to the car, Gigi sitting on the driver's side now. He told Brock to text their imminent arrival to his mom and started rolling forward.

As they drove, the surroundings became more urban and familiar, better-lit, and populated. They passed the gas station, unchanged since the sixties, and saw the houses abruptly close ranks on the streets and beat back the forest. He drove onto the main street, also bizarrely unchanged, though a few stores had replaced the ones he remembered.

Brock huffed. "Oh my God, there's a vegan bakery here."

"Someone in Maney knows what veganism is?"

"And a café. A fancy one." Brock pointed. "Fair-trade organic coffee."

Well, thank fuck for that; Gigi wouldn't be reliant on his parents' store-brand instant to wake up.

He paused at a stoplight. There was very little traffic out. Friday night: everyone would be at Pinky's bar on the other side of town; the twenty-four-hour diner near Pinky's; Warner's, the only nice bar in town; or the "club" that was really a bar with a dancefloor, the one that kept changing ownership and name and had a closing time of midnight.

The town looked pretty much as he remembered it, but somehow smaller and more worn. The stores on Main seemed to be sagging, and as the light changed and he drove past the post office at the end of Main, he wondered if it had always been that squat and old.

Ditto for the public library, which was a few blocks away from the centre of town. And the Metro, its small (and only) competitor Lee's Independent Grocers, the salon, Scotiabank, the animal hospital . . . the school.

The silence in the car took on a special quality as they drove past their high school. Gigi might've made a cutting remark about it, but honestly, the energy just wasn't there. Not for that place.

A few blocks later, he pulled into the driveway of his childhood home. Despite not having been home in years, it looked exactly the same. The porch light was on, and as he parked, he saw curtains in the dining room windows twitch.

"Home sweet home." Gigi glanced at Brock.

Brock looked ready to throw up again.

Oh God, it was actually happening.

He was here. Back in this stupid town, with his stupid old friends and his *family*. Brock wondered how long it would be before they heard through the grapevine that he was here with Toby Rosenberg for Sophie Rosenberg's wedding. He wondered if maybe he should call them first rather than let them hear from someone else. Yeah, that was a great idea, be yelled at on the phone, then marched back home and yelled at there. Or worse. Likely worse. *Fuck*.

To say nothing of meeting the Rosenbergs, plural. Brock had met Sophie and Alan a bunch of times, but Gigi's parents exactly once. They'd come to Toronto to spend Christmas with Gigi, who always had an excuse not to go back for holidays, and Brock had met them when he'd come by for dinner. That had been a nice meal, but now he was sharing a *house* with them *and* their relatives.

He had no idea what to expect. His family was small, so his idea of big families came from movies and TV. Stuff like kids running around underfoot and screaming, while adults talked over each other as they watched TV or ate, and dogs (always dogs) lay around drooling on things, and the elderly grandmother or grandfather misheard everything. If they were anything like Gigi, he could expect a chorus line every ten minutes.

And of course they were late because he'd chickened out of going in the first place, then needed to literally puke his guts out. Oh man, he had to forget that ever happened. So embarrassing. Gigi must think he was pathetic, because they shared opinions on most things and Brock was definitely one hundred percent pathetic. Total wimp.

He should never have come here.

Gigi gripped his shoulder, and Brock stared at him in surprise.

"Ready to go?" Gigi asked, eyes bright.

"No." Seeing as he couldn't imagine this trip turning out to be anything but a shit show, he might as well be honest.

The grip tightened. "I believe in you, boyfriend. We can do this." A quick peck on the cheek, then Gigi exited the car, bringing in the scent of cold night air and autumn leaves. Numbly, Brock unbuckled his belt and got out.

Mrs. Rosenberg stood on the porch, waving at them. "Hi, boys! We're in the middle of eating." She was round and soft, with dirty-blonde hair that swung around her shoulders and a big smile that shone like a beacon at them. Brock could see Gigi in her face and hair, and the resemblance almost made him smile. She looked really happy to see them.

Gigi strode up to her and gave her a hug. Brock looked away, uncertain if he should grab bags or go say hi first. When he saw Gigi gesturing, the decision was made for him.

He joined them on the porch, aware his tread was heavy on the wooden steps. "Hi, Mrs. Rosenberg."

She let Gigi go and turned to him. "Brock! So nice to see you again. And it's Naomi, remember?" Then it was his turn for a hug, and he tried to relax as her arms came around him. She was warm and smelled like savoury, delicious things.

He gingerly hugged back, then stepped aside. "I'll get the bags." He turned away and walked back to the car, a dark worry pushing him to move their stuff into the house before any of the neighbours recognized him.

Gigi helped him muscle their gear inside to the front hall, where they basked for a moment in the warmth and light. Naomi fussed over Gigi as though he were a teenager again, her hands ruffling his dyed red hair. "Why do you keep changing your hair like this? It was beautiful as it was."

Gigi ducked away. "Mom! It's fine!"

Brock looked around. They were in a hallway with one open door leading to what sounded like the dining room—judging by the talking and laughing—a staircase, and more doors leading to other parts of the house. Lining the walls were family portraits and funny photos and a few prints of trees in the local park. A bright-green rug on the floor added another burst of colour to the scene. Lights blazed, and garlic and rosemary scented the air.

Everything he'd expected of the Rosenberg house, yet somehow more.

"Leave your stuff for now. Come eat," Naomi was saying.

"We're blocking the door, Mom. It's totally a fire hazard."

"Toby's enough of a fire hazard already!" someone (Sophie, it sounded like) shouted from the dining room, followed by laughter.

Gigi straightened, eyes ablaze, and stormed into the room. "Ooohhh, *someone* doesn't want her wedding present."

See? Siblings. Brock suddenly ached for that kind of easy connection. The last time Gigi and Sophie had been together was months ago, but it was like they'd never been apart.

Naomi smiled at Brock, the edges of her eyes crinkling. "Come on. We won't bite."

He knew that. Logically, he knew that. He pulled a smile from somewhere and followed her in.

A large table took up the majority of the room, laden with so much food and drink Brock almost threw up again at the sight of it all. Mr. Rosenberg sat next to Sophie and an elderly lady; Sophie's fiancé, Alan, sat opposite Sophie; and the other chairs were taken up by adults and children Brock didn't know.

Gigi stood by the table, finger pointing at Sophie. "You. I literally walk through the door and you're already giving me shit."

"It's like childhood never ended," Mr. Rosenberg said to the elderly lady next to him, who snorted agreement.

"You literally walk through the door in the middle of dinner and expect us to be happy about it?" Sophie countered, standing up. "Rude."

Gigi gasped. "*You're* rude for making everyone come to the middle of nowhere for your stupid wedding!"

A round of snorts and exclamations faded as Gigi and Sophie hugged.

Mr. Rosenberg rose. "Does your old man get a hug too?"

Gigi let go of Sophie and turned to wrap his arms around his dad.

A lump rose in Brock's throat.

"Nice to see you again, Brock." Sophie nodded at him as she sat back down.

Gigi and his dad let go and grinned at each other. Brock relaxed— and when had he tensed up?—then was steered by Naomi to an empty spot next to Alan.

"This is Brock," Naomi announced. "Toby's boyfriend."

Suddenly all eyes were on him, and he swallowed nervously. "Hi."

"Hi!" Yup, they knew how to chorus. And how to smile at him as though they were completely okay with him joining their family meal, even though he'd made Gigi late and he wasn't family. Though why wouldn't they be okay? He was being stupid.

Brock sat down. Alan smiled at him. "Hey, man."

"Hey."

Brock had only met Alan Wong a handful of times before now, but he'd always seemed pretty cool. Then again, he was a lawyer, like Sophie, and cut an intimidating figure in a suit. Alan wasn't in a suit now—he was in a fitted plaid shirt, chinos with the cuffs rolled up, and blocky glasses. Way more relaxed. Still cool. Nothing like Brock, who was pretty sure he'd caught some vomit on his sleeve and was ready to drive right back to Toronto.

"Good drive up?" Alan asked.

"Yeah."

"Glad you're here."

The guy on the other side of Alan leaned over. "Yeah—now he's not the only non-Rosenberg in the house."

Brock wasn't sure whether to laugh at that, but Alan rolled his eyes. "That wasn't my point, but yeah, that's true." He grinned at Brock. "I'll give you some tips for surviving here. My family's coming tomorrow, and I'll be staying with them until the wedding."

Tips? For surviving here? Would he really need those? He'd expected to be the only non-Rosenberg in the house straightaway, so Alan being here already was a nice surprise. Gazing around the table at an array of people with similar face shapes and smiles, Brock was hit by an image of a troop of angry Rosenbergs. *Ugh. No.* An angry Gigi was hard enough to deal with.

Alan introduced the guy on his other side as Gigi's cousin, Ed. Then they went around the table, Brock promptly forgetting everyone's names except Ed, Sophie, Alan, and Gigi's parents, John and Naomi. The elderly lady sitting next to John was Gigi's grandmother, who told him to call her Grandma.

Gigi squeezed a chair in between Sophie and some other cousin of his. Ed passed Brock a plate of creamed potatoes, and Brock slowly dumped a spoonful onto his plate. People kept passing him food, and he added to his plate until there was a mound of food in front of him. His stomach roiled just looking at it.

"How was the drive up?" John asked him.

Brock was instantly aware of Gigi's eyes on him. And Naomi's and Grandma's and Sophie's and that cousin whose name he'd already forgotten.

"Good," he said.

"He means boring," Gigi jumped in. "Nothing but *trees* between Toronto and Sudbury."

"We normally play games in that stretch," Naomi said.

Gigi and Sophie rolled their eyes and groaned loudly. Evidently they knew their parents' car games very well.

"We went over the wedding schedule on our way up," Alan said.

"*So* much better than playing I Spy for three hours," Sophie added with a pointed look at her dad, who dug into his casserole without a word.

The conversation turned into the kids teasing the parents for crappy car journeys of the past, and Brock watched in amazement as no one got snippy or tense. He turned to his food and took a tentative bite of chicken. It tasted amazing, but his stomach clenched around it.

Seriously, he had to relax. He knew the Rosenbergs were good people. Wasn't this scene almost exactly what he'd pictured when he thought of their family? Minus the dogs underfoot. Granted he hadn't realized just how *many* people would be here, or just how loud it would be, or how hot this number of people made a room . . .

"Brock."

He looked up. John met his gaze evenly, and Brock straightened. "Yes, sir?"

John smiled warmly. "It's John. The last time we met, you were about to graduate and were looking for work. You find something?"

Brock nodded. "Advertising."

"Oh nice. Lucrative field."

"Depends what we're advertising, but yeah, it can be."

Alan grinned. "It can be? You tell people what they need to buy. Guy, you'll end up making more than me without the heinous hours."

Gigi rolled his eyes. "His hours are heinous already. He spends all his time at the office."

John cast a fond smile at his son. "That's working life."

"*My* working life keeps me plenty busy without trapping me in an office all night."

"Yeah, but your pay sucks," Sophie pointed out.

"*Oh*. So it's all about the money." Gigi snorted. "Like I could expect anything else from a *lawyer*."

"Are you enjoying it?" John asked Brock as Sophie and Gigi continued snapping at each other.

"Yeah." Brock raised his voice over the argument.

"Glad to hear it. So you're pretty settled in Toronto?"

"Yes."

"I heard from your mom that your gap years took you through a lot of countries," Naomi said. "You done with travelling?"

Brock could feel his face heating up. Naomi had spoken to his mom? When? What had she said? "No, but I like having a home base."

"Oh yeah, I hear that," John said affably.

"Oh, I'm sorry." Sophie rolled her eyes at Gigi. "I didn't realize wanting to *own a house* was a stupid idea."

"If you save up for it, you'll never get there," Gigi declared. "Not in Toronto. *My* plan is to become so famous that someone gifts me a mansion. Or marry a rich octogenarian right before he kicks the bucket, whatever happens first."

"Brock might have something to say about that." Sophie winked at him, and Brock's stomach twisted.

"Or not." Gigi skewered vegetables with his fork. "Brock wouldn't mind if I went after a dying rich guy with too much property."

Uh, he kind of would.

And, oh no, everyone at their end of the table was looking at him now. Gigi put a forkful of vegetables in his mouth and began chewing, his eyes stony.

"You do you," Brock replied.

There was a small gap before Sophie sighed loudly. "You're so full of shit, Toby. Call me in twenty years' time and tell me just how that works out for you."

Alan bumped Brock's shoulder. "I'll make sure you get to live in the mansion too."

"Thanks." Brock pushed food around on his plate, aware he'd said the wrong thing. Gigi didn't look like he'd been joking, but Brock knew it would've been better to treat it like he had been. He wasn't like Gigi though; he couldn't just come up with something off the cuff. Any minute now about five humorous responses were going to come to him, and he'd kick himself for not giving those.

The kids at the other end of the table ducked away and ran out of the room, and the adults began collecting plates as if by unspoken signal. Brock realized he'd swirled his food into oddly coloured mush and set his fork aside, ashamed at wasting it.

"Not hungry?" Naomi asked him.

He shook his head. "We— Uh, I snacked a lot on the trip."

"I can imagine." She inclined her head at Gigi. "This one used to get through a pack of Hickory Sticks every thirty kilometres."

"*Mom!*"

"Sophie preferred Cheezies though."

"When Toby didn't steal them from me," Sophie said.

Gigi slumped in his chair. "Oh. My. God. I didn't come here for abuse."

Sophie turned and threw her arms around him. "No, you came because you *love me.*"

"Do I? Do I actually love you?"

Naomi reached for Brock's plate, and he hurriedly picked it up and stood. "I'll, uh, I'll help clear."

"Me too." Alan popped up next to him.

Naomi seriously had the best smile. "That's sweet. Thank you."

"Such handsome boys," Grandma said suddenly. Her sharp eyes regarded them through thick glasses from across the table, and she jabbed a finger at Brock. "Toby, he reminds me of your grandpa's best friend. Big arms, big hands, big feet. You know what they say."

John ducked his head, and Naomi's jaw dropped. "*Mom!*"

Gigi made a choking noise from within Sophie's arms. Beside Brock, Alan was trying hard not to laugh.

"Uh, thanks, Grandma," Brock said. "Can I take your plate?"

"Thank you, dear."

He reached across and took it, then hustled out with Alan behind him. He stopped short when he realized he didn't know where he was going.

Alan took the lead. "Oh my God. That was great. She told *me* she'd never met a Chinese lawyer before."

Brock winced. "Ugh. Sorry. You been here long?"

Alan pushed open the kitchen door, and they walked in. Alan went straight to the dishwasher. "Three days. Sophie and I have been putting the final pieces together. Assembling the wedding favours, collecting deliveries, organizing people's travel, checking in with the food, all that stuff. Apart from that Chinese-lawyer crack, Grandma's been a hoot." Alan began stacking plates in the dishwasher. "Her scrambled eggs are amazing. Make sure she cooks you breakfast at least once. Soph and I are trying to do the vegan thing, but it's not going so well here."

"Vegan?"

"Yeah, man. Seriously, you should try it. I've never had this much energy in my life. We've got a vegetarian spread with vegan options organized for the wedding reception. Homemade booze too. Sophie makes her own gin, and my best man started a microbrewery last year. He's bringing batches of his IPAs."

Brock's head was spinning now. "Oh. Sounds . . . good."

"Totally." Alan's eyes gleamed. "It's gonna be sweet."

Brock looked around the kitchen for more to clean up. He didn't really want to return to that hectic dining room, so he began moving dirty pots into the sink.

"Hey, uh," Alan leaned a little too casually against the counter, "you and Toby. Sophie says you've been together over a year, eh?"

"Yeah." A year and three months, but who was counting?

"Things serious?"

Seriously out of touch or *seriously messed up*. Both of those descriptions had *serious* in them. He shrugged. "I guess."

"You're both from this town, right? Man, what are the odds? Did you know each other at school?"

Did we know each other at school? What a question. Brock plugged the sink and ran the tap. "I knew of him, but we weren't friends or anything." That was true.

"Crazy how that happens. I bet you never expected to end up with someone from your hometown. I hear Toby practically choked this place in his dust, he was so happy to leave."

Brock snorted. They'd both done that.

"It's cool of you guys to come back." Alan's voice was low. "Soph might joke a lot, but I know it means a lot to her. And to me."

Brock pulled a smile. "No problem. Happy to be here." He hoped he sounded sincere.

Alan nodded, then started scraping leftovers into Tupperware dishes. A few moments later, Naomi, John, and a few cousins drifted in with more plates and a lot more conversation.

John joined Brock at the sink. "Appreciate it, Brock, but you've had a long trip. Go take a load off." He pulled on rubber gloves, and Brock backed away.

Naomi immediately ushered him and Alan out, telling them they didn't need to tidy up the kitchen. Brock glanced behind him at the sight of John and several elderly relatives cleaning together. That would never happen in his family's place. His dad wouldn't be caught dead near dirty dishes.

In the hallway, Brock paused at the sight of other family members dispersing around the house and Gigi with a large glass of wine heading for the couch in the rec room with Sophie. Alan followed them, leaving Brock by himself next to his and Gigi's luggage.

No one was watching him. No one was waiting for him. He could just leave if he really wanted.

He mentally winced. That wasn't a good idea or a good sign, if he was having ideas like that.

Be logical, Brock. You're in the Rosenberg house. Your parents don't know you're here. You're safe.

But Naomi Rosenberg had spoken to Brock's mom about him.

That meant . . . well, it could mean a lot of things. They could've discussed the wedding. Their sons. Brock wondered if his mom had told Naomi he hadn't spoken to his parents since starting university. He'd simply changed numbers and never called the house anymore. Definitely bad-son activity, cutting off contact like that. Maybe Naomi *did* know about it and was only being nice to him because he was dating *her* son.

Orrr he could remember what his mom was actually like and how his family had always operated: *keep it in the family.* So no, his mom wouldn't have mentioned to outsiders that her son hadn't spoken to her or her husband in five years.

She might not have mentioned him at all. In which case, his parents probably weren't aware he was in town.

Yet.

And that *was* something Brock could count on. Naomi had probably said he'd be there, but even if she hadn't, at some point someone would see him, recognize him, and mention it to one of his parents. Small-town grapevines were ridiculous and real. The Stubbses would hear he was around, and they'd hear he was gay and dating Toby Rosenberg and staying here—like he would willingly go back to their place—and they'd be angry, and they'd come around to this bright, warm house, and oh God he absolutely could not let them near the Rosenbergs—especially Gi—and *shit* his dad meeting Gi . . .

Blood roared in his ears. He had to stop *that* at all costs. No way was he letting his dad anywhere near Gigi.

But what could he do? Look at him—he was standing in the middle of someone else's hallway like a silent, crazy statue. He could barely make a decision about staying or going, moving to the rec room with his boyfriend or hiding in the bathroom until he could think clearly again. Someone would eventually notice that—

"Hello."

Oh. There was a little girl looking up at him with a confused expression on her face.

Brock blinked. How long had she been there? "Hi."

"Are you okay?"

She was tiny, barely coming up to Brock's waist, and had the same grey eyes as Gigi. A cousin, maybe?

"Um," he replied.

"Because you're just standing there."

"I'm thinking."

Her head tilted. "About what?"

Being afraid. *Yeah, totally share your batshit feelings with a little girl. She's, what, six?* "Stuff. What's your name?"

She grinned. "Rosie. I'm *five*." She held up her hand, fingers outstretched. "What's your name?"

"Brock." What the hell. "I'm twenty-four."

Her eyes widened. "You're so *old*."

A laugh burst out of him.

"You had a sad face just now so I thought you forgot how to walk."

That surprised another laugh out of him. "I think you're right."

She grinned. "My mom says that to me a lot. Maybe you should stop thinking, and then you won't have the sad face and you can remember how to walk again."

That made a weird kind of sense. He took a big, dramatic step and feigned shock. "Oh hey, I remembered!"

She giggled, which sent a rush of delight through him.

"There you are!"

He looked up. Gigi stood at the door of the rec room, wine in one hand and other hand on hip.

Rosie spun around and ran at him. "Hiii, Toby!"

Gigi grinned and bent down to give her a one-armed hug, then she was distracted by something in the rec room and disappeared inside. Gigi gazed after her with an affectionate smile, and Brock gazed at *him*, struck by a realization.

Gigi looked kind of . . . *good* with a kid.

It was weird. Brock had written off having kids, especially after the stuff he'd gone through with *his* family, and he'd never seen either himself or Gi as a parent at all—considering some of the very adult and sometimes loosely irresponsible stuff they got up to in clubs and late at night, definitely *not*. But one hug with a small person and Brock could really see Gigi as a dad.

It was a nice picture.

And Brock thought he might fit into a picture like that one. Not right now, no way, but . . . suddenly *written off* had turned to *maybe*.

"You okay?" Gigi asked.

Brock mentally shook himself. "Yeah." To his surprise, he was. Whether it had been the injection of silliness for a little girl or something else, he did feel better. Calmer.

And just *done* with worrying. Like, so what if his parents were going to find out he was there? They didn't know right this very moment. So he could chill out and enjoy being here tonight and deal with whatever was gonna happen tomorrow.

If anything did happen. After all, he wouldn't put it past his parents to be so pissed off with him they refused to contact him in return. A guy could dream, right?

"You gonna come in here and talk to us?" Gigi's tone was casual, but there was a hard core to it, the same one that had reared its head during dinner.

The thing was, Brock knew his boyfriend just wanted this weekend to go well. They'd promised, hadn't they? So Brock smiled and gestured. "Lead on."

Gigi turned and Brock followed him into the rec room, which was wide and held three large sofas, a huge TV, several shelves of books and DVDs, and was cluttered with family photographs. Brock stopped to take in pictures of Sophie and Gigi as kids—skating on Maney Lake in winter, cheeks red from the cold; on a beach somewhere with ice cream, squinting at the camera; in a family portrait at Easter, baskets of chocolate eggs held up proudly.

"Oh my God, don't look at those!" Gigi grabbed his hand and tugged him over to the sofas. Brock was shoved into a space between Grandma and the armrest of the sofa, which Gigi perched on, and found himself staring at Sophie and Alan, who sat on the floor with glasses in hand. The rest of the sofas were occupied with adults chatting, and kids occasionally streaked past in a blur of legs and laughter.

"So, Brock," Sophie said, tilting her glass at Gigi, "how much are Mom and Dad paying you to date this loser?"

Gigi made an exasperated noise, and Brock automatically touched his leg to soothe him before saying, "If I told you, I'd have to kill you."

Gigi turned on him. "Don't encourage her!"

Sophie leaned forward. "Totally encourage me. I have all the juicy growing-up stories." She grinned as Gigi groaned. "So spill. I wanna hear Toronto stories!"

"Uh . . ." Brock wouldn't know where to start. Gigi practising his routine—no, *her* routine—was always funny. The drag shows were good. Some of their nights out with friends, drag and otherwise, had been pretty wild—maybe too wild to retell with kids around.

But the fun Gigi stories Brock tended to think of were the dumb shit that happened when they were cooking together or having sex or doing something with friends. Gigi would say or do something hilarious and Brock would laugh, or Brock would do something dumb and Gigi would make it funny so they both laughed. A lot of that stuff was personal, though.

Like how Gigi had handled Brock's scars. He had a whole bunch of them on his back, sides, and arms, but they'd healed really well and weren't that noticeable anymore. Gigi hadn't even picked up on them until a few weeks into their relationship, and when he had, he'd totally taken them in stride. He'd been *really* chill about it, and they'd ended up laughing over something again. Then having sex.

Brock had forgotten that.

Problem though: that wasn't the kind of story Brock thought he could tell these people.

And would they want to hear about their life together anyway? This family *seemed* cool with him and Gigi, but Brock doubted that extended to hearing sex stories about them. Even the sweet ones.

"You want funny Toronto stories?" Gigi cut in. "There was this asshole heckler I got during my drag act . . ."

And just like that, Brock was relieved from having to say anything.

Next to him, Grandma made a huffing noise and stood up. Brock watched her walk to one of the shelves.

Gigi stood up, handed his wineglass to Brock, and began reenacting the heckler story, swanning around as LaMore tearing the heckler to shreds. Sophie, Alan, and the cousins on the sofas laughed, rapt as they watched Gigi.

He really was an amazing performer. Even without the wig, face, padding, shoes, or dress, Gigi could channel his queen. Brock was so lost in him he didn't notice Grandma had returned until she'd sat next to him and tapped his arm.

Brock turned to her and saw she had a photo album on her lap. She smiled at him, held one finger to her lips, and opened it.

A birth certificate for Toby James Rosenberg and a picture of what had to be newborn Toby stared back at Brock from the first page.

Oh. My. God. Brock wanted to pull the album over to him, curl up in a corner, and leaf through the entire thing for the rest of the evening.

Instead, he turned the page to see more pictures. A younger, tired Naomi holding a tiny Toby and a very small Sophie grinning at her little brother, the entire family with Naomi on the hospital bed. A lump rose in Brock's throat.

Grandma quietly murmured the names of grandparents and relatives as they turned the pages. Brock watched Toby—and it was hard to connect this adorable baby with the man currently miming throwing boob pads at a heckler—grow from a wrinkly faced newborn into a toddler in the space of several pages.

So many pictures. It was kind of scary how many there were. Not that Brock was complaining, because this was honestly worth the entire drama of getting here, but he couldn't remember his parents ever taking casual, multiple pics of him like this. Was it normal for families to document their kids this much?

They reached Toby at five years old, and it was crazy to see the similarities to adult Toby. Gigi. Facial expressions and obvious signs of personality: Toby covered in crayon, Toby playing dress-up with his sister, Toby hugging his dad fiercely. Brock got those same fierce hugs now.

A loud gasp announced the photo album's discovery. "What the *hell* is going on here?"

Brock looked up in time to see Sophie, Alan, and one of the cousins—Ed?—tackle Gigi to the ground. Gigi reached towards Brock and Grandma, fingers clawing at the carpet and eyes wide. "Don't you *dare* look at those pictures, Brock, so help me—"

"Oh hush, Toby." Grandma waved him away. "Your young man loves these pictures."

"I really do."

Gigi choked and struggled against his relatives.

Sophie was on his back and cursed when he tried to roll over. "Goddamn— Toby, just let it happen."

"Nooo."

"She did it to me too. Believe me, it's better not to fight it."

Alan, who was sitting on Gigi's legs, gave a thumbs-up. "Ten out of ten, would secretly look through adorable baby pics with Grandma again."

Ed chortled, and they high-fived.

Around them, the other Rosenbergs were laughing like this was the funniest shit they'd ever seen. Generally Brock tried not to do anything that prompted Gigi into angry-diva mode—and seeing old pictures of him definitely edged that territory—but it *was* hilarious to watch his wrath being foiled by his sister and entourage.

Brock turned back to the album and ignored Gigi's grunts and swearing. By the time Gigi got free, Brock had almost made it to the end of the album, which was around the start of high school.

Gigi reached for the album, but Brock put down the wineglass so he could grab Gigi's hands and stare up at him.

Gigi was red and panting slightly, hair askew and shirt crushed. "You don't want to look at those."

Brock knew he hated reminders of his high school days, especially visual ones, but Brock thought teenage Toby was adorable. He'd thought that at the time too. So he smiled. "They're awesome, Gi."

Gigi frowned. "I wasn't at my best back then. That wasn't me."

Grandma *pshaw*ed. "Toby, don't be ridiculous. You were so handsome. So much like your dad at that age too."

Brock glanced around, suddenly self-conscious. He was holding his boyfriend's hands in front of Brock's family . . . but no one seemed to care? Everyone was either smiling or distracted by something else.

"*Brock.*"

Brock stared back up at him. Man, he really didn't want people looking at those pics. *Awww.* Brock couldn't do this to him. "We can stop if you want, but I'm really enjoying the album." He pulled Gigi closer, twining their fingers together and trying not to glance around to see people's reactions. "Besides," he said in a low voice, "I liked you back then too, remember?"

Gigi made a strange face, something between happiness and disbelief. "Yeah, well." His voice was slightly shaky. "Your taste always was a little weird."

He gave a deep sigh, then swept up the glass of wine and perched on the arm of the sofa again. This time he leaned against Brock's shoulders so he could look down at the album. Brock tried not to move away from the contact—*this is fine, family is okay*—but he did flinch slightly.

Gigi didn't seem to notice. "You can keep looking, but *just* this one album." He pointed at Grandma. "You hear that, Grandma? No showing him the others when I'm not around."

She wagged her finger at him. "Don't tell me what to do, young man." Then she winked and pointed out a picture of young Gigi dressed up as the Tin Man from the *Wizard of Oz* for Halloween.

Brock took a deep breath. *Okay. We're okay.* "Nice costume."

"I wanted to go as Dorothy, but I knew better." Gigi took a big gulp of wine.

Ed, Sophie, and Alan grinned at them from the floor. Brock wasn't sure what was so funny until Grandma finished showing them the album. Gigi left the room for more wine, and Sophie took the opportunity to perch on the sofa arm.

"You two are cute, you know." Sophie had a knowing smile on her face.

Brock shifted, not sure what to say to that. "Uh-huh?"

"I was totally expecting him to lose his shit when the photos came out, but he didn't. Much." She lightly touched Brock's shoulder. "He let you finish seeing them. True love, Brock, true love."

Somehow he doubted that, given recent events. "Did you let Alan see yours?"

"Once Ed stopped wrestling me, no, of course not." She made a face. "He still got through most of the album though. Grandma's sneaky."

Grandma rolled her eyes and huffed.

Alan raised his glass. "I love you, sweetie. Even with braces and zits."

She covered her face with one hand. "Oh my *God*."

This family was nuts. No one in Brock's family would sneak photo albums or drink wine on the floor or be amused by drag stories. He barely knew his distant relatives, so he thought this was maybe the first time he'd ever seen this many related people in one room. How did Gigi and Sophie cope with them all?

Granted, there weren't so many people in his family that they'd take up all the sofa space in the living room. He had a few cousins who lived in Saskatchewan, and out of all of Brock's grandparents, only one grandmother survived, and he wasn't sure she even had photos of him. When the family *was* together, she'd sit down in the best chair with a Screwdriver and a cigarette to cackle throatily through the conversation. Brock liked his grandmother, but she wasn't anything like Gigi's.

He realized with a jolt that he hadn't spoken with his grandmother in years. He had no idea how she was doing.

Gigi returned and demanded his spot back. Sophie returned to the floor, and Brock forced himself *not* to care when Gigi rested against him again.

"So, lover, when am I going to see your baby pics?" Gigi asked.

Oh God. Even Brock could see the implications. *I just embarrassed myself, so I expect the same thing back. Also: when am I meeting your family?* He had to ask here? In front of all these people?

At a loss, Brock shrugged and went for a neutral answer. "I don't know."

Gigi's eyes narrowed, but when he spoke, his voice was teasing. "Are they that bad?"

See? He always knew what to say. "Yeah."

"Worse than me at two hundred pounds with zits and a bad haircut? I doubt it, boyfriend."

Ohhh shit. There was that steely note in his voice again. He hadn't been teasing, then. Brock watched him sip his wine, acutely aware of how easy it would be to make him happy: *Yeah, I'll show you pictures of me as a kid. Yes, I want you to meet my parents. Yes, I'm glad to be here.*

Experience had taught Brock that easy wasn't ever good or even that easy. Not in the end.

Shit, he was going to have to talk about his family, wasn't he?

The room suddenly seemed way too warm. Like, *really* stuffy. And the Rosenbergs were being really loud. The smells of food and wine and people were way too thick and sour, and Brock felt his stomach twist again.

"I need some air." He lurched to his feet.

Gigi said something in warning, but Brock ignored him and headed for the front door. He paused there, not wanting to go anywhere he could potentially be seen, though he doubted the neighbours would recognize him at this time of night. Maybe he could walk out and duck around the side of the house?

"Babe."

Brock turned around.

Gigi stepped over their bags, which still sat in the entrance, and joined him next to the door. "What's going on with you?"

"Nothing." Brock winced. That was nearly always the wrong thing to say. "I mean . . ." Jesus, he sucked at this. Talking about shit. Especially family shit.

Gigi crossed his arms, wine tucked into one elbow, and waited.

Brock grasped for something. "I like your family." There, that was something, and it was even true. "And all the pictures they have. I mean, they have a *lot*, like a disturbing amount, but when you think about it, it's actually awesome they have so many. And I'm really glad your grandma showed me you as a kid because I loved seeing that."

"Your point?"

"My family doesn't do that. Any of it." Brock hoped Gi would read between the lines. He was usually good at doing that—great, in fact, as sometimes he read stuff between lines that didn't exist, and pissed Brock off in the process.

Gigi frowned, unfolded his arms, and took another slow sip of wine. One long, frowny, unblinking moment later, he said, "I don't follow."

Brock gestured at the living room. "My family's different about those kinds of things. I mean, I don't even know where pictures of me are."

Gigi shifted weight to his other foot and gave a sigh. "Uh-huh. And this meant you needed air?"

"My family isn't like yours."

"No shit, babe." Gigi stepped forward. "You never mention your family, but I get the impression that they're not exactly the never-ending source of laughs and total humiliation that mine is." His free hand reached out and rested on Brock's chest. "Here's the thing though—they raised *you*. So I'm sure they're not as bad as you think, you know?"

There was a lump in Brock's throat. Gigi looked so certain. "Uhhh—"

"So let's try this again." He smiled and his hand moved up to gently squeeze Brock's shoulder. "We're in our crap-hole town for the weekend and you haven't introduced me to your parents. So when am I seeing your baby pics?"

"Um. Never?"

Gigi's face blackened with anger, and his hand tightened on Brock's shoulder. "Oh?"

"Boys?"

Brock turned to see John and Naomi standing there, smiling and flushed with food and wine. Clearly the washing up was done.

"You just standing there for fun?" Naomi asked.

Brock cleared his throat. "Uh, we were, uh . . ."

Gigi turned abruptly and went back into the living room. Flounced, really (he did the hip thing).

Brock refused to be distracted. "*I* was about to take our bags upstairs."

Naomi nodded. "Sure! John will help." She patted her husband's shoulder and followed Gi into the living room.

Oh man. That could've gone better. He still had a lot of stuff to explain to Gigi. But first . . .

Brock looked up at John Rosenberg. He was a tall man, solid but lean, with a defined jaw and silver-threaded sandy hair. There was a brief moment when Gigi's face appeared in John's, and Brock could see how Gigi would look when he reached John's age. The vision made his heart ache.

"You're staying in Toby's old room," John said.

Brock nodded. "Cool. Great. Awesome." *Shut* up, *holy shit.*

John grunted and bent down to pick up several bags. Brock collected what he could, then followed John up the creaking stairs. The stairs and landing were lined with more family pictures, and the floorboards creaked underfoot. On the landing, John led him to the room and pointed out where the bathroom was. Inside, Brock dumped the bags before surveying the space.

"Things are more or less as he left it," John said. "We're hoping you can help him clear it out this weekend. Put in a good word for us."

Brock nodded, a lump in his throat. "You gonna join us downstairs?"

Brock suddenly wanted nothing more than to lie down on the bed and sleep until the weekend was over. No way was he going back down to a pissed-off Gi and a room full of happy, loud people. "Ah, I'm kind of bushed after the drive."

John nodded and clapped Brock's shoulder. "Fair. If you change your mind, you're welcome. Feel free to shower. We'll see you downstairs for breakfast in the morning, but if you need anything, just shout. Sleep well."

Then John left, and Brock was supremely grateful for at least one chill Rosenberg.

So here he was. Gigi's old room. Toby's room. When Brock had been in high school, he'd wondered what it looked like.

The room was medium-sized, with a slight slope in the ceiling near the window. It was too tidy to have been completely frozen at eighteen-year-old Toby, but he got an immediate sense of what teenage Gigi had been like when he was at home. The walls were papered with posters from musicals and movies, a bookcase held multiple DVDs, books, trophies, and video games, and a desk still had folders and notepads on top of it. A few plush toys rested on top of the books, one of which looked like Luna from Sailor Moon.

The thought that he could have seen this room while it was still in use annoyed him a little.

The bed was a twin, and on the floor next to it was an air mattress, sheets and pillows already arranged. This family had put them together without any questions. A lump rose in his throat. Gigi was so lucky.

He began searching through his bag for the sleep shirt, but the room was distracting. His eye kept being caught by a poster or the title of a DVD. When he found his shirt, he gave in and went to the bookcase. Books on theatre and movies, YA and fantasy, and a few children's books fought for space with Mario Kart and Legend of Zelda. The trophies and medals were interesting—mostly drama club–related stuff, but there were a few third-place medals for street dancing dated from Gigi's last year in high school. Brock picked one up: blunt, fake bronze, heavy and meaningful. Had winning this prompted Toby towards dance in university?

The familiar image of teenage Toby came to mind, all hair and acne and big mouth, singing and dancing. A firecracker, sizzling, then erupting when lit. This town had given him shit for his weight, his breathy voice, his theatrical tastes, and his orientation, but he'd given it right back.

Nowadays he was slimmer and his skin was better, but the essentials were still there. If anything, they'd become more pronounced now that he had Gigi LaMore. Now that he *was* Gigi. That teenage wit had sharpened with experience and education; Brock knew because he'd been on the receiving end of it more times than he liked to remember.

But Brock knew him better now, and knew how much it took to take on that shit in the first place, let alone turn it around and give it back.

Coming here had been a mistake. Staying up here to sleep was a mistake. Gigi would see this as the retreat it was and become angrier.

Fuck. Everything Brock did was wrong. Standing here getting all nostalgic over toys and books wasn't going to help with anything.

He used the bathroom, then returned to Gigi's room and changed. He pulled the air mattress away from the bed and put his phone on to charge. Turned out the light and made himself comfy on the mattress while unfamiliar laughter drifted through the floor from below.

Brock woke up as the door opened. When had he fallen asleep? Blearily, he watched Gigi come in, close the door, then strip off and aim for him and his mattress.

This was a surprise.

Brock inched back as Gigi sidled in next to him, moving close so that Gigi's face met his. Wine furred his breath, and his body burned against Brock's. Gigi only wore briefs, his dick so hard it threatened to break free of them. An arm wormed its way around Brock's waist, and Gigi bent to suck on Brock's neck.

"Gi?" Brock murmured in disbelief.

"Mmm. Hey, boyfriend." That arm tightened, and Gigi sucked fiercely.

"What're you doing here?"

That wide mouth split into a smile against Brock's skin. "Wha' does it *feel* like 'm doing?"

Was he serious? After today? "Go sleep in your own bed, Gi."

A hand latched onto Brock's shoulder. "'M pissed off. Still." Gigi's knee rubbed along Brock's leg, working its way between his thighs. "Buh I wanna fuck. An' I know"—fingers fanned on Brock's abdomen—"you're up for tha.'"

True. No matter what arguments they'd had, sex had never been a problem. Brock always loved fucking Gigi, always wanted to touch him and hear his moans and taste his skin. Even now, as Brock let his thighs open and Gigi worked his knee up to press against Brock's balls and dick, Brock could feel the familiar heady rush of knowing it was him, *his* guy, and that his guy wanted him. Usually he gave in to it.

Tonight felt different though. Tonight felt totally disjointed. Like Gigi wanted him, but not in the way he usually wanted him. It was all intertwined with today—how he'd wanted Brock to come here, and how he'd wanted Brock to be funny and chill in front of his family, and how he'd suddenly wanted to know Brock's family, and now *this*? Brock was sick of trying. He couldn't do this as well.

Brock eased back from Gigi's face, gently pushing the knee away. "Not tonight, Gi."

Gigi stopped attacking his neck, head tilting up to stare Brock in the face. "Wha'?"

"You're drunk."

"Not thah drunk. An' we've been drunk before." He leered.

"I don't want to."

Gigi's hands tightened on Brock's skin before he hissed angrily and pulled away. "*Fine.*"

Brock's heart sank. He knew that tone. "Don't . . ."

"Don' *what*, boyfriend? Be mad? You don' wanna be here an' don' wan' me t'meet your family an' now I can't even blow you? *Uggghhh*, 'm *so* mad." Gigi rolled over and stood.

Brock sat up. "Gigi."

"Don't *Gigi* me. I *got* it." He somehow managed the four steps to his bed and got in, back towards Brock. "You can sleep aaall by yourself this weekend. The shop is *closed*."

"Gi . . ."

Gigi waved. "No, no, you sleep withou' me an' *like* it, boyfriend." He shifted around before giving a deep, sad sigh.

Brock was torn between joining him and flipping him the finger. He did neither—just lay back down and rolled the sheets around him. Regret and anger roiled inside him, clenching his stomach tighter. It took a long time for him to fall asleep again.

CHAPTER FOUR

Three months ago

Gigi gave herself one last look in the mirror, checking her curves were in place, her boobs were sitting well, and her tuck was neat. Leotards hid nothing, and the stage at Woody's was tiny.

A twenties chorus girl gazed back at her. Stylized, of course, because LaMore wasn't simply a cardboard cutout from a line of identical girls. Sparkly leotard and matching heels, feather boa and headpiece, accentuated rosebud lips, come-fuck-me eyes, and enough diamonds to see her through to retirement.

Well . . . "Diamonds." Chorus girls only earned so much. But damn, she was looking fierce! Channelling chorus-girl chic tonight, honey! Marilyn Monroe and Jane Russell would shrivel in their heels if they could see LaMore. Gigi gave a wiggle, just to see the right things jiggle, then executed a perfect turn and strode from the dressing room to the wings.

Her friend, Miss Molly Maneater, was just stepping off the stage as Gigi approached it from the wings.

"Oooh, girl, you look like you're husband hunting tonight," Molly said.

Gigi arched one elegantly shaped brow. "Who says I'm not?"

"Your boyfriend might have something to say about that," one of the bar staff, Jason, muttered.

Awww, cute. "Keeps him on his toes."

Molly laughed and whacked Gigi with a fan. "You're terrible."

"What's the crowd like? You warm them up for me?"

"Please. Enjoy my sloppy seconds and I'll try not to embarrass you at the bar later."

Gigi cackled. "You nasty bitch."

"I'll have a cosmo waiting for you."

Molly stepped away, and Jason gestured Gigi forward. The host for this evening was wrapping up one of his awful jokes, and Gigi danced a little on the spot to keep up her energy. She liked the chorus girl routine, but it needed her to be warmed up, flexible, and to keep her wits about her.

The host got a round of groans and applause, then Gigi was introduced. She double-checked her wig and headpiece, tossed back her shoulders, and danced onto the stage.

Here's how the routine went down: she danced on like she was part of a chorus line, then was surprised to find she'd gone on stage without the other girls and was *so* embarrassed, and would you believe those bitches? Like, maybe she could perform for the audience anyway because working girls like her were always looking for their big break. Cue the big startled eyes and fluttery eyelashes, work the room, work the room, then segue into a song and dance routine, can-can, because that was always expected and appreciated, and finish off, ideally draped over a willing audience member. And they were *always* willing.

Tonight's song was Eartha Kitt's "An Englishman Needs Time," only Gigi had changed up *Englishman* for *Canadian* and adjusted a few lyrics to be more relevant to her fellow Canucks. It usually went down like Molly on a fireman—loud and enjoyable for everyone concerned.

She got through to the part where she was surprised at being alone on stage, then minced forward to pick up the microphone where the host had nicely left it for her—downstage, front and centre, on the floor. As she bent over and picked it up, whistles erupted.

"Now, now, boys," she breathed into the microphone. "Behave."

"Bend over again!" someone shouted.

"Are you hung like a god and able to lift me with one arm?" Gigi asked. "Because if not, pay me." Laughter from the crowd. "I'm supposed to be up here with a whole line of girls, but somehow I'm here all on my own-some." She pouted and there was a resounding

Awww. "I mean, what's a girl to do? I work so *hard*—" yells and whistles "—and I go home simply *aching*, you know, from all this *hard work*, and then this shady shit happens." She tossed her head. "Well, don't you know, I can perform on my own! I'll show those bitches. I've been working on a thing. You wanna see my thing?" Roars of affirmation. "You do? Oh my *gosh*, you're too sweet! It's just a little thing."

She lowered her voice back to its normal level. "Well, actually, it's a *big* thing. The rumours are true. I feel like I have a roll of loonies between my legs."

Back to her higher pitch. "I hope you like it!" She turned around, wiggled a little as she took her place, then made a sign to Jason. "This is a small number I've been working on, and I'm singing it for my favourite kind of man." She waited a beat. "Alive." Laughter. "I mean *Canadian*, sillies!" Whoops and cheers. Such a patriotic bunch.

Gigi loved this. The innuendo, the playacting, the freedom to deliberately camp it up and be her sexy feminine self. She'd never had this as a kid, and every time she was on stage, she revelled in it. It was like breathing. Sort of. Hiding herself away since being a baby queen meant she deserved her moments here. Dancing in glitter and heels, in front of an audience of gorgeous men, was where she was born to be.

She was a performer. An entertainer. Nothing like the beauty queens waiting in the wings for their slots, bedecked in their perfect costumes and flawless contouring, here for the attention and the clothes without acknowledging the *performance*, the history. A lot of them had the personality of a clothes hanger. Appropriate, considering that was all they essentially were. Drag as art was all well and good, but connecting with your audience was art*work*, baby. And Gigi knew how to *work*.

So she did. She sashayed, she spun, she danced around, she flirted with the audience, she made them laugh, she gathered *muhneh bitches*, then she left them wanting more. That was how LaMore rolled.

And by the time she reached the bar—still in leotard and heels and batting away drinks offers on the way—to find Molly and the promised cosmo, she was feeling pretty damn amazing.

Molly handed her the cosmo, and they saluted each other with their drinks. "Good set, hunty."

Gigi preened. "Oh, that old thing?"

They took ladylike sips of their drinks.

Molly gestured at the stage and the young queen speaking vacuously on it. "Look at this tone-dead cow. Jesus Christ. Which do you think she smoked first—pot or meth?"

"It's inexcusable." The queen was lovely, but in the pre-twenty-two way. Girl was going to pack it on once she grew up. "Especially after you showed them how it's done."

Molly was one of the blessed drag queens—beautiful *and* funny. Right now, she wasn't looking so hot: one eye was smudged slightly from sweating under the lights, and the curls in her black hair were falling out already. She was forever complaining about how Asian hair just did not curl well, and Gigi kept telling her to get a haircut and buy some more damn wigs already if her own hair was so difficult. Not that Gigi could be too bitchy—wigs were expensive, and Molly's natural hair *was* gorgeous.

"I wonder how long we'll be doing this," Molly said. The sass had dropped from her voice, and Gigi glanced at her. She looked super serious.

"Queens can go for decades, baby. You know that."

"Yeah. It's just . . . I don't know. So tiring, you know? And these upstarts don't give me hope for the future."

"Hey, bitch, some of us upstarts *are* the hope for the future."

Molly smiled at her, then sipped her martini. "It's just . . . I wonder what else is out there, you know?"

What had brought this on? This wasn't normally Molly. Gigi glanced her over, glanced around the bar, then hit on it. "Your beau broke up with you?"

Molly grimaced. "Third one this year. Kinda makes you think there's something wrong with you."

"Nope. You're looking fine and everyone here wants you. Go out and get another." Gigi pointed out a particularly fine specimen of shirtless man.

"Baby, wanting *me* isn't the problem. I'm not Molly all the time—*that's* the problem." She gave a deep sigh, then shimmied in her chair as if to shake off her funk. "But you're right! Plenty of fish to be had." She smiled at Gigi. "Speaking of fish, where's your guppy?"

Good question. Gigi dug into her handbag for her phone and found a message from Brock: *Running late. Sorry.*

"Not here."

Molly raised her eyebrows. "But he will be?"

"Yeah." Suddenly in a sour mood, Gigi drained her cosmo and turned around to order another. A nearby guy paid for her drink (of course), and she and Molly began the terribly easy task of reading the other queens while flirting with the guys lingering near them for attention.

In the back of her mind, though, Gigi wasn't enjoying it. Like, it wasn't difficult to get to Church Street from Brock's fancy hipster workplace in downtown. This was, what, the fifth time Brock had come late? And this time he'd actually missed her routine. Gigi LaMore didn't come out to play every week, so if he missed the show, he missed the point of being here—well, apart from spending time with his incredible queen, which totally went without saying.

Like, wasn't the whole point of being in a relationship with someone to *be* with them? To spend time doing the stuff they liked to do? Supporting them? Brock had been great at that until his stupid job. What the hell was he doing there that was so much more interesting than being here? Because Gigi wasn't sure *anything* outdid bitchy queens for entertainment.

Not least, he was missing Molly's superb takedowns. God, the girl's vocabulary was so extensive it should have its own condom size.

She glanced at her phone again. At this rate, he'd get there when LaMore was about to wilt into a bucket of streaky makeup and eyelash glue, at which point Rosenberg would rise up and fret. LaMore wasn't the type to *fret*. No. Not at all. She'd cool her heels, then strike—

"Sorry I'm late."

Oh my goodness, that voice. If she weren't tucked, she'd have an embarrassing costume problem to deal with. As it was, she just had a painful costume problem.

But wait, she wasn't supposed to be turned on just from hearing him. She was supposed to be angry with him for being so late. Okay, here was the plan: Chill. Grace. Serenity. Professionalism.

She flipped her hair and turned around. "Glad you decided . . . to . . ."

He was wearing a tight tank that showed off his arms, jeans that showed off his dick, and eyeliner. Combined with a light sheen of sweat from the summer heat covering his skin, and the evil smile on his face as he eyed her up and down, Gigi was ready to *swoon* into that bucket.

That expression should be criminal. So should those jeans. Goddamn her baby for looking so good.

Fuck it. She was only human.

She jumped at him and wrapped her arms around his amazing shoulders. Serenity and grace was for later in life, right? Wisdom and age, blah, blah, blah.

Oooh. Strong arms pressed her against a hard body, sending fireworks through her. *Come to Mama.*

His breath was hot on her ear. "Hey, beautiful."

She'd heard those words so many times before, but damn it if they didn't make her feel all warm and bubbly anyway. "Hel*lo* handsome."

He huffed in amusement, then tilted his head to kiss her cheek. Carefully, so he didn't smear the inch or two of makeup on there. Boy had learned well. "When are you going on?"

Oh, right.

Molly was shaking her head when Gigi pulled away from him and clocked him with her best icy glare. "Already happened, sweetie. You missed it."

Brock's face fell.

Oh. Shit. That hadn't been his intention.

And it looked like Gi had done the chorus girl routine too. Damn it. He liked that one.

Brock tried to figure out just how mad she was, but it was sometimes difficult because she was so good at pretending to be mad. "I'm sorry. I had this one last thing to wrap up, and it took longer than I thought and—"

He was cut off by one elegantly manicured finger placed on his lips. Gigi's eyes glinted in the bar lights. "I'm not angry, honey."

Uh-huh, she was *really* mad.

"I'm just disappointed."

Nail-scratchingly mad.

"I expected better of you."

Brock tried not to wince. He hated disappointing his boyfriend, especially when he was his girlfriend. LaMore's anger was just *so* much worse than Rosenberg's. Brock wasn't sure if it was because she could be so much more cutting, but it was totally scary being on the receiving end of it.

Honestly, he wasn't sure if he was up to dealing with it tonight. Working a full-time job was on a whole other level to studying, and he was tired in a way he'd never been before. He'd just wanted to come here and hang out with his queen. And okay, he'd missed the performance part, but he'd seen it already. It wasn't like Gi had time to look for *him* especially while she was on stage, so why did it matter?

He knew better than to say any of that out loud.

But she did look amazing, even when she was lecturing him. Sometimes *especially* when she was lecturing him. Brock didn't know what it was about her—the makeup should've been weird, but was sexy and artistic in a way he still didn't understand. The way Gi could slither, dance, and just *move* differently according to who was in control was also sexy. The sheer fuss of the dresses and feathers and glitter was overwhelming, but awesome in a fancy, bright, fun way. All that, the feminine mannerisms and the occasional male edge freaking *got* to Brock. He loved how the whole gender thing played out in drag. There was something really powerful about it, and about Gigi, no matter whether she was LaMore or Rosenberg.

Man, he was so lucky. He *needed* Gi on levels he was still trying to understand.

So, no, he couldn't let her be seriously angry with him. That was the last thing he wanted.

He opened his lips and mouthed her finger, sucking it and rolling his tongue around it.

Gigi narrowed her eyes, the grey of them barely visible through the curtain of fake lashes. "What are you doing?"

Brock reached up and took her hand, keeping it near his mouth. "Saying sorry." Then he sucked her finger some more, keeping his eyes on hers.

Sometimes it was difficult to tell, but he *thought* she was blushing.

"You think good tongue is gonna save you?" Her voice had gone slightly breathy.

"If you need help making a decision," Molly remarked, "I volunteer as very willing tribute."

"That's not how these games work," Gigi snapped.

"Fuckin' shame."

Brock teased another finger into his mouth and tried not to smile when he saw her swallow. Yup. He'd rescued this.

"You," she cooed, "are a very bad boy."

"'M sorry."

"And you're talking with your mouth full."

"Mmffmm."

She leaned in closer. "Madame is going to teach you a lesson tonight."

Brock couldn't *wait*.

He slipped her fingers out of his mouth and kissed her hand. "I hope so, madame."

She lifted her chin. "Got anything else to say?"

He tugged her closer to him so he could run his hands along her waist and hips. Knowing that under the padding and cloth and mascara and lingerie there was a very toned and hard male body was *such* a goddamn turn on. "Can I buy you and your sister a drink?"

Molly fanned herself. "Oh my days, he's well trained."

Gigi tilted her head slightly, a small puzzled line appearing between her brows. Brock wasn't sure what that look meant. Had he said the wrong thing? Asking to buy a queen a drink was never a wrong move though. Never. Well, almost never. It looked like Gigi had been expecting him to say something else. But what? What more could Brock do except be there and be sorry?

Gigi suddenly grinned, sending relief swimming through Brock. "You can indeed, boyfriend."

He leaned forward and gently kissed her, then got their drinks orders and leaned on the bar. Disaster was averted tonight, but man, he needed a drink now. He'd have to be on time for the next performance. Brock could totally handle that.

CHAPTER FIVE

Gigi woke up to a dry mouth, deep headache, and full bladder, and he burrowed his face into his pillow with a groan. His mom's infamous wine cabinet had struck again. Ugh. Had he even made it to the bathroom last night? Had he brushed his teeth and washed the journey off him?

Wait.

No. No, he had not.

Not that he remembered much, but he *did* remember his top priority when going to bed, and it sure as hell wasn't getting clean.

He forced his eyes open. His clothes were where he'd left them last night, crumpled over his suitcase. Brock wasn't where he'd left him though. The air mattress was slightly deflated and the sheets on it were crumpled. Gigi was alone in his room.

He'd epically fucked up. All he could remember was wanting Brock, the smell and feel of him. He'd gotten that, but he'd also been pushed back. Brock hadn't wanted to fuck him, because why would he? Drunk and desperate was *such* a good look on a queen. Especially when it was followed by drunk and sad. Real classy.

Damn it, Brock had worn that hurt expression again, hadn't he? Bitching had happened, so probably.

Gigi groaned again and covered his face. He was stupid. *So stupid.* What the hell was wrong with him? What was he doing?

Being back with his family felt way better than he'd anticipated. Unbelievably, he'd missed all the teasing and the affection. It was good to see Sophie happy with Alan. And having Brock at the table had left a small glow in Gigi's chest. His people, all around one table.

Even if Brock had barely eaten or said anything and looked perpetually trapped in the headlights. Ugh, awkward. Would it kill the guy to relax?

Then the small glow had been totally wiped out when Brock said he didn't want Gigi to meet his family, then avoided him by going to bed early. Sure. Right. Like Gigi hadn't seen straight through that, the idiot. How were they supposed to deal with this weekend together if they weren't actually together? Though Gigi could tell the guy was trying. He'd said he liked Gigi's family, which was something. After all, Gigi's family wasn't that bad. Gigi's family weren't the people to be wary of in Maney. They both knew that.

Though, Gigi had to admit that after three hours of *Toby this* and *Toby that* and *Toby, you've sure lost a lot of weight*, he'd been ready to get away from them too. He'd braced himself for being called Toby again, and okay it wasn't exactly wrong because, hey, *it was his name*, but it just wasn't who he was anymore. So he'd climbed the stairs absolutely aching to hear his name, and Brock had delivered right away.

Of course he had. Gigi had been very clear on that from the start. Right from the first time Brock approached him in QS Dance, Gigi's dance school.

Gigi had wrapped up his first lesson with Mark, his hetebro competition partner, and had bumped into Brock in the hallway. Brock had recognized him by then, but it had taken like two days. Gigi wasn't sure how he'd felt about that. Queen lost a bit of weight and dyed her hair, and suddenly she was unrecognizable? After *their* history? Hmmm. In any case, the first time Brock had called him out as Toby had been then, in that hallway, when Gigi was all tired and sweaty after a practice session, and Gigi had instantly replied, "It's *Gigi* now."

Brock had blinked, then warily said, "Gigi. You remember me?"

Of course he had. How could he not? The high school crush who'd crushed him. Gigi couldn't decide what was worse: that he was back or that he was so fucking hot. How could a T-shirt and jeans be so sexy on someone. *How*?

He still looked good in a T-shirt and jeans, but he'd put on a little weight since starting his job. Gigi suspected that same shirt would be tighter now. Not that that was necessarily a *bad* thing.

The second and last time they'd "discussed" his name, they'd been dating for two months. Brock had stayed over, and they had been lying in bed in a post-sex, pre-breakfast haze. Gigi had been trying not to stare at the scars slashing down Brock's side when Brock had retrieved the pillows from the floor in order for them to lie comfortably.

Once they'd resettled, Brock had begun stroking his fingers along Gigi's shoulder and arm. One long, delicious sweep down, then back up. Gigi closed his eyes, ready to be lulled back to sleep by the sensation.

"Can I ask you a question?" Brock said quietly.

"You just did."

The sweeping paused, and Gigi's skin was lightly flicked. "Hey."

"Course, sugarplum."

"Why do you prefer being called 'Gigi' now?"

Gigi opened his eyes to look at Brock. He was staring at the ceiling, face calm and nonchalant. Avoiding his gaze? No good. Gigi reached over and gently pulled Brock's chin towards him. "Gigi is who I am. Toby is who I was."

A small crease appeared between Brock's brows. "But . . . your drag performance is Gigi LaMore. Right? You don't do drag all the time. You're not her all the time."

What the hell was he talking about? Gigi LaMore was like an amplification of who he was. She dazzled and preened and danced the way he sometimes didn't let himself do as a male dancer. She played and brought out deep parts of himself that he'd refused to keep hidden any longer. She was fierce. Beautiful. Rude. Unapologetic.

Gigi Rosenberg was those things too, but he was less rude and more apologetic. Gigi LaMore had adorers and a stage; Gigi Rosenberg had friends and three jobs.

Toby, on the other hand, had a weight problem and hated attention. Toby raged. Toby hid. Toby was no fucking more, not if Gigi had anything to do with it.

"No, but she's me, and I'm her." Gigi rubbed his thumb along Brock's jaw, enjoying the stubble prickle. "We're different sides of the same person."

"I get that, but your sister called you Toby the other week, and you didn't care about that."

And now Gigi regretted putting Sophie on speakerphone so she could meet Brock. "Family's different."

"How?"

Gigi shrugged. "They know all of me and love me. And they always have."

Brock's mouth twisted. "I . . . Oh."

"Plus my parents wouldn't really get it, even though they love me and what I do. And I don't mind *them* calling me by the name they gave me. I put them through enough shit." He really had. Sometimes Gigi wondered how they'd put up with him, especially through all that trouble at school and his *Rent* phase.

"But no one else calls you that?"

Gigi gripped Brock's jaw, making sure they stared into each other's eyes. "No one," he enunciated clearly.

Brock's lips thinned.

Aww. He didn't look happy. Time to fix that. "You know what else no one else calls me?" Gigi inclined his head forward and kissed Brock on that tense mouth. "Their boyfriend."

Brock's face had cleared into a smile. He'd pulled Gigi closer for more kissing, which had led to more touching and then to one of the best morning blowjobs Gigi had ever had.

And Brock had never raised the question again. He'd never needed to. Instead it had been Gigi, and on occasion *Ms. LaMore*, and on very special occasions *madame*, but no more mentions of *Toby*.

Being back here, surrounded by family members, Gigi was rethinking that whole "family's different" thing. Because it did feel strange now.

It's only for a weekend. Like it even matters that *much.*

Inside, LaMore shook her head.

Gigi rolled to a sitting position and groaned when his head complained. Jesus. *Jesus.* He was never drinking again.

Along with being a drunk asshole last night, there was one other little problem he definitely had to talk to Brock about: Brock's family. Brock hadn't mentioned them much—at all? Gigi couldn't remember—since they'd started dating, which in retrospect was raising all sorts of alarms for Gigi. Like, he'd never seen Brock calling them or arranging stuff with them, which *was* weird.

Gigi remembered Brock's mom and dad. He'd seen them at school sports days and occasionally around town, and Gigi's mom went to a book club with Brock's mom. They seemed pretty quiet and nice. So what was the deal there? Obviously Brock was uncomfortable with them . . . right? This wasn't a thing where he was ashamed of Gigi?

Wait.

Brock *was* out to them, right? Right. Like, how could he not be?

See, this was why they had to talk shit out. Otherwise Gigi just reacted (like last night) and didn't understand what was going on.

He stood, pulled on his *EXPERT READER* shirt so he wore something more appropriate than boxers and regret, and made his way downstairs to the kitchen. In it were his cousins Ed and Sarah, eating at the table, and Grandma making scrambled eggs on the stove.

"Morning, Toby," Ed and Sarah choroused.

"Hey. Where's Brock?"

They both shrugged. Grandma turned from the stove. "Your young man was up with the lark. I made him eggs. You want some eggs?"

He knew Grandma's eggs. They were buttery and creamy and cheesy and had bacon bits. His stomach screamed, *Yes*, while his head bit down with a vicious, *Girl, hell no.* "Not today, Grandma."

She fixed him with a familiar glare. "You're a growing boy."

Gigi went digging in the fridge for something healthy. "Twenty-five is when most people stop growing. I'm officially on the road to death, Grandma." He pulled out fruit and yogurt while Ed and Sarah scoffed behind him.

"'The road to death'? You talk about death to *me*? Oh, Toby," Grandma sighed.

"Grandma, you still got a *long* way to go." Gigi kissed her cheek before moving to the blender.

"See? I'd never get away with that," Ed said to Sarah.

"Good morning, honey." Mom had come into the kitchen.

Gigi waved at her before creating a breakfast smoothie. When he was done, she was pouring herself a cup of coffee. He turned to her. "Mom, have you seen Brock?"

She nodded. "He went out to get groceries with Alan and Sophie."

"He . . . did?"

"Yeah. We needed extra for lunch with the Wongs. They're arriving today."

Gigi frowned. "Lunch?"

Mom looked exasperated. "You didn't read the emails, did you?"

Emails?

"There's a schedule," Ed said.

Schedule?

"Your job this morning is to help your dad clean the rec and dining rooms."

Job?

"But I—"

"After that, you're having lunch with all of us." Mom sipped her coffee. "Then it's the bachelor party in the afternoon and evening, while Sophie has a girls' night here."

Bachelor party? "Mom, what the hell?" Gigi burst out.

Mom rolled her eyes. "Honey, you really have to stay on top of these things."

"It's after ten! Why didn't anyone wake me up earlier?"

"Brock said you were sleeping."

"I was, but *bachelor party*? I might want more warning than *three hours* for a bachelor party!"

"Chill, coz," Ed said. "It's no big deal. It's only orienteering, then dinner."

Orienteering? Orien-fucking-teering? Weren't there better options for partying than tromping around nature with a compass and no dignity?

Mom's mouth twitched. "Read your emails, Tobias, then hop to it. We need to clean this place up." She topped up her coffee, then walked out, leaving Gigi with his jaw open and a smoothie in hand.

Bachelor party?

Bachelor party?

Since when were he and Brock invited to straight bachelor parties? Gigi set his smoothie down, afraid he'd drop it. Oh fuck no. What was it going to involve? Strippers? Pinky's, the dive bar? What did straight guys do on bachelor nights besides bellow at each other and drink shots? Would he have to bellow at them too?

Fuck. Damn it. *Fuck.* Hell in a handbasket.

"I think he might want those eggs now, Grandma," Ed remarked.

"If you're not going to be helpful, go away," Gigi snapped.

What he wanted was advice on how to deal with a straight bachelor party. Seeing as his family would be useless on principle, that left Gigi with only one person he trusted to give him the real deal on straight dude herd behaviour. Gigi downed his smoothie in one go, washed up, then returned to his bedroom and his phone.

There were a few texts from friends, which he ignored in favour of finding Mark's number and calling it. Mark was straight. Mark would have the answers to everything. Mark would also take Gigi seriously, unlike certain cousins downstairs or Gigi's friend Tyler, who'd just laugh at him. Mark had let Gigi whip him into shape for the dance routine last summer—not literally whip, though Gigi had been tempted at times—and Gigi figured if anyone could help him in this, his hour of need, it would be the Most Hetero of Heteros, Mark.

"Bro!" Mark cried. "Nice to hear from you! But, dude, is your sister's wedding a slow burn or something?"

"Huh?"

"Why are you calling me?" There was a rustle like Mark had settled against something soft. "Not that I don't appreciate it, bro, but I totally thought you'd be, like, blasted the entire weekend."

"That part's coming." Gigi paced around his room. "The bachelor party is the rest of today. I had no idea it was happening or that I'd be *invited* to it."

"Didn't read the emails, eh?"

Gigi huffed. What the hell was with everyone and this email-reading thing? "I've never been to a straight bachelor party and I don't know what to do. Help me out, Marky Mark."

"Dude. *Dude.*" Gigi could tell Mark had a huge grin on his face. "I'm like legit touched. I don't think anyone's called me for advice before. Except for Cal, when he was trying to write an economics paper this one time."

Cal being Mark's little brother. Gigi snapped his fingers. "Stay on track, sweetie, I don't have much time. What do straight guys do? Do they do hetero versions of gay stuff or what?"

"I have like *no* idea what gay bachelor parties are like, so what am I supposed to compare against?"

"*Mark*. Focus."

Mark chuckled. "Sometimes we go do manly things together, like paintball or hockey or go-karting. Mostly we get drunk and hit up bars or clubs and talk about girls."

Gigi shut his eyes. "Hnnn. No. I mean, okay, I figured about the drinking and girl talk, but what else? Do straight guys fight?"

"Not unless there's an asshole in the group."

"Is there always a stripper?"

"Dude, there is never a stripper. That's, like, a total stereotype."

"What do I do if there *is* a stripper?"

"Uh. Watch, then tip her?"

"Do straight guys bellow?"

"What?"

A door opened below, and Sophie shouted, "We're baaack!"

Gigi winced. Shit. The walls were thin here. Maybe it was just as well sex hadn't happened last night.

"Duuude," Mark said excitedly, "was that your sister? She sounds hot."

Gigi gasped. "Oh. My. God. You didn't just say that."

"I totally did."

"My *sister*, dude!" Gigi was hissing now. "You can't say that about my very happily engaged sister! The one whose *wedding* I'm here for! Take it back!"

"Tell her congrats. Relax, Gi, you'll be fine. I mean, I wouldn't go all drag queen on them and start talking about tucking—actually, yeah, totally nix any talk about *that* unless they, like, ask—but hey, maybe they'd be cool with that anyway? Feel them out. You're a dude too, you know. Dudes can be dudes together, even if they're different kinds of dude. And if anyone gets, like, homophobic or starts shit, text me their names and I'll take care of it."

Oh, what could Mark do from Toronto? Absolutely sweet nothing, that was what. But the gesture did make Gigi feel better. Mark was right after all. He was a man, and straight guys were men too. And if he could squeeze into a glittery minidress and dance on stage in heels, he could do this. "Okay. Okay. Thanks, Marky Mark."

"No probs, Gi. You got Brock as your plus one, bud?"

Gigi froze. "Yeah."

"See, you're golden. He's got your back. Good talk, bro. Go drink." Mark hung up on him. Gigi stared at his phone, then took a deep breath and went downstairs.

He found Sophie, Alan, and Brock unpacking groceries in the kitchen, food littered around the kitchen and their coats still on. Their faces were slightly pink from the exercise and they all looked *happy*, the traitors. They stopped short, eyes uniformly wide.

"Hey, bro," Sophie said after a beat. "Nice shirt."

"*Bachelor party?*"

Brock sighed deeply while Sophie victory-punched the air and Alan cursed.

"I told you to read the emails," Brock told him.

Gigi's jaw dropped. "You did *not*, you big fat liar."

"I did. Multiple times."

When? When had Brock told him that? Was it when he was plotting to *not come at all* or when he'd decided to deny his boyfriend baby pics? Oooh, Gigi was going to—

Wait. Alan had been digging in his wallet; he now handed a ten-dollar note to Sophie. What the hell? "You *bet* on me?" Gigi heard his voice squeak. Oh, *ugh*.

Sophie grinned. "Yup."

"Have you had breakfast?" Alan asked. "Your grandma made the awesome eggs."

Brock was frowning. "Aren't you cold like that?"

Gigi flung his hands wide. "Maybe one of you could tell me why the hell someone invited me to a straight bachelor party?"

Sophie rolled her eyes. "See, babe, this is what I was talking about. I can put him in time-out if you don't want him to go."

Alan shook his head. "Nah. All the men in our families are going." He smiled at Gigi. "I want you there too. It's just orienteering, food, and drinking. Nothing crazy. No stress."

But that sounded like it was *the rest of the day*. This was so unfair. He hadn't signed up for this. Gigi thought he'd get his boyfriend alone and talk out last night, then shower and eat and be fussed over by his parents and hide from Maney until the actual wedding. He'd imagined walking in the woods *a little* with Brock and bitching about people they both knew. He'd imagined having time for a few quickies when there weren't people in the house. Now it sounded like he wasn't going to get any downtime at all. This was unreal.

He still had to talk to Brock, family and bachelor shenanigans or not.

"We need to get this food put away." Brock held up two large bags of milk, his big arms lifting them easily. Gigi glared at him; how *dare* he remind Gigi of his sexiness right now? Gigi grabbed them from him and headed to the fridge.

"I'm looking forward to lunch," Sophie chattered as she gathered their reusable bags. She shared a sickeningly sweet smile with Alan. "Our families eating together for the first time."

Ugh. Spare him. Like this place needed more people in it.

Gigi somehow found space for the milk bags, then returned to Brock. "I need to talk to you."

Brock kept his eyes on the groceries he was unpacking. "In a minute."

The landline phone rang, and Sophie pounced on it. "Hello?"

"How about now?"

Brock tightened his jaw. "In a *minute*."

Sophie turned around. "Brock, it's for you."

Brock went *white*. He stared at Sophie like she'd spoken in an alien language, then walked over to the phone and took it. "Hi?"

Gigi glared at him. Talk about fortunate timing. He turned around and began stacking vegetables, totally listening in on his boyfriend's side of the conversation.

"Good." Pause. "Yeah. Last-minute trip. Um. For a wedding?" Pause. "It's good." Pause. "Good." Pause. "Uh, with a friend." Pause. "Sorry, it's been—" Long pause. "I can't really—" Another long pause. "No, that's not what— Dad, come on—" Pause. "Sure. No, I'll come to you. See you soon."

He hung up, gave a sigh, then said, "I'm going to my parents' for lunch."

Gigi turned around. "What?"

"Oh, that's a shame." Sophie was standing with a bag of onions in hand. "We'll miss you here."

Brock looked tired. All the flushed happiness that had been there when he'd walked into the kitchen was now gone.

God, *what* was the big deal? Gigi walked over to him. "I thought you didn't speak to your parents."

"I . . ."

"Uh-huh. I'm coming with you."

Sophie made a noise of protest but was totally drowned out by Brock's firm, "No."

"*Excuse me?*"

There was a beat where no one said anything. Gigi stared at him, waiting, and when Brock cursed quietly, Sophie and Alan left the kitchen with some excuse that Gigi didn't bother listening to.

"It's complicated." Brock's voice was quiet.

"You never talk about them, and you don't speak to them, and suddenly you're dropping our stuff to see them? And you don't want me to come. Explain it to me."

Brock dragged his hand through his hair. "Look, they're not nice people, okay?"

Gigi glanced out the kitchen door, certain his mom and half his family was there eavesdropping. "So what? They're still your parents. That's like a thing. You've met mine, why can't I meet yours? If you want to have lunch with them, can't they come here?"

"No!" Brock's eyes were wide. He shut them and took a deep breath. When he spoke, his voice was lower. "No. They can't."

What the fuck? "Why not?"

Brock's fingers tightened around two cans of chopped tomatoes. "Because they're *really* not nice people. You should be here with your family. You'll have more fun."

"What the literal fuck? Don't *I* get a say in this? How about I don't listen to this crap and come along anyway?"

Brock glared at him, letting go of the cans. "This is lunch, Gi, not the end of the world."

Gigi leaned in so they were face-to-face. "You are staying in *my parents'* house. You have met *my family* multiple times. You have met my *entire* family now. And you're telling me that I can't meet *your parents?*"

"That's exactly what I'm saying." Brock's mouth twisted. "Seriously, this is not a big deal, and it's better if you—"

"Fuck you. It *is* a big deal. What is it? Is it me?" Gigi gestured to himself, aware his T-shirt was maybe not the best choice for a conversation like this. "Are you ashamed of me? Don't want to introduce a flaming queen as your boyfriend? Am I too *queer* for your parents? You *are* at least out to them, right?"

"Shut *up,*" Brock snarled, making Gigi take a step back. "Have you *ever* thought that maybe not everything is about *you*? I want to see *my* parents by *my*self. This is *my* business. There is *nothing* more to it than that. Why the fuck is that so difficult for you? Get your head out your ass, Gi, and leave me the *fuck* alone." He turned around and stomped out.

Gigi stood in his boxers, T-shirt, and bare feet, abruptly cold.

What the fuck.

Where had that come from?

Was he that pissed off at being here that he'd be this harsh?

Because he had another think coming if he thought this was the end of it.

Gigi went after him, only to be brought up short at the door by Mom stepping in his way. She was frowning, and her hand was firm as she gripped Gigi's shoulder to stop him ducking around her. "Honey, I couldn't help overhearing—"

"Mom, I need to—"

"Stop, Toby."

He stopped, focusing on her now.

She put both her hands on his shoulders. "Listen to me. I know you're upset. And I get why. But you need to calm down."

Calm down? *Calm down*? "My so-called *boyfriend*—"

"Is also very upset. You won't reach any kind of understanding if you're both this angry." Mom looked sad and worried. Last night Gigi had noticed grey in her hair and how there seemed to be more lines around her face, but right now she resembled the mom he remembered from high school, the one who told him he'd get through all the bad times and be better for them.

"But I haven't even *spoken* to his parents, Mom!"

"I know. It sounds like you have a lot to talk about. But you have to *talk* about it, not hiss at each other in the kitchen." Her hands came off his shoulders. "I think Brock has a lot on his plate. When you speak to him, be the kind young man I know you can be, all right?" She brushed her fingers through his hair. "You're all bedhead. It's like you're a teenager again."

Gigi rolled his eyes. "You think *Brock* has a lot on his plate? Mom, he's not the one who has to balance like three jobs and is perpetually broke and whose hometown remembers him as the fat gay kid. He wasn't even *out* when he was here."

"Toby, everyone has problems. And you have to move on from all that. It's in the past." She smiled. "Remember, this weekend is about your sister and your new brother-in-law."

Oh. *Oh*. Was that *so*? Gigi glared. "Don't worry, Mom. I'll make sure my gay drama doesn't interrupt the straights' happy day."

Her mouth dropped open. "Toby. No. That's not what I meant and you know it. We're your family. *Alan* is your family. We love you and we'll help both of you through this if you want us to. But Brock did have a point: this weekend is not about you."

Yup, that was the mother he remembered from his teen years. She was right—of course she was right—but now he felt like Toby again. Pissed off and frustrated. Guilt sunk in, and he felt himself finally calm down.

Well, Toby might be surfacing, but there was still a fully-bloomed Gigi in control. He could be pissed off and frustrated, but *gracefully*.

"Mom, I'll be lucky to age as well as you have," he informed her.

She scoffed. "Is that a compliment? I've had better."

"Thanks for the advice."

She stroked his hair back. "Anything for my favourite son."

"I'm your only son."

"Not for much longer." She smiled as he began spluttering. "Go shower, and if you see Brock, tell him it's safe to help me prepare food before he goes."

Free to move now, Gigi went looking for his boyfriend. He wasn't in the dining room, rec room, laundry room, or in Gigi's old room. He didn't seem to be in the house at all. Gigi glanced out the front door to see their rental car missing from the driveway.

What.

The.

Actual.

Shit.

He'd just skipped out? Without telling anyone?

What was going on with him? That wasn't like him. Seriously, he was turning into someone Gigi barely recognized. The Brock of their first six months wouldn't have just left like that or pushed him away last night or flipped out on him in the kitchen just now.

Though, that Brock was also the quiet one who hadn't ever mentioned his parents. What he *had* said was he didn't talk to them much and they weren't nice people, but that didn't seem true if he was going to their place for lunch.

So what was going on? Now that Gigi was staring at an empty driveway instead of his boyfriend's face, it all seemed totally weird. Especially since Brock didn't do things he didn't want to.

Well. Except come here. That was kind of a big one.

What if he *didn't* want to introduce Gigi to his parents? The prejudice against loud campy guys was real. Thing was, he hadn't actually meant it when he'd said that just now. It just didn't make sense with him and Brock. Brock had never been ashamed of him before. He'd been to LaMore's shows, which totally epitomized gayness, and never said a word when Rosenberg felt the need to throw on some makeup or nail polish or a glittery scarf or frilly top. He seemed to like it, actually. Especially when Gigi wore lacy lingerie.

Mmm. He *really* liked that.

Argh, thoughts like this weren't helpful. No, Gigi didn't think Brock was ashamed of him. He didn't *think* so. But if his parents weren't nice people, then maybe it would be too difficult to bring an effeminate queen to their front door.

But Brock didn't strike him as the kind of guy who'd completely back down from doing that. Like, Brock was *out*. He'd made a point of it, sometimes really uncomfortably so. Like, even to the point where *Gigi* was standing there thinking, *Dude, come on.* Which wasn't often, or even something Gigi had thought would ever happen, but it had. So even if it had been uncomfortable to introduce him to his parents, Brock would've done that by now anyway.

So. Something else was wrong here.

"My family isn't like yours."

A suspicion wormed its way to the front of his mind. A memory. The first time he and Brock had spent the night together.

Gigi closed the front door and went up the stairs, frowning.

Brock had cornered him in a nightclub, helped by Tyler and Evie, the reprobates Gigi deigned to call friends. Gigi had spent the entire week avoiding him due to, well, *feelings*, and suddenly he'd found himself in Brock's muscly arms and staring into Brock's puppy-dog brown eyes. It would've been a crime against gaykind if Gigi hadn't taken him home and fucked him speechless. So he had.

But the morning after had delivered a surprise. He'd woken up, aware that Brock Stubbs—*the* Brock Stubbs—was in his bed, and Gigi had turned to watch him.

Brock lay asleep, breathing softly, one arm flung above his head and miles of skin stretched out across Gigi's sheets. He'd shoved the duvet down to his waist in his sleep. Gigi traced the broad lines of his face, the sweep of his neck and shoulder, the hard curves of his biceps and armpit where it joined his torso, silvery with scars, and—

Hold the fucking phone.

Scars? He leaned forward and looked closer. Brock's underarm and a small area along his side were dense with scars. Gigi swallowed. They looked like razor and knife scars laid on top of thicker ones, wheals where ones hadn't healed well, and thick pearly masses where they had. There were hundreds of them, all localized within strict bounded areas that would be hidden under shirts. The edges of the areas were feathery with slices, and he followed one with horror as the pearly skin ran down the length of his underarm from his armpit to his elbow.

Gigi shifted up so he could examine the rest of the arm flung above Brock's head. Clear, unscarred skin from elbow to palm.

His head reeled. Brock had hurt himself like this? When? Why? And why under his armpit and sides and not in the usual places people cut themselves? The careful, deliberate violence of the scars didn't match up at all with the steady, sweet man he'd fucked last night. What had happened?

Then Brock stirred and opened his eyes. "M'ello," he murmured.

Shit. Adorable. Gigi's heart ached. "Morning, you."

"Timizzit?"

Gigi made himself check. "Seven thirty."

"Zirly." Brock closed his eyes and burrowed into the pillow. His arm, however, snaked around Gigi's waist and pulled him closer.

Gigi didn't know what to do. He'd seen those scars on other people, but not on someone like Brock. Not someone who'd chased Gigi for a week, who'd gotten on his knees for Gigi, who shared the history they did. Should he mention them? Would Brock care?

"Some of us have places to be," Gigi said.

"Mm-hmm." Brock burrowed in and kissed him, morning breath and all.

Gigi closed his eyes and sank into that kiss. Giving into Brock felt so good. When Gigi had been seventeen, he'd dreamed of doing this with Brock. Not just sex, but waking up together. Cuddling. Freaking *cuddling*. Reality was so much better than his awkward little teenage fantasies.

Not that it meant anything. Much. Gigi had lost all his cherries as soon as he could after moving to Toronto, along with eighty pounds and any delusions about boyfriends being good things. Judging from how Brock had gone down on him, it had been a long time since Brock'd been a virgin too. Honestly? Good. *Awesome.* They knew sex. They could be chill about this.

But last night had been different. And this morning was different. *Chill* wasn't the right word anymore, because this boy had chased him and had scars in secret places.

If they were important, Brock would've mentioned them, right? He seemed totally at ease being naked in front of Gigi.

Gigi's chest hurt, so he ended the kiss. "I have to get up."

Brock opened his eyes and a slow smile spread across his face. "You sure?" His hand moved down Gigi's back to his ass, fingers rubbing the divots Gigi knew were there and teasing the top of his crack.

So cute. *So* cute. But . . . scars. Gigi was in over his head.

Therefore, he hadn't asked. And he'd kept not asking, even when he noticed other faded scars along Brock's back—not as thick as his sides, but wide and painful looking. It was actually a few weeks later before Gigi finally drummed up the courage to ask Brock about them. Brock had paused in peeling off his shirt to stare at the ones on his sides in surprise.

"Oh." His face had gone carefully calm. "They're nothing."

"Nothing? *Nothing*? You sure about that, boyfriend?"

"Yeah."

Gigi reached out and deliberately pressed one finger against the worst part of the slashes, where the skin was scar tissue and totally white. "Did you have an emo phase I wasn't aware of?"

Brock laughed. "Nope." He flung his shirt aside and reached for Gigi's. "Black hair doesn't suit me."

Gigi had scoffed, then been distracted by getting naked with the man who was definitely his boyfriend by then. Too distracted to follow up about the scars.

The third time had been in Syracuse, when they had been lying in bed, drowsy and sexed out. Gigi had turned to him and asked, "So, you ever going to tell me about these scars?"

Brock had yawned. "Nope. It's in the past."

And Gigi had been used to them by then, so he'd dropped it.

Only now, here, with his boyfriend having disappeared somewhere in Maney, he was wondering if maybe that had been a bad idea. If maybe those scars and Brock's "not nice" parents were somehow connected.

Or maybe he was overthinking things. If family stuff had been that bad, or was still that bad, Brock would've told him, right? That was the kind of shit people in serious relationships told each other. So if Brock hadn't told him, it wasn't anything like that. He'd even said so.

Maybe this running-away-with-the-car thing was just another stage of Brock Being Pissed At Gigi.

But Gigi wasn't sure about that anymore.

Goddamn it.

Whatever. What the hell could he do about it now? Maybe he *should* remember why he was here and who he was really here for. He needed to shower, shave, brush his teeth, and make sure he looked as ready for a goddamn straight-boy bachelor party as he could with what clothes he had. And maybe he wasn't straight, maybe his boyfriend was losing his mind, and maybe this bachelor party was going to be the next circle of hell, but Gigi would be damned if he wasn't going to look like a true queen throughout it all.

Before he did all that, though, he sent Brock a text. Partly because he wanted Brock to know this wasn't over, and partly because he wanted Brock to know he could come back. There was an unsettled feeling lodged in Gigi's gut now, and a girl knew when to trust that feeling.

Brock had driven to the parking lot for the national park segment of the forest that edged the north side of town. Why this place, he had no idea. It was quiet, at least. Not many cars around. No one to see him being there, in town. Not that it mattered anymore.

He sat in the car, staring at the tree line. The colours were turning, and he knew the forest would smell of autumn—crisp and woody, mulch and dry leaves. Around this time of year, that smell seeped into the town and lingered. Autumn in Maney didn't smell like autumn in Toronto, and it was honestly amazing to breathe in the air here. So clear.

Like anyone else who'd grown up in this town, he knew if he took the main path from the parking lot into the forest, he'd soon find a three-way fork in the road. The main route led left to the lake where people skated in winter, swam in the summer, and canoed most of the year. A second route led to a quarry about five kilometres in, and the third route meandered prettily until it intersected with a hiking route that circled the town. There were masses of unofficial tracks crisscrossing all those main routes, leading to clearings and funny-shaped trees and gorgeous views over the town. He knew because he'd walked most of them, trekking with his dad and then for school trips and campouts with friends, then alone because he had thoughts he couldn't share with anyone else and it was better than being home.

The forest looked as he remembered it, but somehow different. That was something he'd forgotten about nature, how the same exact forest could look different each and every day. Whether it was because it had physically changed, aging with every day, or because he had changed, he couldn't say.

His cell dinged an incoming message. It had to be Gigi. He braced himself and opened it: *Omg I cannot believe you ran out like that. Come back, okay? I'm sorry. My mom wants you to help her with lunch. You're so in my orienteering group later.*

Naomi had overheard them and said something to Brock as he'd left, but he hadn't stopped to listen. Clearly she'd spoken to Gi. No mention of meeting Brock's parents, but Gi wouldn't let that drop for long.

His parents.

His *fucking* parents.

Brock put the phone down and leaned forward to rest his chin on the steering wheel, eyes on the oranges and reds of the forest. If he wanted to be poetic, the forest looked like it was on fire. Like, a nice kind of fire, the kind that soothed and warmed. Simple and safe.

Why the hell couldn't other things be that simple?

His parents weren't happy with him. Brock hadn't expected them to be, but reality was visceral in a way imagination could never match up to. The town grapevine had pulled through after all. His mom had sounded disappointed, and his dad had wanted to know why the hell Brock hadn't called them in so long. So far, so standard, but the worst part was his dad informing him he was to report in and "explain himself."

Jesus. Brock hated that phrase. It had been a long time since he'd heard it.

His dad had said he'd come by and pick him up, but Brock knew better. No, he was going to take the car and have an exit strategy. Because he *had* somewhere else to go now.

The eggs Grandma had made him for breakfast sat heavy in his stomach, and he shifted his weight in the seat. The day was laid out for him: go back to the Rosenberg place and try to look Naomi in the eye while helping with lunch; go to his parents' place and . . . well, confront them and probably come out; meet the bachelors here in this very car park for orienteering and pretending that he'd always been out; take a quick shower and change for dinner and drinks; then get through dinner and drinks. Not forgetting to try to be the guy Gigi expected him to be throughout it all, which meant being friendly with the relatives, fun and easygoing, and *out.*

Oh man. Explaining himself to his parents. Coming out to his parents. It wasn't like Brock had never imagined returning and confronting them, but the idea that he had the opportunity to do it was . . . not as exciting as it had been in his imagination.

But it would be a moment, right? To really declare himself to them and to, like, *be* himself. He could do that. He was *good* at coming out by now. His parents would react badly, but as long as he had a way of leaving, it would be okay. And then he wouldn't have to worry about them anymore, and he could enjoy this weekend, and he could explain everything to Gi, and it would all be okay again.

So. Get through lunch, and he'd be solid.

Someone knocked on his window.

He almost jumped into the passenger seat in surprise, letting out a somewhat unmasculine gasp. When he settled back, he saw a woman staring through the window. He frowned. She seemed kind of familiar.

"Brock Stubbs?" she asked through the glass.

Oh *wow*. The voice helped—she was Marjorie Pine, a girl from his high school theatre group. She'd performed opposite Gigi in a number of productions and had graduated in the same year as Gigi. Last he'd heard, she'd moved to Edmonton, so her being here had to be unusual. She looked good. She'd filled in and changed her hair, and the result was more maturity than the last time he'd seen her.

Brock opened his door and stepped out the car. "Marjorie?"

A big smile burst across her face. "I thought it was you! Hi!" She gave him a big hug, and he hesitantly hugged her back. They hadn't spoken much in theatre group—he'd been part of the tech crew, not the actors—but he had good memories of sharing spliffs with her and Aditya after rehearsals. He was pretty sure she'd hated Gigi though, and Gigi had definitely hated her back. They'd fought constantly on stage when they weren't delivering lines.

"It's good to see you." Brock let her go.

"Likewise!" She spread her hands wide. "I mean, I didn't expect to see *you* back here. I thought you went off to Guam or somewhere."

"Indonesia. And that was only for a year. Then I went to Europe." He shifted his weight. "I've been back in Canada for years now. Toronto. I thought you were in Edmonton?"

She nodded. "Yup. Still am! I'm here for a long weekend to see my parents and help them with a big group of guests." Her parents ran one of Maney's two B&Bs.

"Oh."

"The guests are here for Sophie Rosenberg's wedding—have you heard about that? Fancy-ass wedding on the lake."

This was it: the grapevine in action. "Yeah."

Her smile turned knowing. "Which means *Toby* is in town too. Some coincidence, huh?"

That was his cue. "Not really a coincidence. I'm in town for the wedding. I'm, um, Toby's plus one."

Marjorie's eyes widened. "No. *Shut up.*" She smacked his shoulder lightly. "You two got back together? That's awesome!"

Brock blinked. They'd never *been* together except for . . . "Uh, we weren't really—"

"Oh hey, I knew about you two making out after rehearsals." She said it like it was nothing.

But it wasn't nothing. Brock's vision narrowed to just her smiling face. She'd known? Back then? About them? *What?* They'd taken such care to hide it. Brock had been certain no one had known. He'd been *sure* of it.

"You did?" he asked, feeling light-headed.

"Oh yeah. Adi did too. We didn't talk about it much because you hung out with Josh, and Toby got enough shit as it was. Plus I liked you too much to rat you out." She peered at him. "You okay? You look ready to faint."

No kidding. Fainting would be preferable to this belated embarrassment—and slight frisson of fear. Who else had known? Had anyone gossiped? Had his dad's eventual reaction been based on hearing the true version of events?

Brock sucked in a deep, wood-scented breath. "Yup. I'm good. I'm great." He leaned against the car for support. "I didn't know anyone knew we were doing that." Not until they'd been caught.

"I noticed you and him lingering a bunch of times and figured it out." She shook her head. "Sorry it ended like that. I felt super bad for you two. Well, for Toby; I judged *you* super harshly for a long time, but I think I understand now why you did what you did."

Shit. Brock just wanted to curl up in a hole and die. Oh man, this sucked. "I, uh, wasn't in a good place."

"You're telling *me*. This was a shitty place to grow up. I've been here for four days and I'm already itching to get out. The woods are great to ramble in, but it's not like I can walk through them all day." She flipped her hair over her shoulder with an unconscious toss of her head. "You and Toby free for drinks or coffee while you're here? It would be awesome to catch up with you both."

Brock wasn't sure Gigi would be up for that. Besides, the schedule the Rosenbergs had emailed around didn't give them much free time. The wedding was tomorrow, and they were returning to Toronto the day after.

"I don't know that we can," he said apologetically. "We're pretty busy."

Her face fell. "Oh. Sure, yeah. I get it."

"I'm sorry."

"No, I should've figured you'd have family stuff to do."

Damn it. Now he felt bad for disappointing her as well.

"But actually, we're, uh, we're doing a bachelor thing tonight," he said. "We'll be at Warner's for drinks from 9 p.m. onwards. If you're free..."

Her face split in a grin. "Yeah! Absolutely! I'll see you there."

She left after that, explaining she had to return to the B&B, and Brock watched her go from the side of his car. What a blast from the past. He'd avoided thinking about that theatre group for years, as what had happened between him and Toby had been so painful it had coloured the last year and a half he'd been at school. Before he'd kissed Toby for the first time, he'd had a lot of fun learning the stage lighting, sound and curtain set up, and hanging out with the rest of the group. Even though he'd only joined it for an excuse to be around Toby, and to linger at school, it had taught him a ton of skills and given him a few new friends.

And now look at him. Still around Toby, still lingering, only outside the damn forest instead of in an aging auditorium. Didn't want to go to his parents', didn't want to return to the Rosenbergs', didn't want to move at all.

But he had to. He was here, and he had no real choice except to see this through. He wouldn't run away—couldn't, not if he wanted to be able to look himself and Gigi in the eye again.

His arms were crossed, and he found himself absently rubbing the scars along one triceps. Fuck. He pulled his arms apart, looked up, and took a big, deep breath, easing his shoulders back and down. It was a posture Gigi did to calm his nerves before a performance.

He could do this. He'd gone through worse. There were the three months he'd eaten nothing but rice and fruit in Indonesia, and the time he'd been stranded in the Netherlands at a rural train station somewhere between Utrecht and the German border with five Euros to his name. Seven hours spent on a bus in Cambodia. His adolescence here.

Yeah. He could do this.

Then he got back in the car and drove to the Rosenbergs'.

The house was in a state of chaos as people rushed in and out the front door. Several of the aunts were bundling the younger kids into a car, presumably to get them out of the way until lunchtime, and Brock got a wave from Rosie as he walked by. Inside, there were more people carrying around food, and he saw Gigi helping his dad carry cots from the rec and dining rooms to the laundry room. Brock received a nod from John and raised eyebrows from Gigi. Gigi was clearly busy, and Brock didn't know what to say to him anyway, so he went to help Naomi.

She didn't mention the fight or the fact he'd left, only welcomed him back, handed him an apron, and set him to washing rice, then chopping vegetables. People ducked in and out of the kitchen in bursts of chatter to steal food and ask questions, but the conversation in the kitchen remained limited to the food. It was nice. Peaceful. Relaxed.

All too soon, the time came for him to leave. He untied the apron and passed it to Naomi, who took it with a tomato-y hand. "Thanks for the help."

"No problem, M—Naomi."

"Toby's good with prep, but it's nice to spend time with you." She paused a moment, then smiled at him. "Have fun with your parents."

Unlikely. *Very* unlikely. In fact, if the way his stomach was threatening to return breakfast, it was possible that he might give them an actual reason to be angry with him for once.

He nodded. "Thanks."

"Brock." She paused, clearly conflicted. "I know my son isn't the calmest person in our family, but I hope you know he cares deeply about you. We all do."

Oh God. Not this. Not sympathy. That was the last fucking thing he needed.

A lump rose in his throat, and he forced it down. "Yeah. Sure."

She had grey eyes—Gigi's eyes—and a kind but worried expression. "If you need us, any of us, please call, okay? You won't interrupt anything. Lunch is just food."

Damn it, now he was embarrassed. "Got it. Thanks, Naomi."

She gently brushed his arm. "I'll see you later."

He didn't see Gigi on his way out—not that he went looking. If Brock lived in another universe where his parents were nice people who hadn't hurt him for years, then he'd have brought Gigi home a lot earlier, and gladly. He'd have shown Gigi off. He'd have *demanded* they meet and like each other.

But that wasn't the universe he lived in. No, this was the universe where his nervousness had him barely able to start the car, continually wiping his hands on his jeans on the drive over to his parents' place, and taking calming breaths the entire way.

When he drew up outside his old house, he needed a few moments to sit and prepare himself. There was a weird feeling that every action he took was beyond his control—as though he was a windup toy, and someone had set him in action, so he was stuck until the mechanism had played out.

Granted, it had been a long time in coming. And if he'd done it before now, he wouldn't be in this situation. Despite the feeling of predestiny, he *knew* he could resist it. He could simply drive away and not stop until he reached Toronto. He could drive in the opposite direction and not stop until he reached *Vancouver*. He could keep going—fly back to Europe or to South America or Antarctica. Never come back.

Thoughts like this were stupid. He *had* come back. Maybe even to do this very thing.

The house looked the same as it ever had, though a little older and faded. Paint peeled around the corners and edges, and the gutter looked like it needed clearing. His stomach clenched at the sight of it. When he had been a teenager walking the long way from school, his stomach would drop and his pace would slow to a dawdle as soon as he'd turned the corner into this street.

No dawdling could happen in a car outside the place.

He took a deep breath and turned the car off.

Keys out. Step out. Lock. Check it's locked. Keys in pocket. Check for phone. Check for wallet. Check again for keys. Check for . . . Stop fucking around.

Without him telling it to, his body walked the twenty steps to the front door. His hand raised and knocked because his dad hated the doorbell. The welcome mat was the one his mom had bought when he was in high school, still in surprisingly good condition despite being over ten years old.

Footsteps sounded behind the door. It swung open to reveal his mom, Fiona Stubbs. His heart ached at the sight of her: rounder, a little more hunched, comfortable jeans and blouse buttoned up to her neck, her big brown eyes peering warily. Still his mom.

She brightened as she recognized him. "Brock! Oh honey, welcome home!" She opened her arms wide, and he stepped into them, bending slightly so he could hug her back—gently, tentatively. She smelled as he remembered: floral, with an underlying tang of antiseptic.

"Hey, Mom." He let her go. At closer range, he could see more lines in her face and grey strands in her blonde hair. Was that a healing cut on her lip?

"It's wonderful to see you." She pressed a papery palm to his cheek, and his heart turned over. The last time he'd seen his parents had been after returning from overseas, before he'd moved to Toronto and essentially cut off contact. Years. Literal years. If he were a parent, he'd have been understandably furious.

His mom didn't look it, but then again, his mom had stopped showing anger a long time ago. Even if she was angry, she also looked genuinely happy to see him. There *was* love there, right? Maybe he could've kept in contact with her without involving his dad. Somehow.

But she didn't go anywhere or do anything without telling his dad. Brock doubted that had changed if she was still here.

"You too." It was almost true.

"Is that the prodigal son returned home?"

Brock stiffened and looked beyond his mother's shoulder. His dad stood in the shadows of the hallway. Of course the curtains were partly drawn during the day, like it would kill the people in this house to have some sunlight in there. Like it would kill his dad to be visible from the front door.

Pete Stubbs also looked older, a little smaller, and rounder. A bigger beer belly than Brock remembered preceded the rest of him as he stepped forward with a smile and an extended hand.

"Hey, Dad." Brock warily shook his hand.

"Good to see you. Glad you're in town." Brock's hand was clenched painfully tight for a moment, then let go. "Your mother's prepared lunch for us."

Heart thumping, Brock stepped inside the house, ensuring he closed the door quietly behind him.

Being back was surreal. The place looked unchanged. Still the lone, posed glossy family photo hanging by the front door, the rack of coats, the hardwood floors and cream wallpaper. Still the chemical smells of a clean house, with an added faint odour of something cooking. Brock toed off his shoes and followed his parents through the dim hallway to the living room.

There were changes here. The flat-screen TV was bigger and the sofa was new. The wallpaper had changed, and there weren't as many tchotchkes on the sideboard and furniture. Dad's framed Stanley Cup ticket from 1967 was above the fireplace now.

There were lots of memories here. Watching TV. Presenting his report card. Playing on a rug in front of the fireplace. Being shoved so close to the open fire in that fireplace as a child that his eyebrows singed. Huddling on the carpet as screams raged overhead. Beatings. Running away.

He shook his head to clear it. He needed to be focused on the here and now, to be alert and ready.

They moved to the table in the kitchen, the informal one that sat four and had been the scene of family meals for years. The formal table in the official dining room was hand-carved maple, sat eight, and was only used for guests. Brock had been in that room maybe five times in his life.

"Have a seat, boys," Mom trilled as she bustled over to the oven.

Pete sat at his usual place at the head of the table, and Brock automatically went to sit next to him, but paused. "Can I help you, Mom?" He thought he heard a snort from his dad.

She flapped an oven mitt at him. "No, no, honey."

He sat.

"How long've you been in town, son?" his dad asked.

Was that a loaded question? Maybe. Brock never knew with his dad. Ah, shit, he could feel his nervousness making him sweat. *Don't overthink this.* He made sure his face was still and his voice casual as he said, "Oh, only since yesterday."

"Right, right, *last-minute trip.*"

Pete sat in his chair, legs wide and forearms proprietorially on the table near his cutlery. The regal position sent an abrupt wave of hate through Brock, and he turned his attention to the settings. They were already laid out with their usual military precision. Knives facing the right way and in the correct right-hand position, fork on the left, sparkling clean, all lined up at the bottom.

God, it was like he'd never left.

What was he doing here? Why did he have to be here? Eating lunch like this again?

He wasn't a kid anymore.

He was taller than his dad now.

Brock was pretty certain he was stronger now too.

And Pete honestly looked older than Brock remembered. Fragile. It was kind of a shock.

Okay, so when Brock had imagined something like this happening, he'd figured there would be a grand declaration of who he was and his sexuality—but right now, all that was going through his head was *You both can go fuck yourselves.* He hadn't thought about saying that to people who seemed much older and weaker than he remembered.

Reality wasn't as noble and easy as his imagination.

In any case, this moment wasn't a good time to come out with anything. Past experience said there was *no* good time for breaking news, but after food was better. Fewer things his dad could throw at him.

Time to change the subject. "How's the office?" Brock asked. Pete was a legal clerk in the local practice.

"Same old. People keep dying and leaving their junk to their kids. Some of whom are less deserving than others." Hard stare.

Here we go. "Uh-huh."

"I never thought I'd find myself being jealous of the idiots who walk through the office door, but . . ." His dad warmed to the subject, as he always did, and Brock resisted the urge to fidget as he heard the usual spiel. *Kids these days have no gratitude or respect. People are fucking morons. The world is going to shit. You will get nowhere unless you work hard and listen to me. If only everyone thought the same way. I could turn that practice around in weeks. I know what's best. I have built this family up from nothing. I, I, I.*

Mom came over and placed food in front of Dad, then came back with Brock's and her portions and sat down. They waited while Pete scanned the food, then picked up his fork and began eating. Brock resisted sighing in relief as he followed suit. If Dad hated the food—

"This tastes burnt."

On Brock's right, his mom stilled. "It does?"

It didn't.

"Tastes fine to me." Brock shovelled a big mouthful in.

Dad picked over the food. "You left it in the oven too long."

"I followed the recipe. Maybe it's the bacon? I used a different kind of bacon."

"No kind of bacon tastes like this unless it's burnt."

Brock wanted to duck under the table, the way he used to when he was a kid and could feel the tension building in the air. Instead, he stared at his plate. What even was this? Noodle casserole? If anything, it looked undercooked. The cheese was barely browned.

His mom straightened as if to rise. "You want something else?"

Pete shoved the plate away. "Yeah."

That was Brock's cue to stop eating. No one ate unless his father did. Because they were a *family*, and families ate *together*. His stomach clenched, and his hands gripped his cutlery tighter. Why were things like this? Why did they have to be so fucking tense? Why couldn't he just eat, say his thing, and leave?

What was stopping him?

He rebelliously shovelled in another forkful and chewed, eyes still on his food. Pain exploded across the back of his head, and he grunted as he jerked his head away. Shit. He might be older, his dad might look weaker, but he still had a hefty palm. Brock should've seen his dad's hand coming.

A mistake to rebel. He knew better.

"You forget your manners?" his dad growled.

Brock dropped his fork, and his mom hesitated by him as she rounded the table. "You want something else too?"

"Nah, I'm good."

"Give him something else," his dad snapped. "No one wants to eat burnt food, Fiona."

His plate was moved from in front of him. Brock had also forgotten how his dad loved to drag shit out like this. If it wasn't the food, it was the cutlery. If it wasn't the cutlery, it was the cleanliness of the table, or the plate, or Brock's hands. If it wasn't any of those things, it was the goddamn lighting or the time or his mom's hair or . . . something. Always *something*. Even if there was nothing, it was only a matter of time until he found something.

How the hell had he lived like this? He could remember when things had been good, when he was young and had loved playing with his parents. Somewhere, somehow, things had gotten bad, but he'd only really woken up to that around the age of ten, when his dad had slammed his mom against a wall and threatened to kill her if Brock told anyone. That had been the first really bad thing.

But afterwards, he'd been fine for a long time. Everything had been okay. Then Brock lost his pocket money and his dad had hurled a mug through the TV. Then he'd seemed better again, and they bought a new TV, but Mom spilt tea on the couch, so that had gotten her slapped so hard she fell to the floor. And so it went, months of happy family times before Pete snapped. Slowly it had turned to weeks of sunny behaviour before his dad lost his temper, then days. As Brock entered his final year of high school, it had reached a stage where his dad was liable to lose his shit at any time at all. Brock and his mom had had no idea what would set him off or when. Opening or closing doors. Cleaning dishes loudly. Not picking up groceries when asked. Correcting him. Fighting back.

What was almost worse was his mom's excuses. *Dad was stressed. He doesn't mean it. You shouldn't have done that. Don't provoke him. It was my fault.*

It couldn't be her fault every time. Or Brock's. Not *every* time.

Fuck this place. Seriously, fuck it. Why the hell had he come back? Why had he let Gigi talk him into coming here? Why was Brock doing this to himself? This wasn't some grand, empowering exercise in standing his ground—this was walking into a war zone and expecting to deflect shrapnel with the sheer force of self-belief.

"So how's your job?" his dad asked him. "I assume you have one."

His mom walked back into the kitchen and began looking through the cupboards.

Brock gritted his teeth. "Good. Earning." He had to leave. Say his thing and leave.

"Big city treating you well?"

"Yeah."

His dad shook his head. "Don't know how you do it. The place is expensive. All that noise and crime. Full of fags and immigrants too. Going to the dogs."

Such an asshole. *Such* an asshole. Brock felt less and less like a person, and more like a pulsating sack of pure anger the longer he sat there not saying anything.

"Guess I fit right in, then."

Wait.

Who said that? Did *he* say that?

He'd said it.

Oh fuck. Fuck fuck fuck fuck *fuck*.

In his peripheral vision, his mom's movements stopped.

Beside him, Pete went very, very still. "Care to repeat that?"

Brock forced himself to look at his dad, if only to be prepared for whatever he would do next. "The reason I'm in town is because my boyfriend's sister is getting married."

His dad was expressionless.

"We knew that, sweetie," his mom said slowly. "Why would . . . Oh, *boyfriend*?" She blinked. "*Toby Rosenberg*."

Brock didn't move his gaze from his father.

"This better be a joke." Pete's voice was low and calm. A shudder ran up Brock's spine at that tone. It was one of the worst ones.

"It's not," he ground out.

"Honey," his mom said, "are you—"

"Shut up." Pete's eyes bored into his. "Don't say things you'll regret, boy. We discussed this back in high school, remember? No son of mine is a fag."

Brock remembered that "discussion." Once the rumour mill had picked up the discovery of him with Toby—because of course it had—Brock had known his dad would have something to say about it. He'd prepared his story, the same one he'd told Josh and anyone else who'd cared to listen, and had it ready when he came home late one night and found his dad waiting for him in the living room. He'd managed to convince him he wasn't gay, that it had been entirely Toby's fault, but it hadn't spared him the belt or kicking.

His mother had said nothing at all, simply haunted the doorway and rushed in to pick him up and ice his back and sides once it was all over.

But this wasn't the same. Brock was older and stronger. Not a child, not a lanky teenager. An adult.

Somehow it didn't seem to matter now that he was here, in this house, facing the man who'd tormented him for almost as long as Brock could remember.

No. Fuck that shit. It *did* matter. This stopped here.

He braced himself. "I *am* gay. So I guess that means I'm not your son."

He saw the fist coming and scooted his chair backwards out of the way. Pete still slammed into him with all the heaviness of a brick wall, and Brock brought his arms up in time to shelter his face from blows. He kicked out and twisted off the chair, landing in a heap on the floor, Pete on top of him.

"The fuck you say?" Pete grunted, lurching off him.

Brock rolled to his feet and grabbed the chair, holding it between him and Pete. His dad stood too, clenching his fists.

Brock would never consider himself a quick thinker, but his mind very clearly mapped the route to the front door. He knew he could get there before his dad could. Whether he could do it without wetting himself or throwing up was another matter.

"After all I've done for you," Pete snarled. "I fed you"—he picked up a fork and flung it at Brock, who deflected it with the chair—"I clothed you"—more cutlery followed—"I put a roof over your head for *years*"—a ceramic mug that Brock didn't manage to deflect thudded into his collarbone before shattering on the floor—"put you through school, and *this* is the thanks I get?"

To Brock's surprise, a bout of hysterical laughter bubbled up from nowhere. *In for a penny* . . . "I've *always* been gay. It has nothing to do with you."

"You're not too old for a whipping."

Brock glanced down at Pete's belt, then grunted as another mug shattered against his chair. He turned his face aside instinctively, but in his distraction, a fist followed.

Brock saw red. He *felt* red—a hot, hazy rush of fury that surged through him when another punch caused pain to explode across his face. The chair. He swung the chair almost like a baseball bat, aiming high.

The next thing he knew, his dad was collapsed on the floor, clutching his head and groaning. One leg of the chair lay next to him, and there was a small crack in the seat of the chair in Brock's hands. Cheap, uncomfortable piece of shit.

His mom stood frozen in the kitchen, hands over her mouth.

Brock threw down the chair. "Fuck. You."

In this position, his father looked especially fragile. Way past old, almost *elderly*. A twinge of guilt ran through Brock, but he ignored it.

"Oh no. Oh no," his mom whispered. She inched around the kitchen counter, then gasped at the sight of Pete.

Pete slowly uncurled, his face a warped, furious caricature of his usual features—but there was a new hint of wariness there. "Stop fucking around, Brock. If you ever want to see this house or money from me, you will stand down." His eyes narrowed. "That goes double for seeing anyone in our family ever again."

Like Brock gave a shit about the goddamn house or his father's money. And it wasn't like he'd seen anyone in his family lately either. If Pete thought that was what it took to make him panic, he was so wildly off-base it was almost funny.

And in any case, there was nothing to stop his mom or his relatives from contacting him. Nothing. Not even Pete. So he was lying. Everything that came out of his dad's mouth was pure, noxious shit.

He hadn't even gotten off the floor yet. Brock had hit him hard, but he hadn't hit anything vital.

"Brock, honey, take a moment to think about this," his mom started.

"This is *your* fault," Pete snapped at her, his eyes never leaving Brock's. "I tried my best with him. I knew that incident with that Rosenberg faggot didn't seem right. I knew Brock was lying. I *knew* it, but *you* said it had to be a mistake." He shook his head. "I should've known something was wrong when you didn't come home, boy. You think we didn't notice you changed your number? Ungrateful, dishonest piece of crap. No real man turns his back on family."

"You're such a fucking asshole." Brock's voice sounded strange; it was coming out all twisted and raspy. "I never wanted to come back. Why the fuck would I want to come back *here*? I'm only here to tell you my life is better without you, and that I'm never going to see you again."

"Oh, Brock. Don't do this. Listen to your father." His mom took a few steps towards him, and Brock took a few steps back, hating the lost, confused look on her face. Why couldn't she ever fucking take his side?

"*That's* why you came here today?" his dad asked. "To hurt us? To make your mother and me a laughingstock in our community? You think you can do this to me and not face consequences?"

Brock swallowed. *Just words, just words.* "I came here today to tell you I'm gay, and that I'm not afraid of you." That last one was a lie, and might always be, but fuck it sounded good to say it. It *felt* good to say it. "You can keep the fucking house. And back in high school *I* kissed Toby, not the other way around."

There. Done. He pivoted and sprinted through the living room, into the front hallway.

"Brock! Get back here!"

His shoes. He needed his shoes. He scooped them up.

"This isn't over, boy!"

Brock left the house, slamming the door behind him as he burst into the cool, open air. He ran to the rental car and dove in, heart beating so fast it was a buzz in his temples and chest. He tossed his shoes into the passenger seat and fumbled with the keys to start the car. All he could hear were his desperate pants, loud in the space of the car. He dropped the keys twice, his hands were shaking so much, but by the time he'd picked them up the second time, he realized no one had followed him outside. He managed to start the car and shifted into drive. One socked foot on the accelerator and he was gone.

Brock watched the house recede behind him in the rearview mirror. A shudder ran up his spine, then another, and then he turned the corner and navigated towards Main Street.

Oh fuck. Oh God. Ohhh, *shit*.

Oookay, so, unbelievably, that had gone way better than expected. Being older and stronger was an improvement on being a kid.

He'd fought back—and *won*.

He forced himself to breathe deeply, marking each exhalation with a slow, "*Fuuuck*."

He'd done it.

He'd come out.

And he'd fought his dad.

Holy shit, he'd *beat his dad up*. What the hell? That wasn't who he was. Didn't that make him the same as Pete?

Wait, he'd done it in self-defence. In total self-defence, actually. His face and chest throbbed. That made it . . . not *okay*, but better.

At a red light, he checked his face in the mirror. Red marks on his cheek and jaw and near his eye. Those were going to be nasty bruises by the end of the day. People were going to ask questions. Ugh. Just what he needed.

And injuries there were unusual. In the past, his dad had largely left faces alone. Didn't leave anything that would draw attention. Either he was getting sloppy or he'd been so furious he hadn't thought about where to land his fists. Not that Brock had given him any chance to aim, with him fighting back and all.

His hands were still shaking, but gripping the wheel helped a lot.

He exhaled, long and loud. That actually hadn't been so bad. He'd forgotten how much worse the buildup could be than the actual encounter. So, he was definitely totally completely disowned—but he'd done it. He'd come out. And not only was he out, he was also *out*. Like, of the family. He'd completely pissed off his parents right? That meant no more pressure to face them. No more awkward thoughts about maybe calling them on major holidays (just to see if his mom was okay, just to check they were still in Maney, just to . . . do something about the silence). No more pretending he liked his family. No more sniping, critical comments from his dad, and no more pathetic apologizing from his mom. No more *anything* with the Stubbses.

His chest lightened. He suddenly whooped, pounding his hands against the steering wheel. He felt *amazing*. He could do anything he wanted now. He was *free*.

When the light turned, he kept driving and saw the high school appear on his left. The *high school*. Where he and Gigi had started. Holy shit. Talk about visiting the past.

It seemed like an excellent idea to pull into the parking lot and stop for a moment. So he did that.

He turned off the engine but left the car on so he could keep the stereo playing.

Gigi's RuPaul album blasted into the car. Brock thought the song was "Champion," but he wasn't sure. The auto-tune kind of made all the songs on that album run together.

He sat back, hands still shaking slightly. Only slightly. He crossed his arms so he didn't have to see them. Drank in the realization he'd done it. He'd *finally* done it. He'd come out. He'd stood up to them. He'd . . . *hit his dad with a chair*.

But it was okay. The world hadn't ended, and he was still sitting there. He was safe. He would never have to deal with his parents again. He didn't have to hide anything from anyone anymore. This was the kind of moment in movies where people cheered, where the hero quipped an awesome one-liner, smiled, and walked into a newer, better life.

All Brock did was burst into tears.

CHAPTER SIX

Eight years ago

Toby blinked as the spotlight hit his face. He shifted his weight to one foot and waited while the tech crew adjusted it. *Tech crew* meaning Brock, hopefully. He could just picture those amazing large hands steadying the heavy lamp in place and that frankly *adorable* frown Brock got when he was concentrating.

God. Toby was about to pop a boner right here on stage, for real. Cute guys should be banned from tech crew. *Stop thinking about him. Think about . . . think about math. Yeah. Freaking binomial functions should be banned.*

"That's perfect!" Ms. Vankampp shouted from the stalls. She strode down to the stage. "Brock, Tina, get a secondary in position, upstage right."

Another light flickered on behind Toby. He shifted his weight back to the other foot. He desperately wanted to *do* something, like practise the pirouettes he'd been learning or turn and shout lines at his costar, Marjorie, who stood upstage from him looking as bored as he felt. But they were supposed to stay quiet and still so Ms. Vankampp could communicate with the tech crew.

"We're almost done," she said to them before whirling around. "Brock! Your *other* right!"

The secondary light flickered on over Marjorie, who hissed and pretended to shy away from the weight of the glare. "Nooo! It burrnnnsss."

And Toby thought *he* was a drama queen. He arched an eyebrow—which was exciting because he'd practised it for months until he could do it perfectly. Not that Marjorie would appreciate the subtle art of a raised eyebrow. "Wow, Marj. Dying undead bloodsucker comes so naturally to you."

She flipped him the finger as she sank to the floor, breathing heavily.

"There is no need for dramatics, Marjorie." Ms. Vankampp regarded the stage carefully, then raised a thumb. "Good enough! Mark those positions down for Reno and Billy in scene five."

"Ms. Vankampp, do we *have* to be here for this?" Toby asked, ignoring Marjorie's rattling gasps behind him.

"Yes, Tobias, you do." Her gaze flickered between him and Marjorie. "Practise your lines."

Toby sighed loudly and side-eyed Marjorie. "You learn your lines yet?"

"No," her undead corpse said.

"Of course you haven't."

"I have a *life*," she sneered. "It gets in the way of lines."

Toby refused to visibly bristle. "Well, Reno, you might want to get on that instead of on your boyfriend."

She surged to her feet, her face furious. "You'd know all about having a boyfriend," she hissed, "*wouldn't* you, fag?"

Toby felt himself blush. He wouldn't, actually. Truth was, he hadn't even kissed a boy. Didn't seem like he'd ever kiss anyone at this rate. But if the truth hadn't stopped rumours and bullying when he'd started high school, it wouldn't stop them now. And actually, it was okay. He was seventeen now and in his final year. After this, he was off to Toronto and a way better, way gayer life. *This is the last year I have to put up with this shit from her. From anybody.*

"At least my cocksucking skills are only rumours," he deadpanned.

Her jaw dropped.

"Ms. Vankampp?"

That was Brock's low voice. Toby had to stop himself from turning around, even though he itched to look at him. The guy was the hottest thing this side of the Georgian Bay. Biceps like a god's from hauling around stage equipment, curly brown hair that Tobias wanted to wind his fingers through, and a smile that lit up the stage brighter than this fucking spotlight currently blinding Toby.

He couldn't help it. He could never help it.

Face burning, he turned around and stepped out of the light so he could see them. Brock and Ms. Vankampp were poring over lighting diagrams in front of the stage. Brock was marking the paper with a pen. Toby tried not to actively drool because Brock was wearing the blue sweater today, the one that set off his colouring so freaking well. It wasn't cool to be caught staring, so he moved around, going over a few dance steps while trying not to look like he was ogling Brock. As he moved back into the beam of light, Brock and Ms. Vankampp turned into shadowy outlines. He executed a spin to find himself face-to-face with Marjorie.

"Are we gonna have problems here?" she hissed.

"How about you knock it off with the fag bullshit and I won't mention what you smoke with Aditya backstage when Ms. Vankampp isn't watching?" he replied archly.

She went red. "Deal." She took a step back and eyed him up and down. "I *cannot* believe you're playing Billy. Fattest Billy ever." She turned and flounced off the stage.

The bitch. How dare she upstage him? And the weight remark was just *low*.

But it had happened in front of the theatre group leader and Toby's long-term, doomed crush. Oh man. Had they heard? He and Marjorie had been quiet, but maybe they'd heard anyway. Acoustics were a thing. *Fuuuck*. He could feel himself getting hot in the face, and just freaking *knew* Ms. Vankampp and Brock were watching him. He quickly barrelled offstage too, needing to get away from their scrutiny. Particularly from *him*.

And there is nothing *wrong with me playing the lead. Goddamn Marjorie. I'm good at this. There's nothing wrong with liking boys. There's nothing wrong with being overweight*. Like Marjorie could even talk anyway; her hips had to be as big as her fat mouth. He wasn't fucking *fat* anyway.

Not *that* much.

He tugged at his shirt and tried not to think about all the fries he'd eaten at lunch. Tried not to imagine what Brock saw, really, when he looked at him.

"Tobias?" Ms. Vankampp said behind him.

He froze. *Now what?* He turned around to look at her. She had her arms crossed and was giving him that *I'm so sorry* look. "Is Marjorie giving you problems?"

This whole hick school is giving me problems, lady. "No."

"If she is, let me know," she said. "I cast you as Billy because you're the best triple threat this province has. You were born to play him."

He resisted rolling his eyes. *Yeah, it means so much to me to play the lead in yet another hick school production.*

Okay, that was actually a lie—it totally did mean something, just not as much as if he were in a theatre school. Even though Ms. Vankampp was totally overstating it—and probably *had* to say nice things because she was a teacher—hearing her say that was still awesome. And Toby's mom thought all these school plays proved he had a chance at the acting thing. Which, okay, she was his *mom*, so whatever. But sometimes Toby believed her and it felt really good. Like, it could actually happen one day he *would* get out of here and live the life he wanted.

"Thanks, Ms. Vankampp."

"Good." She checked her watch. "We've run over time. You all right to get home?"

"Yes, Ms. Vankampp."

"Good job today, Tobias." She smiled encouragingly and walked towards Marjorie and the cast members playing Hope and Evelyn. They hung around in the backstage area, poking props at each other. Toby slunk away to the hidden depths of backstage, where he'd stashed his bag. If he didn't hide it every rehearsal, he couldn't guarantee getting it back in one piece.

In middle school, Toby had joined the theatre club because he loved performing. When he found himself staring at Aditya's ass during a production of *A Midsummer Night's Dream*, he'd had to face some hard facts, not least about what a total cliché he was.

Unfortunately, the moment he realized he liked guys and that his penchant for drama wasn't something he was going to grow out of, everyone else seemed to pick up on it too. He couldn't seem to hide it, much as he tried not to be obvious. Whatever *that* meant, because literally all he did was breathe and walk around and maybe dance and sing a bit, and suddenly that meant he was gay. He didn't even *tell* people he was. Wasn't coming out meant to happen on his terms?

Then Turk Rogers saw him looking through men's health magazines in the general store one weekend, and as Turk was the hockey captain and walking popular jock cliché of the school, that meant everyone knew for certain by the time Toby rolled into school and into the new hell that was his academic life. Three years later, he no longer put anything in his locker, didn't look at other guys beyond theatre roles and group projects, knew how to weasel out of a fight, and had put on fifty pounds.

Granted, things had calmed down a ton after Turk graduated. Now he was playing hockey for some university in Ottawa, and Toby regularly hoped there was a puck with Turk's front teeth written on it. And maybe a faulty helmet. Okay, at least a crappy mouth guard.

He checked his bag. Everything was still there, including his stash of candy. He was reaching for a Coffee Crisp when someone stepped behind him. He whirled instinctively, dropping his bag.

"Whoa, hey there." Brock raised his hands. "Just me."

Toby blinked in disbelief. *Just him?* Brock Stubbs couldn't be *just* anybody. He was the underappreciated tech crew buff. The cute junior that no one else seemed to notice. The shy guy with a sweet smile. Oh man, Toby finally had an excuse to look at his face and could barely stand how *completely gorgeous* he was. What was he doing back here? Away from everyone else?

You're alone in a secluded place with the cute shy guy who's never ever spoken to you before. But this is your school, and this is real life. You know how this ends, Toby.

"Hey," he said warily. His guard went up even as his heart sang like a lovesick diva.

Brock smiled, sending a shock straight to Toby's groin. "I saw you come back here, and I, uh, wanted to make sure you were okay."

What?

His disbelief must've shown because Brock dragged a hand through his cropped hair. "Marjorie looked like she was giving you shit, and that spotlight was pretty bright . . ."

This was directly out of Toby's daydreams, the ones he let himself have late at night when there wasn't anyone to taunt him for having a dopey look on his face. In them, the cute guy in a secluded place scenario always turned out really nicely for him.

Reality, Toby!

"I'm good," he said.

Brock shifted weight. "Yeah?"

"Yeah." Toby picked up his bag. "I've had worse."

Brock winced. "Oh. Yeah."

"Yeah," he echoed, wincing at himself. *Behold, the eloquence of teenage masculinity.* Shit, he really was a total failure—like, on a crush level *and* on the smart-ass-gay level. "I gotta go, so . . ." He pointed past Brock towards the front of the stage.

Brock glanced over his shoulder quickly. "Oh, right, yeah. Yeah." He suddenly looked nervous. "I kinda wanted to ask you something else." Those gorgeous brown eyes flickered to Toby's, then away. He blushed.

Blushed.

Toby froze. Was this what he thought it was? It had to be. Even if Brock was pulling some awful elaborate joke, Toby couldn't move. Hell, even if someone had come up from the side with something nasty like, oh, a hockey stick, he still wouldn't move. Especially since Brock was coming closer now, his eyes glittering in the sparse backstage light.

"Oh yeah?" Toby gulped.

"Yeah." Brock came forward another step. "I, um, saw you looking at me during rehearsal one day."

Toby's heart stopped. "What?"

Brock smiled uncertainly. "Last year. *Hedda Gabler.*"

Toby remembered the very rehearsal. Brock had been helping put up the set and had been sweating through his shirt from hauling shit around. Like Toby could've *not* perved. Most of the girls on set had. Brock was so *freaking* hot.

"Really?" His voice was breathy. Shit, he sounded so *girly*.

"Yeah. And I've been thinking about that. About you. And I noticed you kept watching me. So I thought . . . I wondered maybe . . ." His eyes were flickering between the floor, his hands, and Toby's gaze. He reached out and touched Toby's hand.

Omigod.

Toby swallowed. They stared at each other before Brock quickly leaned in and kissed him.

Omigod.

Toby didn't even have time to close his eyes before Brock stepped back. His face was red, eyes wide.

"Is this a joke?" Toby's voice went hoarse.

"No," Brock said quickly. "Swear on my life it isn't."

Toby glanced around. No one seemed to be nearby—the coast was clear.

"I promise." Brock's hand dragged at his hair. "I, uh, I've been meaning to do that for a while. Waited until a quiet rehearsal so we could be alone."

"Seriously?" Toby's heart was doing flip-flops in his chest. His face was warm, and his dick seemed about as stunned as his brain, but he could feel it starting to clue in to events.

"Yeah."

Moments like this demanded a line. Something amazing and suave. Toby couldn't think of a single thing to say. "Could you do that again?" came out of his mouth, and he felt his face go even warmer.

Brock's smile turned Toby's chest inside out. "Yeah." He stepped forward and kissed him again.

Toby closed his eyes and let his senses go into overdrive.

Holy shit.

This was amazing. Like, this was better than anything he'd imagined, and Toby had imagined a *lot*.

Brock's lips were dry but soft. He smelled like sweat and lamp dust and it was the sexiest thing ever. Brock's hand cupped Toby's cheek, and maybe it was Toby's stupid daydreams or his complete lack of experience, but this felt perfect. A feeling of sheer *right* tingled through him all the way to his toes. His hands somehow made their way to Brock and gripped his shirt, and even *that* felt wonderful.

Brock stepped closer, his breath huffing gently across Toby's face. Toby jerked as their groins brushed each other, breaking the kiss. He stared at Brock, shocked and so fucking turned on his mind played static.

Our dicks touched. My dick. His dick. Holy shit, he has a dick and he's hard. Omigod, Toby, of fucking course *he's got a—*

"Brock? You backstage?" Tina called from behind the curtain.

Her voice was like an icy bucket of water. Toby blinked and Brock backed up. Toby waited to see what he would do, what he would say, eyeing him until Brock turned to the side. "Back here," he called.

Toby tried to speak, but no words were coming out. Words were unnecessary, right? *First kiss. First kiss. With* Brock Stubbs.

Wait, wait, did this mean Brock was gay too? It totally meant Brock was gay too. Or bi. At least queer. Hell yeah. Toby wished there was someone he could thank for this glorious bounty he'd just received. His little heart diva was singing a fucking aria.

"I, uh, I guess I'll . . . um . . ." Brock seemed at a loss too.

Tina jerked aside a nearby curtain and smiled at them. "Hey, Toby! You chewing Brock out for keeping that spotlight so bright?"

Toby forced a smile. "Something like that."

"He totally did." She whacked Brock's shoulder lightly, making Brock wince. "Juniors. Think they know it all."

"Hey, what gives?" Brock joked, pulling his shoulder away from her.

Toby hoisted his bag back onto his shoulder. "I gotta run. I'll see you two tomorrow." He moved past them, careful not to brush against Brock in case that somehow released gay rainbows into the air and told Tina they'd been making out and that their dicks had touched.

"See you!" Tina called after him.

Toby rushed out of the auditorium and to the school parking lot where his dad waited like normal. This was their routine after he'd been jumped after school a few years ago, but today he didn't register the usual annoyance he felt at still having to be picked up. Today he barely registered the ground.

Best day ever.

The next day was a busier rehearsal, and Toby tried his best not to get his hopes up. That morning he'd woken up after a particularly bad dream and remembered that this was still his hick school. It might've been a prank. A really horrible prank. Or it was just a magical limited-time-offer-only experience. Brock would wake up and realize this was a mistake, he was just curious, and only wanted to experiment with the one out gay kid. He wasn't serious.

No way could a guy that hot be seriously into a guy like Toby.

But for once Toby's paranoia was wrong, and he was cornered by Brock after the rehearsal again. They hid themselves behind the blackout curtain and made out for what felt like hours. It happened again after the next rehearsal, behind unused scenery and with full-body contact this time. When it kept happening, Toby had to tell his dad that rehearsals were running longer so they didn't have to leave right away, then he revelled in the sweet planetary alignment that allowed Toby to *finally* get some action.

After a few weeks of making out and increasingly bold groping, Toby started thinking that maybe this was a Thing. He wasn't sure what kind of Thing, but it wasn't nothing. They'd felt each other up and panted curse words into each other's shoulders, given hidden handjobs and hickeys while other cast members tromped around packing away props. It wasn't exactly romantic, but something about the way they were so aware of each other, the way they read each other, was totally beyond the physical stuff. True, Brock didn't acknowledge him if they passed each other in the hallways, and if anyone was hanging around after rehearsal, their sessions were always way shorter, and Brock *always* left first, but Toby wasn't going to complain. Not when the alternative was not kissing him at all.

So, to find out if he was the only one thinking this might be a Thing, he needed to ask the guy. They'd held whispered conversations about the play and random shit like Zelda and anime and hockey, but they'd both skirted the topic of what *this* was between them. After one particularly hectic rehearsal Toby hung out near the blackout curtain like usual and gave Brock a small smile when he walked into view.

Brock quirked an eyebrow when he didn't burrow into a dark corner straight away. "What's up, Toby?"

"You know what," Toby said instantly, then grinned.

Brock ducked his head, blushing. He glanced around, then moved closer. "You okay?"

Toby nodded. He drank in the sight of Brock—his lean, ropey body, his arms in that tight shirt, his curly hair—then took a deep breath. "I was wondering what this is."

"This?"

Toby gestured between them. "This. What we're doing."

Brock ran his fingers through his hair. Toby reached forward and took his hand. The guy would be bald before forty if he kept that up. Brock snatched it away, and Toby understood, he really did, but he couldn't help feeling a little hurt.

"We're, uh, we're just messing around, right?" Brock said a little breathlessly.

Messing around.

Um. Okay. That wasn't . . . It was realistic though. Still pretty good. And like Toby was an awesome catch? *Please*. Even *he* wasn't that delusional.

Toby slowly nodded. "Okay." He could work with messing around. He had less than a year left before graduation anyway. Only, his stomach hurt a little bit at the thought of leaving this school while Brock was still here, and he didn't think it was due to the Mars bar he'd inhaled in his nervousness before meeting Brock today.

"Cuz, I mean, I'm not . . ." Brock glanced around again, then whispered, "gay."

His stomach turned.

Come again?

"Huh?" he managed.

Brock frowned. "I'm not, man. I just, I dunno, I like you. You're like an, an exception or something."

"Liking another guy is pretty gay," Toby said. "Kissing another guy is gay. So's pinching another guy's nipple while he gives you a hand—"

"Shhh!" Brock rushed up to him, hand held out as if to keep him quiet. Toby had images of Brock covering his mouth while jerking him off and his knees went a little wobbly.

Focus, Toby.

"I get it," Brock whispered urgently, "but I'm *not*, all right?"

His knees straightened. "Whatever."

He felt disappointed, though he wasn't entirely sure why. If he had a choice, he wouldn't be out in Maney either. So what if it wasn't a Thing? The hot guy wanted to mess around. That meant more kissing and handjobs, which was a total win-win. Maybe they'd even get around to blowjobs if they could go somewhere more private. Like his bedroom. *Omigod, that's an awesome idea.*

Okay, maybe not his room straight away, but Toby could work them up to meeting outside the auditorium and sort of pretend they were boyfriends, right? Even though he'd probably graduate before that ever happened, he could at least try. And had he just thought the word *boyfriends*? With total seriousness?

He had to lighten up. He was leaving Maney next year. Messing around was good. *Good.*

"You want to stop doing this?" Brock asked. He looked disappointed too. Uncertain. His brown eyes were doing that cute worried-frown thing they did. Toby loved that look. It meant Brock would let him push things a little.

"No," he said, honestly.

Brock's face lit up. "Good. I don't either."

Toby moved forward and rested the palm of his hand on Brock's chest. Brock leaned in and pressed his lips against Toby's, which, *mmm*—

"The fuck?"

Toby froze. They both looked over. There stood Aditya, with Josh Rogers.

Josh Rogers, baby brother of Turk Rogers. The Turk Rogers who'd outed Toby and made his life hell since middle school.

Josh Rogers, who Toby just remembered was also kind of friends with Brock.

Josh Rogers, clenching his fists, scowling, and *looming* like he was ready to punch something. Toby swallowed. Or some*one*.

Brock shoved Toby.

He stumbled back. *Huh?*

Brock was glaring at him. *What the flying hell?*

"What the fuck is this?" Josh demanded. Loudly. Like, totally unnecessary loudly. "Is this fag coming *on* to you, man?"

Um, excuse him? They'd *both* been caught.

"Don't worry." Brock stepped back, eyes on a point somewhere beyond Toby's shoulder. "I can handle him."

What?

Josh went to Brock's side. "You okay, bro?" Adi frowned, and Josh pointed a stubby finger straight at Toby. "Leave him alone, you fat fuck. This might be the fucking theatre, but they're not all fags."

Oh. Oh, now he got it. They hadn't caught *them* together. They'd caught *him* hitting on Brock.

The realization made him go cold.

Oh, *fuck*. He'd been so *stupid*.

Toby looked at Brock. He'd gone stone-faced, his arms crossed, eyes on the floor. Where was the smiley guy who'd been so nervous about kissing him?

"Are you for fucking real?" He hated how his voice cracked just a little at the end.

Josh started at him, but Brock and Adi grabbed his arms.

"No, Josh," Adi cautioned. "Don't—"

"If I see you anywhere near this guy again," Josh bellowed, "or if I see you pull this homo bullshit again with *anyone*, I'm getting my brother back into town and we'll pay you a special fucking visit, you hear?"

"Josh, leave it," Adi said warningly. Marjorie appeared behind him, drawn by the loud voices. Her eyes were wide.

"Don't bother. You and your brother don't have a thing to worry about," Toby heard himself say. His voice didn't really sound like him.

He defaulted to his usual reaction whenever homophobic shit like this happened: he picked up his bag and walked away.

"Damn fucking right we don't," Josh shouted behind him.

"Calm down, dude." Adi at least sounded like all he wanted was peace.

"Seriously, bro," Josh said, "you all right?"

"I'm fine." Was it Toby's imagination or did Brock sound sad? "Nothing happened."

Oh. *Really* his imagination.

Toby's eyes met Marjorie's just as he heard that. Shit, he wished she hadn't seen this. He felt light-headed. Suddenly it seemed like there wasn't any oxygen around him. He took a deep breath and forced himself to keep walking. Off the stage, through the auditorium, out the door. He was an actor. He was a *queen*. Well, he was going to be, one day. And one thing people like him could do well was act gracefully in moments like this.

But.

"Nothing happened."

He managed to make it to the hallway before the tears spilled over.

Brock Stubbs left school feeling a lot of things. One of those things was intense relief that Josh hadn't suspected him of being gay—had, in fact, fulfilled his duty of friendship and backed him up. Having seen what had and still did happen to Toby—the shoves, the insults, that one time Turk Rogers and some of his hockey buddies had waited for him after school with a hockey stick—Brock had no desire to bring that down on his own head. Especially since Brock had a year and a half left and still lived at home. Toby was graduating in less than a year. He'd be fine.

No, this wasn't big deal. It would all blow over. Even if word did get to his parents, he'd be able to cover himself. No one knew how long they'd been doing each—doing things. He'd lost his mind for a few weeks, was all. He'd forgotten himself and now it was over and he could put the wickedly adorable Toby Rosenberg out of his mind. No harm, no foul.

Maybe if he told himself that enough, he'd believe it.

Because the last few weeks had been among the best of his life. Approaching Toby like that had taken every single paltry ounce of courage he'd had. He'd been pretty certain Toby liked *looking* at him, but whether he'd be open to doing more hadn't been so clear.

After all, Toby was *Toby*. He was fearless and creative and magnificent. Insults rolled off his tongue as easily as poetry. Whether he was acting, singing, or dancing, Toby was incredible on the stage. He was absolutely everything Brock wished he could be—fiercely independent, proud, sassy, and so, *so* strong.

Not to forget gorgeous. His eyes were grey and intense, and his mouth was super soft and wide. He had this cute breathy giggle, and he made these whimpers when they kissed that drove Brock crazy.

Kissing him had been his deepest daydream come true; being kissed *back* had been beyond dreams. As time had gone on, Brock had had little sprouts of hope that Toby had seemed to like him back. All the time they'd spent behind that blackout curtain had lit this happy little glow inside Brock, because it seemed as though his crush *did* like him back.

And Brock had completely and utterly fucked it up, like he always fucked things up.

He stopped outside the drugstore and gazed at the doors for a moment, deliberating.

Today had been unfortunate. He hadn't expected Josh to come looking for him, because Josh thought the theatre scene was totally gay, but he'd wanted to see if Brock needed a ride home. Brock knew he should have been caught as well as Toby, because, really, he was the one who'd started things. Toby didn't deserve any of the shit that had happened to him or any of the shit that *would* happen to him once word of today reached everyone.

But when they had been caught, and Brock'd had the chance to come clean, *should have* hadn't even been in his head. He'd reacted with total fear at being revealed, not realizing what he'd done until he'd seen Toby stumble back, a terrible expression of shock and betrayal on his face. All he could think in the moment was, *People can't know, he can't know, my dad can't know.*

Coward. Total, fucking, useless *coward.*

Toby deserved better than him. Toby deserved better than this town. Brock deserved less than nothing.

He went into the drugstore and bought shampoo and razor blades and shaving cream. As his total was rung up, he saw himself doing this ten years from now. Working some crappy job in Maney, maybe in the same legal office as his dad, kissing men in alleys and behind bars—or never kissing one again—buying shampoo and razor blades and shaving cream, and going home. After today, that was all he was good for.

All of his fear and clawing guilt were dissolving into a familiar monotonous bleakness, which was preferable, if he was honest.

When he arrived home, his dad's car was in the driveway. He sneaked quietly into the house, listening. Raised voices came from the kitchen. Brock tiptoed up the stairs, making as little noise as possible, and deposited the shampoo and shaving cream in the bathroom.

Something smashed downstairs.

Brock paused, closed his eyes, and took a deep breath. Toby's expression of shocked betrayal lingered behind his eyelids. He'd never forget it.

He took the blades into his room and made sure the door clicked very quietly shut behind him.

CHAPTER SEVEN

Okay, so this orienteering thing was starting any minute now, and Gigi had taken great pains to ensure he looked the part—slightly teased hair under his favourite snapback, a tight white T-shirt saying *NOT TODAY SATAN* layered with a flannel shirt of Brock's, stretch denim skinny jeans (so he could walk in comfort but still look fabulous), completed by old hiking boots and a whisper of makeup to even out any blemishes.

But there was the minor problem of his boyfriend *still not being back from his parents'*. Two and a half hours. What was taking him so long? Where the hell could he be? The town could be walked from one side to another in like an hour. It was impossible to get lost.

He was lingering by Ed's car, watching as Rosenbergs and Wongs assembled at the entrance to the park. His dad, Alan's dad, and Alan's grandfather were chatting off to the side, pointing out trees and foliage. Alan's university and work buddies were bellowing (he *knew* it) in a group by one of their cars, while cousins from either side drifted to and from groups. The kids old enough to trek for a few hours were running around yelling in some kind of game that involved sticks. How could there be so many *men* at this wedding?

Gigi returned to his phone. After calling and texting Brock multiple times, he'd given up and started scrolling through several months' worth of unread spam and junk to find an email titled *ALAN'S FINAL HOORAH! FINAL DEETS HOORAH!* Turned out Julian, Alan's best friend, had organized the bachelor party with every guy in mind, including Alan's grandfather and uncles and nephews. Hence the orienteering this afternoon, dinner at some buffet place, then ditching the kids and older folks for "manly entertainment" at Warner's for the rest of the night.

Manly entertainment.

Gigi was pretty sure these guys didn't mean the things Gigi thought of when he heard the words *manly entertainment.*

He called Mark again.

"Hey, bro."

"Mark, honey, you missed a small detail about straight bachelor parties earlier."

"I did?"

"'Manly entertainment.' Kindly explain to me exactly what that means."

Mark chuckled. Someone's voice mumbled in the background. "It's only Gigi, Frannie. He's freaking out about a bachelor party. Yeah, I know, I don't get it either."

Gigi was going to rip Mark's face off the next goddamn time he saw him. "On a time limit, Mark!"

"Bro, chill out. What kind of place are you going to for manly entertainment?"

Warner's was one of the nicer bars in town. Pool tables, good whiskey selection, lots of hunting trophies on the walls, dartboards, and all sorts of other shit Gigi had only heard about because he'd never been in there. "It's a bar. A hick one, but *nice.*"

Mark laughed. "Then, dude, that means drinking, card games, pool, and more drinking."

"You sure?"

"One hundred percent, my man. Total no-brainer."

"If tonight is anything other than drinking and card games, Mark, I'm one hundred percent blaming *you*," he hissed.

"Got it, bro. Have a stellar time."

He hung up just as one of Alan's friends raised a sign saying *STAGS ASSEMBLE.* Oh, *God*, really? Really? *Stags*? Gigi wasn't a stag. He was a motherfucking *gazelle.* Seriously, why the fuck was he even here?

He'd pushed himself off Ed's car and had started walking toward the assembling stags when a familiar car pulled into the park. A very familiar car, considering he and Brock had driven silently in it for like six hours the previous day.

Fucking finally.

Gigi changed route to meet the car. He saw Brock get out and lock it, and he drew up short for a moment. At first glance Brock looked exactly the same: no change into hiking clothes, his hair still a bit bedheady, his usual calm expression on his face—then the *huge-ass fresh bruises* on his face jumped out and went *Hiii, look at us.*

What *happened* to him?

Brock spotted Gigi and made towards him, his face breaking into a smile. Gigi stood stock-still, eyes roving over the clear imprint of knuckles on one side of his jaw. How could he smile with that damage to his face? And who'd done it? Who in this smoky smear-stain on the great Canadian landscape had done this to his boyfriend?

"Oh my God," he said.

"You're wearing my shirt." Brock stopped in front of Gigi.

"I needed something to sweat in," Gigi replied. "What the hell happened to you?"

"It looks good on you."

"*Everything* looks good on me. Answer my question."

Brock hugged him. *What the . . .* This whole morning had been them glaring at each other, so having this snuggly guy instead was awesome, but Gigi didn't like what this meant *at all.*

It felt good to be held again, especially this tightly. Gigi's hands went to Brock's waist, and he breathed in and got a hit of Brock-sweat. Normally that was good, but the guy had to have taken a bath in it to smell this bad.

Gigi pulled himself away, hands lingering a little on Brock's waist. This close, he could see Brock's eyes were clear but looked kind of puffy. Had he been *crying?* Gigi's hands clenched wads of Brock's shirt. Brock didn't cry. Gigi had literally never, ever seen him cry. "Baby? What happened to your face?"

Brock burrowed in close, arms tight around Gigi's shoulders. "Someone hit it."

Gigi rolled his eyes. "No shit. Who? And why? Because if this is some homophobic bullshit, I'll scratch their eyes out. You know I will."

Brock snuffled a laugh into Gigi's shoulder. "No. Please don't do that. I'm fine, okay? Really, I'm good."

The thing was, Gigi knew what it was like to have someone come at you, and no one was ever *fine* afterwards. He pulled his hands away and brought them up to frame Brock's face, forcing him to meet Gigi's gaze. "Babe. Tell me."

Brock's mouth twisted, and he looked away. "My dad."

His . . . *dad*? The fuck? *The fuck?* "I'll make his eyes into earrings."

Brock snorted.

"Seriously. I'll storm into his house and fucking take him apart. He did this to you?" Gigi wanted to pull Brock close and make it all better, but he didn't know how. His brain kept stuttering over the fact that *his dad* had laid into him like this. "Why the hell didn't you call me?"

Brock shrugged. "You had your lunch thing."

"But baby, I'd've helped you. I could've, I don't know, kicked him or something."

Brock was shaking his head. "No. Gi. No. You're brave, but you wouldn't've been able to do much about him. You're safer at home."

What the hell? He wasn't some delicate flower. Gigi had seen shit go down—on *and* off the stage. He'd been on the receiving end of it enough. Had Brock forgotten that?

"Aaayyy, lovebirds! Group's over here!"

See? *Bellowing.* This was too much for Gigi to handle, honestly.

Brock pulled away. "It's over, okay? Let's go hike."

"Orienteer. And how about we go press charges instead? That sounds like more fun to me." Gigi totally meant that.

"*No.* That won't help anything, I promise." Brock let him go. "Come on. I want to do something fun now."

"And you think *this* is gonna be fun?" Gigi could think of all sorts of better alternatives, like sitting on his bed and taking care of his man and never letting him within a four-block radius of his dad again, but apparently that wasn't going to be an option. Not when Brock was walking towards the group of bachelors—sorry, *stags*, ugh, what even *was* this—and decidedly not listening to him.

Gigi fell into step with him. "Can't we at least look after your face?"

"Does it look bad?"

"Uh, yeah? I think you have a black eye coming in."

Brock shrugged. "Nothing's broken. Honestly, I don't want to think about it anymore. It's done. I used to love walking through these woods."

Normally, the strong outdoorsy thing really did it for Gigi, but he couldn't enjoy it now. What the hell was even happening right now? Why was Brock shrugging this off like it wasn't a big deal? It *was* a big deal. The fuck?

They reached the edge of the bachelor party group, and Brock glanced at him. "We'll talk more later."

"Sugarplum, that is a promise."

Ed's eyes widened at the sight of them. "Holy shit, Brock. What happened to the other guy?"

"Got him with a chair."

Ed laughed and fist-bumped him. Gigi felt sick to his stomach; he was pretty sure that wasn't a joke.

"Welcome!" one of Alan's friends bellowed from below that stupid fucking sign. "I'm Julian, Alan's best man, and I—" he whipped out a sheet of paper "—have group assignments!"

Group assignments? Was this school again? No fucking way. Gigi wasn't going into the goddamn woods, through all that goddamn nature, with a bunch of *strangers*.

Brock leaned in close. "Hey. Alan has some hot friends."

Okay, so Gigi might've noticed that too, but it was totally irrelevant because Brock was very taken. He poked Brock in the side—gently—and raised one eyebrow when Brock glanced at him. Brock grinned and winked.

Julian distributed lists and navigation instructions to group leaders and began to direct people to their assigned groups. Brock was sent to a group with Gigi's dad, which had Gigi craning his neck to see how his dad was reacting to Brock's face. People were asking him about it with big grins on their faces, like it was a good thing. Ugh, dudes and fighting. And Brock was totally going to lie about it and say it wasn't anything important.

They really shouldn't be here right now.

Then Gigi found himself directed to his nature comrades, made up of Ed, one of Alan's university friends, and Alan's cousin Luc. He remembered because he was easily the hottest of Alan's cousins who'd attended the lunch. The guys in this group were all in their twenties, which Gigi was kind of relieved about, because then they'd have things like school and jobs and stuff to talk about, right? Right. He wouldn't need to bellow.

A whistle blew for attention. Julian stood on a fence by the park sign and waved. "Listen up! Your group leaders are in charge and I'll be timing you. Keith went ahead this morning to set the control points up, and he swears it's a simple course, so all you have to do is get through it as quickly as you can and have fun! Group One, go!"

And Brock's group set off into the forest.

Shiiit, they were seriously doing this. Should Brock be hiking with injuries? Gigi didn't know.

He felt useless.

Gigi looked at his group. Ed was chatting with Luc. Alan's university friend was tucking sheets of paper and the compass into his pocket, which meant he was their leader. He also had muscly, veiny legs, well-worn hiking boots, a light backpack, and a cap.

Oh hey, was Gigi supposed to have *brought* stuff with him? All he had was a water bottle shoved into his back pocket.

"Hey, everyone," Alan's friend said, "I'm Keith."

Keith? Like, the guy Julian had just mentioned? "As in, the Keith who set up the course?" Gigi blurted.

Keith grinned. "Yup. I love orienteering. I came out here early to set it up and now I am *down* for getting through it with a team. I asked for a group of guys who could win this thing. 'Sup dream team."

"Fuck yeah," Ed whooped, holding his hand up for a high five that Keith immediately clapped.

Fuck me. Gigi wondered just how long it would be before he fell into a worm-filled pit and had to be embarrassingly rescued by these guys, costing them the . . . race? How did anyone even race in orienteering? What was there to win? Had that been in the email? Because when he'd read it, he'd more, like, skimmed it.

The guys were staring at him.

"Woo?" Gigi said.

"I asked if you can hike fast," Keith said.

It would be a miracle if he could hike at all after this much time out of hiking boots. When he was younger, he'd hated it. But Gigi didn't totally break from his younger self to start gauging current hiking abilities by his former dislike of it. "I guess we'll find out?"

It wasn't long before their group was allowed to start. Keith set a punishing pace, striding down the main path like he was trying to beat land-walking records. Gigi sighed and just tried to keep up, which actually didn't turn out to be that difficult.

The forest was quiet and cool, trees creaking in the odd gust of wind. Tall poplar and spruce trees stretched above them, alternating between greens and reds and oranges, and dry leaves crunched underfoot as they walked. It *looked* nicer than he remembered, but Gigi still kept a sharp eye out for any aggressive nature, such as poisonous plants or big sticks or crawly bugs. Not just for himself, mind, but for his injured boyfriend who was being an idiot by exposing himself to nature.

"So where's the first checkpoint?" Ed asked.

"Halfway to the quarry," Keith said. "The route does a zigzag from there to the lake to this amazing huge tree in this section of wood near the parking lot."

"Having you in the group feels a little like cheating," Gigi said.

Keith waved his hand dismissively. "Nah. My knowledge only gives me a small edge. Just follow me and we'll be good."

Twenty minutes later, they'd powerwalked past the fork in the road and two of the other groups and were well on their way to the quarry. They'd gone off the main track and were standing around while Keith consulted his coordinates and instructions in confusion. Apparently they'd gone too far.

Luc and Ed were red-faced and huffing. Gigi, to his surprise, was only slightly out-of-breath despite the punishing pace. Huh.

"I think I ate too much at lunch," Ed panted.

"Me too," Luc said.

Gigi hadn't, not when he'd seen how much butter and mayonnaise had gone into it. "Maybe stick to salad next time."

They groaned.

"Nooo," Ed said. "Look, I love Sophie, believe me, but this vegetarian-wedding bullshit isn't stopping me from loading up on actual food this weekend."

"Word, dude," Luc agreed. "Alan totally shocked us all with that. My aunties went batshit. 'A Chinese wedding with *no meat*?'" he mimicked. "Then he told us it wasn't going to be a Chinese wedding anyway, it was going to be a 'mix of traditions special and unique' to them so what was the big deal?" Luc shook his head. "Kombucha cocktails aren't in *anyone's* traditions, just FYI."

"Is your family okay with a nontraditional wedding?" Gigi asked, curious. Everyone had seemed really happy and eager to get along at lunch. He'd never seen so many people shaking hands and hugging and offering food and eating in one place. So much food. So many people. There hadn't been enough seats at the table, so people had been perched on the stairs and on the kitchen counter and on garden furniture. Complete chaos, but also kind of fun.

Luc nodded. "Yeah, we'll deal. I think my uncle ordered some pork or something via special delivery."

Ed gasped. "Man, my dad did the same thing! Holy shit!" They fist-bumped. "I also heard Sophie's refusing to be given away by Uncle John. That true, Toby?"

Gigi nodded. He'd read *that* email, at least, because he was supposed to be an usher and a witness, and he needed to know the stupid schedule of events. "They're going to walk in from different sides of the ceremony space and meet in the middle. It's supposed to be symbolic."

"Oh, gag," Ed said.

"Hey, I like that," Luc said. "It's a nice idea. Unlike the vegetarian food."

Ed whacked Gigi on the arm. "You gonna let John do his fatherly duty when you and Brock tie the knot?"

Oh *God*. Gigi wasn't ready to answer that question. Marriage? To Brock? Like Brock would even be interested. Nope. Gigi hadn't even *thought* about it. Much. Definitely not when Brock and him had first started dating and Gigi's (no, Toby's) stupid adolescent fantasies had reared back into full technicolour life. And totally not when he mentally catalogued waterfront and bar spaces in Toronto that would be perfect for a reception or a ceremony or wedding pictures. Or eyed up tuxes. Or thought about which club they'd go to afterwards. Nooope. No way.

And even if he *had* thought about it, which he hadn't, he really hadn't thought about it in recent months, because recent months hadn't felt anything like the first few months. Somehow it was hard to dream about a future with a guy who disappeared into his head and job all the time.

Toby would've been really upset about that, but Gigi wasn't Toby anymore. So he just waved those naïve little fantasies bye-bye and went back to work. Which was totally what he was doing right now.

"You're gay?" Luc asked, sparing Gigi from answering.

"Yeah." Did Luc miss Gigi pawing his guy because Brock was hurt? How had he missed that? Normally straight dudes were super on edge about any display of affection, right?

"Do gay guys do stuff like that? Be given away?"

Heaven spare him from ignorant straight boys. See, this was exactly the stuff Gigi *had* expected from this bachelor party. "I think it depends on the guys in question."

"Was your boyfriend at lunch?" Luc asked.

"No. He was visiting his parents." God, Gigi would never be over that. He should've made him stay. Better an awkward-fest than an actual fucking *fight.*

"Lucky guy," Ed said. "I bet he had space to breathe and eat."

Keith let out a strangled, choking noise, and they all looked over at him.

After a beat, Ed asked, "Are we lost?"

"No," Keith ground out.

Luc grinned. "You sure? Because, you know, *Keith*, you mapped the route."

"Yeah, I thought you were the orienteering expert, Keith," Ed said. "Where's that *edge*, Keith?"

Ah. The time-honoured tradition of straight boys giving each other shit. If Gigi joined in, he knew he'd camp it up to eleven, so he didn't.

"We're not lost. We're close to the path." Keith glanced between paper and compass. "It's just, maybe I recorded the checkpoint wrong. I put it by this gigantic fallen tree. Really hard to miss."

Gigi blinked. He knew that tree. It was farther up the main path, but close to where they were. "That's not far from here."

They all looked at him as though he'd just stripped off to a glittery thong.

He straightened and crossed his arms. "Local, remember?"

"Good enough for me." Keith pocketed the compass and coordinates. "Lead on."

Which was how Gigi ended up taking them to the fallen tree and punching their card. Then he led them to the next checkpoint, a clearing between the tree and the lake, then down a shortcut trail to the lake for the next checkpoint, and so on. It turned out Keith had guestimated the coordinates for all the checkpoints and had misjudged the route anyway because he'd jogged it that morning, not walked it.

By the time he'd led them back to the parking lot, Gigi felt on top of the world. He'd taken them through the forest. *He* had. Okay, so maybe orienteering was easy when you knew the landmarks already and didn't have to worry about being sweaty and disgusting because you were so fit from dancing. All that shitty hiking when he was younger *and* his sexy, energetic job had totally paid off.

And by the looks of a very bored and alone Julian, they were the first ones back.

Keith cheered when he realized, punching his fists in the air. "Yeah! Fuck yeah!" He turned to Gigi. "And it's all on you, Local Hero!" He raised his fist and Gigi fist-bumped him. Ed and Luc clapped his back too.

Goddamn. Gigi had had *fun*. In *nature*. With *straight guys*.

What the hell was even happening anymore? Gigi needed some lip gloss or something, because this so wasn't him.

Only, it kind of was.

Not everyone was so lucky as to have a local guy in their group. No one else showed up until the last half hour, emerging from the forest group by group until they were all back. Even Brock's group was amongst the last to arrive, which Gigi found weird, because he was pretty sure Brock and his dad would've known this park better than he did.

Brock shook his head when asked. "Nah, we didn't do the course once we realized the coordinates were wrong. We just went to the quarry and back."

Dad grinned. "It was a good hike."

Brock nodded, and Gigi glanced between the two, wondering what had happened. They seemed to be all . . . *chummy*. They must've talked during the two hours in the forest, and if Dad had let *any* childhood Toby stories slip, Gigi definitely wasn't going to let him give anyone away at any wedding, ever. But maybe Brock had talked to him about the fight as well? Dad was really good to talk to. He'd always been awesome at helping with problems. If his dad knew what was going on, Gigi felt better already. He'd help.

All the other groups were waving the instructions at Keith, yelling about the mistakes. Julian had to step back on the fence and yell at everyone to calm down because, "It's not about the course, it's about having fun and bonding and shit, right, Alan?" (Alan shrugged.) "And anyway I hope you're all hungry because it's time to wash up and head out for food." (Approving roar.)

Gigi drove Brock, his dad, and an uncle back to the Rosenberg house. Brock was looking pale and kind of woozy all of a sudden, the big dummy—nature wasn't kind to the injured, everyone knew that—so Gigi planned to get him home and lie him down on a sofa as soon as possible.

At home, he found his sister amid a gaggle of women in the rec room—right, they were having a girls' evening tonight—which put paid to the idea of stretching his guy out. Brock walked away into the house before Gigi could order him around anyway. His dad waded into the room to give Sophie a sweaty dad hug that made her squeal, and Gigi went to see if the shower was free. It wasn't, so he decided now was probably as good a time as any to Talk To His Boyfriend, and he found Brock with a plate of food on a counter in the kitchen, scarfing it down as though lunch hadn't been three hours ago. Unbelievable.

"We are literally eating in an hour," Gigi said.

Brock swallowed. "I was hungry, and these are almost as good as Grandma's eggs." He took a big bite of mashed potato, and Gigi's stomach roiled at the idea of all that cream and butter.

"Ugh. Your waistline."

Brock winked at Gigi. "You'd still be interested."

"As if."

"You like meat too much."

Oh ha-ha. This reminded him of an evening last year, after they'd had dinner with Tyler and Evie, and Gigi had gone straight to the mirror in his bedroom to guess the age and weight of his food baby. Brock had followed, sighing, and told him he was wasting his time.

Gigi had glared at his stomach in the mirror, slightly distended and *wrong*. God, he was never eating fried anything anymore. Raw, organic food from now on. In tiny portions. Lots of vegetables. Nothing *but* vegetables. And just enough healthy carbs to let him dance. A guy could live off of quinoa, right? Right.

When he told Brock this, Brock leered. "Like you would ever give up meat."

Yeah, he saw the bait, but he didn't bite—just glared at him. "I could! Do you *see* this?" He gestured to his stomach.

"No. I really don't. And I'd love you if you were fat and bald, so it doesn't matter anyway." Brock stood behind him and wrapped his arms around Gigi, pressing a kiss into his neck.

"Maybe, Brock, it's not about your love for me." He angled his neck for another kiss though, and received it.

"Uh-huh," Brock murmured into his skin, slowly dragging his hands up Gigi's chest.

Gigi raised an eyebrow. "Are you listening to me?"

"Sure."

He let Brock pull his shirt completely off. "Somehow I don't think you are." Brock's stubble rasped against Gigi's throat, and he shivered.

"You're so hot," Brock breathed.

Excuse him? Were they even looking at the same person? "Uh, the food baby and fat oozing out my pores right now say otherwise."

Brock drew him in against his chest and rested his chin on Gigi's shoulder, meeting his eyes in the mirror. "Gi. Seriously?"

"Yeah. Seriously."

"One meal isn't going to do shit. Even if it did, it doesn't matter. You're not your weight."

Had Brock completely forgotten the way Toby had looked back in the day? Gigi had tried, and it wasn't so easy. "Uh, do you *remember* what I looked like at seventeen?"

Brock grinned. "Yeah. Cute."

Gigi groaned in frustration. "*Brock.*"

"So you were bigger—"

"I was Fatty McFatfat—"

"—but it didn't matter. You were still amazing. And super cute."

Oh my *God*. This guy. How did he just say these things? Gigi was struggling to hold back a smile.

Brock's hands ran back down Gigi's body. "What's your deal with your weight anyway? As long as you're healthy, that's all that matters. And you exercise so much anyway. Flipping out over one burger doesn't make sense."

Gigi hands raised to Brock's and pressed them against Gigi's abdomen, right next to his waistband. "It's simple, my sweet, loyal subject. When I was a chubby teen stuck in Maney with unenlightened hicks, I was miserable. Now that I'm a smoking-hot queen dancing and acting in Toronto, I'm happy."

Brock frowned. "But you danced and performed in Maney too. Your weight didn't stop you. Weren't you miserable because of all the homophobic shit?"

A lump had risen in Gigi's throat. "Well. Yeah."

"So what does your weight have to do with that?"

"It didn't *help*, Brock. I wanted to be fabulous and beautiful, and everyone *knows* that means crack-whore thin."

Brock didn't laugh. "You'd still be fabulous and beautiful if you gained weight. That stuff's not related to weight."

"Oh my God, are you a closet chubby chaser?"

Brock did laugh then, chest shaking against Gigi's back. "No. Babe. You're just not making sense. I'm bigger than you are, and you find me attractive." His thumbs rubbed Gigi's abdomen, distractingly close to Gigi's dick. "Do you think you'll stop being a smoking-hot happy queen if you gain a few pounds?"

The thought clenched his insides. *Yes*. But actually, no. Because Gigi would never let that happen. And even if he *did* gain a little, it wouldn't matter because he was a queen and he would make it work. "It just doesn't help," he mumbled.

Brock kissed his shoulder. "I get it. You're at your happy weight. Would you love me if I got fat?"

Gigi blinked. "What? Yeah."

"Okay. Same logic applies to you." A hot breath on Gigi's skin made him shiver. "Good to know I won't be dumped because I gained a few pounds."

"Oh my *God*. I am not that shallow."

Brock's thumbs inched closer to Gigi's dick, possibly helped a little by Gigi's hands. "You are totally that shallow."

"Uh, I *was* a fat femme? I don't propagate that shit." Well, he tried not to. There were enough asshole gays out there demanding *no fats, no femmes, no Asians, no bis, no uglies,* etc.

"Then don't think it about yourself." Brock turned back to Gigi's neck as his fingers dug under Gigi's jeans and shorts to brush the head of Gigi's cock. Electricity charged up Gigi's spine, and he closed his eyes in bliss, pushing Brock's hands deeper into his pants.

Damn, that night had been hot.

Here in his parents' kitchen, Brock waved his fork in front of Gigi's face. "Gi? You here?"

Gigi had a semi now. Great. "Yes. Stop distracting me. I'm not here to talk about you stuffing your face. We need to talk about your actual face."

Brock shrugged and went back to his food.

"Your. Parents. What happened?"

Brock's fork paused above his plate. He took a deep breath, then said, "I really don't want to talk about it."

Gigi stared at him.

Brock stared back.

"Not an option, boyfriend. Your face is hurt. *You're* hurt." Gigi reached over to stroke his hair. "You don't get to avoid this."

Brock's throat worked, and he stared back down at his food. "Look . . . this is not a big deal, okay? It was a long time coming."

It was?

Brock shrugged. "But it's okay. I think I've been disowned, which honestly is *such* a relief."

Holy shit. *Holy shit.* Gigi hadn't been expecting *that.* "Why?"

Brock watched him, brown eyes heavy with all sorts of emotions. "Because I'm gay. Because I'm not the son they want." He sighed, his fork trailing through the carby mush on his plate. "I just can't be in that family anymore. I don't want to be."

Gigi's heart ached. How could anyone hurt this guy? *This* one?

"Babe," Gigi breathed. He reached forward and pulled Brock to him, letting Brock's head settle in the curve of Gigi's neck. Gigi ran his fingers through Brock's hair, cursing himself for not being more demanding. He should've ordered Brock to stay here. "You don't ever have to see them again."

Brock chuckled sadly against Gigi's skin. "Thanks." Brock's stomach growled, making them both laugh. Gigi scratched through his hair gently, and Brock closed his eyes. "Sorry about that—" he waved at his stomach and the plate of food "—I didn't have lunch."

"You didn't?"

"Nah. I, uh, didn't have much of an appetite."

"Omigod, Brock." Gigi dropped a kiss on his hair. "Honey. Sugarplum. Why didn't you say? They have these things called smartphones, you know? You could've told me, and I'd've brought you food before orienteering."

Brock shrugged. "I'm telling you now. That feels really good."

Honestly, it was kind of nice to be touching him like this. Like, he'd been mad at Brock for so long that just feeling his hair now was so … *peaceful*. And easy. Easier than being mad. And Gigi was spitting mad. Not at Brock, but at his parents.

Though, something was niggling at him. Gigi kept circling his fingers through Brock's hair. "They disowned you for being gay? They left it kind of late. What a shitty weekend to do it." It seemed so out of the blue. All of this was.

Brock put aside the food, then settled his hands on Gigi's waist and pulled Gigi even closer against the counter, pressing their bodies together, his face against Gigi's clavicle, eyes closed.

"Brock?" Gigi prodded gently.

He exhaled long and deep, breath hot on Gigi's chest. "I hadn't told them before this weekend."

Huh. Well, that was annoying. It meant that over a year ago, when Brock had literally been on his knees in the street, declaring he was out to everyone and begging for a second chance, he'd been lying. And when Gigi had asked him later if he was out to his family, and he said yes, he'd lied again.

The thing was, Gigi couldn't work up any anger at that. Seeing the bruises on his face totally excused Brock. "Because they were going to do this?" He ran his fingers lightly over Brock's cheek. It was more swollen. They really needed to put ice or something on it.

"Or worse. I haven't spoken to them in, I don't know, like five years or something? A long time." Brock opened his eyes and looked up. "I thought you'd be way angrier than this."

The hell? "Are you serious? Babe, we all know the bad coming out stories. I never expected you to be one of them, though. Why would I be angry at you for this?"

"Don't you remember what you said to me when we hooked up again?" Brock asked. "Right afterwards?"

Gigi frowned. "Not . . . really?" He remembered sex. Really hot sex. *Mmm.*

Brock scowled. "Seriously? The talk we had?"

Oh. Maybe?

Their first night, the one that had started with Gigi and Sarah setting Evie and Tyler up and ended with Gigi and Brock getting together, had been fucking magical and of course involved somehow magical fucking. That was literally the only reason Gigi could give for the sex being that amazing—magic.

He'd lain next to Brock afterwards, hand lazily playing with Brock's pecs. He'd finally fucked Brock Stubbs, and been fucked back, and it was everything he'd thought it would be. Exciting. Sexy. Sweet. Gigi'd pressed a hand over his smile, embarrassed at how *pleased* he was that this man was lying there.

This was what he'd wanted at seventeen.

His eyes flew open on that thought, because suddenly it was like he'd never left Maney or aged or slept with another guy. Gone was the ease and sexiness, back was the excitement and stupid, stupid *hope* of adolescence. *Oh shit.*

Toby took a deep breath, then let it out slowly, trying to figure out where his queen had gone and why his dumb awkward teenage self was lying here instead. This was going wrong. He'd wanted to bring Brock back and fuck him crazy several times over, to be witty and sexy and fun and *memorable*, not lie here feeling like he was going to explode from the awkwardness and inadequacy and sweetness of just lying here with this man. Gigi had retreated, actually disappeared, and Toby was on his own, next to the first guy he'd ever done anything with.

Brock, somehow sensing a change in the mood, turned his face and kissed him. Toby's chest swelled, because *Omigod Brock is here and interested and still* likes *me*, but deep in his stomach was this growing sense of it all being too good to be true, too raw and perfect.

He broke the kiss and put his face against Brock's shoulder, trying to figure out what this was, why he felt like this. He'd fucked dozens of men here, just like tonight, and lain here afterwards, just like this, but only as Gigi. Never Toby.

"What's up?" Brock said.

"Nothing," he said.

"Hey, look at me."

"No. Go to sleep."

Brock kissed his hair and gently pushed Toby's face away from his chest so they could look eye to eye. "What's wrong?"

Everything. Nothing. Absolutely nothing. But totally everything because you make me feel things and I don't know why. Why you? Why us? Why me?

"This doesn't make us boyfriends," Toby blurted out.

Brock's eyes widened. "Uh, okay?"

"I sleep with guys all the time. Like, all the time. So this is nothing special. At all. So don't think this is special. Because it's not." Shit. Shit. What was he saying? See, this was why Toby was never in charge. Word vomit, and none of it was even funny.

Brock had given him a searching look. "Can *we* sleep together again?"

"Hell yes."

"But not as boyfriends."

"No." Shit. "Maybe?" He had to rescue this somehow, before he ran his mouth and made sure Brock would never want to see him again, let alone fuck him like he'd done tonight. "Like, it's not that easy."

Brock's expression softened. "Oh. You mean . . . because of what happened? When we were teens?"

"Yeah. Exactly. You don't get to make that up to me by fucking my brains out. I mean, that helps. *Totally* helps. But I'm still pissed about it."

Oh God. Who did that? Who stayed pissed about something that happened like a gazillion years ago? Gigi would never have admitted that.

Brock's thumbs rubbed along the side of Toby's face. "I told you how sorry I am about that. I really am. Gigi, I'll do whatever I have to to make it up to you."

And *why* did Brock have to be so fucking nice about it? How was Toby so lucky? Just coming back here, still wanting him even though he'd seen Toby at the worst point of his life, was kind of enough.

Toby's eyes were starting to get all prickly. The words *No, it's okay, I get it, I'm just glad you're here* were on the tip of his tongue.

Fuck. Abort! Abort! Abort!

He dug deep inside and somehow brought Gigi LaMore up, fitting back into her like a comfy pair of sneakers. No, gloves. LaMore was classy as fuck. Classy, and a little annoyed for some reason, but always ready to help him out.

She tossed her head, mentally squared her shoulders, and prodded Brock's chest. "You better, sugarplum. I don't give second chances to *anyone*. This is it, and you are going to work so hard for this." There, that was more like it. Sassy. In control. Gigi could relax now.

Brock's eyes darkened. "Work *hard*, huh? That a promise?"

"That's a *requirement*."

"You got it, babe."

"That's *madame* to you."

Brock grinned, so devastatingly handsome Gigi wanted to swoon. When he pressed his lips to Gigi's ear and breathed, "*D'accord, madame*," Gigi might've actually done it.

Then they'd fucked again and woken up and blown each other, and somehow had kept doing that for over a year.

But what part of that night was making Brock glare at him now? What had he said? Was it the *making him work for it* part? Maybe. Had Gigi even said exactly that? He'd said something *like* that.

"You might have to jog my memory," Gigi said.

"You told me you don't give second chances." Brock's eyes bored into his. "And I believed you, because in your shoes, I wouldn't give second chances either. Not to me."

"You took that *seriously*?"

"Uh, yeah? I love you. I loved you at the time. I didn't want to screw this up." Brock looked pissed off for some reason.

Not that Gigi was feeling especially calm himself, because what the hell? Did Brock honestly think he was that high-maintenance?

Well, okay, yes, he was high-maintenance, but he wasn't loony-bin high-maintenance.

"Um, hate to break it to you, boyfriend, but if you'd told me you weren't out to your parents because they were going to fucking hurt you, I'd've understood." Gigi stared at him. "Do you seriously think I wouldn't've?"

The expression on Brock's face said yes.

Gigi stepped back and crossed his arms. "Oh my God. Brock. Honestly?"

"You were always so clear about hating closet cases. And I tried super hard to show you I wasn't one. Like, all the freaking time. Every time we were in public, you know? I've tried to make sure you never doubted me, not even for a second." Brock's face was red.

Gigi glared. "It depends on the situation! It always *depends*! Oh my God, you make me sound like I demanded you be out to everyone and her dog, and that I *check* on you. I don't *do* that."

"Don't you? I am *so aware* of our history. I am constantly judged by you. You don't say it, but I can tell you think it. I *know* you watch me with other people, waiting for me to slip up and not mention my boyfriend."

He shook his head. "I don't do that either." He didn't. Much. But he'd seen the judge-y looks from other people, the ones who didn't like loud, femmy boys who enjoyed wearing dresses and could dance in six-inch stilettos. And he'd *preened* every time Brock had said Gigi was his boyfriend, because screw those people. So what if he liked hearing it?

"Maybe not consciously, but I bet if I didn't say it, you'd instantly be in my face."

Anger boiled through Gigi. Where the shit was all this coming from? "Sounds like you're judging yourself way more than I ever did. You think I don't know about bad family situations? I do. We all know about them. If you'd *just told me*, I would have *understood*, baby, and frankly I'm pissed you think I wouldn't."

Brock dragged his hands through his hair but didn't say anything. Which really was fucking typical. "No freaking wonder you didn't want to come back here."

"No *shit*, Gi!" Brock pointed at his bruises. "This is nothing new. I never wanted to come back to this. But no, I *had* to, for you."

Wait, *what*? "Nothing new? What does that mean?"

"It means what I said. My parents are assholes."

A picture clicked into place in Gigi's head. A different one. One where those scars on Brock's skin weren't from self-harm, but from his parents. His stomach plummeted. "You mean . . ."

Brock crossed his arms. "Yeah."

"When you were younger *too*?"

He seemed to hunch in on himself. "Yeah."

Gigi didn't know whether to hug him or shake him. "How come I'm only hearing this now? What the hell? Don't you trust me?"

Brock surged to his feet. "Seriously? Why the hell would I tell you? Our history is bad enough. The last thing I want to be is some victim of violence as well as a messed-up ex-closet case. I know I'm already not good enough. Not out enough, not fun enough, not brave enough. Never, ever enough."

Gigi's jaw dropped. "When have I *ever* said that to you?"

"You don't need to say it."

"What the— Who even *are* you? This isn't the Brock I know."

Brock's face twisted. "Oh yeah? The Brock you know is done trying to be everything for you. You want the truth, *Toby*? I never wanted to come out to my parents. And I never wanted to come back here and pretend like that was okay with me. But I did it because of *you*."

"Do *not* put this on me—"

Brock held up one finger at him. "Oh, I am. I totally am. I didn't want to be here, but you didn't care. You *never* care. You only ever think about yourself and your goddamn feelings, and I am *tired* of all your fucking drama. You *exhaust* me." Brock threw up his hands. "I am *done*. Okay? Done with this, done with you."

He pushed past Gigi. Or, rather, Toby, because that's who was standing with his jaw on the floor in shock.

What did Brock mean, he exhausted him? What the hell was that about?

What had just *happened*?

Brock brushed past him again, picked up his plate of food, then turned and left the kitchen.

Wait. Had Brock *broken up* with him? Then grabbed a *snack*? Oh *hell* no.

Gigi spun and marched after him. He was heading for the stairs, past a group of wide-eyed Rosenbergs standing in the doorway of the rec room.

"You did *not* just break up with me," Gigi yelled at Brock's back. "*You* don't break up with me. That's not how this works! *No one* breaks up with me! *I* break up with *you*!"

Brock flipped him the bird over his shoulder as he took the stairs two at a time. Gigi ran up after him, only to have his own bedroom door slammed in his face. The lock clicked, and Gigi stared at it in shock. Why did that still work? And how come Brock was the one who got to hide in *Gigi's* room?

"Brock!" he started.

Someone cleared their throat behind him. He turned around to see Sophie, her arms crossed and eyes narrowed.

Oh, right. She was here with the bachelorette party. As was most of his family.

Oops.

"Toby. You done?"

"Nope."

She leaned in. "How about you *be* done?"

Like hell. Gigi gestured at the door. "How about I *wait* until my boyfriend decides he's finished *hiding* in my *room* like a *child* before—"

"Oh my God, shut *up*." Sophie grabbed his shoulders. "I wasn't asking. Toby, you have got to calm your tits. Or at least take it outside—I think Uncle Steve almost had a fit from all the gay drama."

Gigi bristled. "It is *relationship* drama, and he'll *handle* it if he wants the usual birthday card from his favourite nephew."

She winced. "Tobes, that fight sounded terrible. *None* of us downstairs can really handle it. If things were going this badly, why did you both come here?"

He glanced at the door, certain Brock was listening in. "I don't know. I guess I didn't know things were this bad. All I was expecting was my boyfriend to *show up* for my sister's wedding and *not* be a total head case."

Sophie shook him gently. "Toby. There's been this weird vibe around you two since you got here. You're fine one moment, then you can't seem to stop bitching at each other the next. Come on."

Gigi rolled his eyes. "Don't worry, we're not going to start catfighting in the fucking aisle."

"I can't see Brock doing that, no."

"That's not how— Wait, what do you mean, you can't see *Brock* doing that?"

She pulled him in close. "Tobes. Seriously. I thought you two were cool."

Her hands were warm on his shoulders and her grey eyes were steady on his. It was just the two of them, like it used to be when they were kids and Toby was freaking out over something that had happened at school. A rush of affection for her swamped him, helping to wash away part of the anger.

And what was left were more crawly, awful gut feelings. Like, worse than preperformance nerves. Worse than anything Gigi had felt since leaving Maney.

"I loved you." Loved. Past tense.

"We weren't perfect, but I didn't expect this," he admitted.

"Okay. Whatever's going on, you need to figure it out and make up. I love you and I want you to be happy, whether that's with or without him"—she nodded her head at the door—"but so help me God, if you ruin this for me and Alan, I will tear your balls off."

He laughed. "Don't worry, loser, your perfect day will be perfect."

She nodded, her expression serious. "I hope so." She drew back from him. "For what it's worth, I think you should give him some space right now."

Gigi threw up his hands. "I am literally trying to fix things. How is *space* going to fix things?"

"Try it. Come on." She took his arm and gently pulled him away from the door.

Across the landing from them, the bathroom door opened with a billow of steam, and Ed stepped out in a towel, hair plastered to his head. "Oh, hey, guys! Shower's free!"

Gigi scowled at him. Fucking Ed. If he hadn't been in the shower, *Gigi* could've showered, and then he and Brock wouldn't've had that stupid fight. Brock would be talking to him downstairs, and they'd be all loved up like they'd just been, and Gigi wouldn't be having a freaking identity crisis brought on by being back in this town and his boyfriend possibly *breaking up* with him. *Again.*

This was worse than Lifetime.

He shrugged Sophie off and stomped down the stairs. Behind him he heard Ed ask her, "What's with the face? What did I miss?"

After pacing Gigi's room and resisting temptations to destroy everything in it, Brock finally calmed down enough to eat and pull another set of clothes together. Once Ed and Sophie had moved away from the bedroom door, he gathered his clothes and a towel and dashed into the bathroom. Under the shower's excellent spray, he could let himself unravel a little.

Today was officially the worst day.

He and Gigi had had fights before, but nothing like today. Other fights had been about dumb shit, like cancelling a date or getting a little too flirtatious with other men or simply being tired and hungry, and had nearly always been fixed by the end of the day with someone being fucked.

This time, Brock was too livid to see straight, let alone think about fucking. He didn't want Gigi anywhere near him. He didn't even want to look at his face. That entitled, demanding, arrogant, self-involved, utterly *fucking ridiculous*—

He sighed into the wet, tiled space of the shower. The heat of the water made his face ache.

What was he doing here? He should just go. Pack his stuff and drive back to Toronto. Gigi could figure out his own ride. There was nothing here for Brock, not anymore. His parents were finally done with him, and why would the Rosenbergs want him here after that fight? No. Time to leave and *never* come back. And this time he'd keep that promise.

Making that decision felt like the first good thing he'd done in a long time.

He turned the shower off, stepped out, dried and dressed himself, then returned to Gigi's room to pack. Throwing down the towel, his eye was caught by the trophy section on Gigi's shelves. How had Brock ever thought those were amazing signs of early success? Why did Gigi still keep those? Wasn't it fucking *narcissistic* to keep shit like this?

He picked one up at random and glanced it over. *Excellence in Drama, Maney High School.* It was dated the year Gigi had graduated. Right. Drama. The two plays he'd been in that year had earned the theatre group a trip to some Ontario-wide school theatre thing in Toronto, and Gigi had won something for his lead in *Anything Goes*, so the school had given him this as recognition of his ability. Totally over the top.

Anything Goes. They'd had their first kiss during rehearsals for that.

He shoved the trophy back on the shelf and went to his bag. As he rolled clothes up and tossed them in his bag, someone knocked gently on the doorframe.

"Brock?"

He looked up. Naomi stood in the doorway, her face concerned. "Can I come in?"

It was literally her house. Brock resisted the urge to shrug and said, "Sure."

She stepped in and leaned against Gigi's desk. Brock continued packing. Whatever she was going to say, it wouldn't change his mind.

"I love my son deeply, but he can be a total pain in the ass."

Brock paused, jeans in hand. He looked at her again. She gazed back, totally serious. *Okay. Wow.*

"I guess you heard us," he said.

"A lot of us did. Are you packing?"

He nodded.

"I'm not going to stop you, Brock, but please don't think you're unwelcome just because my son can be immensely selfish and shortsighted."

He let out a bark of laughter. "Should you be saying that?"

"I raised him, so I'm allowed to say it. I got all of it. Years of singing and dancing and tantrums about stuff I barely understood." She shook her head. "Sometimes the way he swung between loving something and hating it drove me nuts. The way he's so open, so completely free with his emotions, it's an incredibly wonderful and beautiful thing, but it *is* tiring to the rest of us who maybe don't need to share everything all the time."

Brock winced. Guilt radiated through him at the memory of actually saying, *"I am tired. You exhaust me."* He knew that wouldn't go down well.

"Living here was rough for him, and because it was rough for him, it was rough for all of us." She crossed her arms and gazed out of Gigi's window. "I can only imagine what it was like for you, growing up here."

"I didn't have his problems at school."

She turned to him. "No. But I imagine that staying quiet to avoid those problems created new ones, right?"

He shrugged. "It's in the past."

"And maybe you had problems of your own?" Her grey eyes stared into his, and Brock was abruptly certain that she *knew*. Somehow she knew his father was an abusive asshole and his mother was a shell of a person and Brock was caught somewhere between the two of them. Sure, he had bruises on his face as evidence, but Naomi didn't seem surprised at all by them.

A lump rose in his throat. "Earlier you mentioned you talked to my mom."

"I know her from a book club a few years back. There *were* problems, right?"

Wasn't it obvious?

He nodded.

She sighed. "I thought there might be. There were signs. She never said anything or asked for help, so I just . . . Anyway. I'm sorry, honey."

He couldn't deal with this. Not right now. "Doesn't matter. I'm over it."

She raised an eyebrow. "Really? It might all be in the past, and you might try to let it go, but sometimes it's hard to do that. Sometimes other people don't let you do that." She pushed away from the desk. "I know you didn't want to come here, but something made you feel like you had to. Maybe it was my son, but maybe it was something else."

Maybe she didn't know shit.

"And I know you don't think you have a place here, but it's my opinion that you do."

Nice opinion to have. Too bad it was totally wrong. He stared down at his bag, open and messy, unsure if he should tell her how wrong she was about him. She was trying to be nice, though. Sure all of this sounded good, but he didn't believe it.

"I don't know what sparked the fight between you two today. But if I know anything about my son, he said stuff he didn't mean and he needs time to think. I hope you're the same way." She abruptly crouched next to him so they could look at each other face-to-face. "Brock, we're not going to stop you leaving, not if you really want to go. But you make my son happy, and I think he needs you here."

"Sorry, Naomi, but I don't care what he needs anymore."

She made a face but touched his shoulder. "Okay, that's understandable. But listen: we also like *you*. We're all happy to have you here. Please stay and celebrate with us."

Brock stared at her in surprise. "Are you serious?"

She cocked her head to one side. "Why wouldn't I be?"

"Do you know our history? What I did to him in high school?"

Her mouth pursed. "I know pieces of the story. Isn't all that behind you? Toby mentioned some of it when he told us you two were dating."

"He . . . did?" Brock thought Gi had just given his family the basics—they'd known each other and they'd crushed on each other. So Naomi *knew* what Brock had done?

"Yes. He said you had changed, so none of it mattered anymore."

Funny. That wasn't what he'd said just now. Clearly it *did* matter.

She smiled at him and squeezed his shoulder. "Look, how about you take a little time to think this over? If you leave now, it'll be past midnight when you get back to Toronto. Stay the night and leave in the morning if that's what you want to do."

Okay, so maybe she had a point there, but Brock didn't exactly care about arriving home at midnight if it meant being away from this fucking town and his insensitive boyfriend.

Who probably wasn't his boyfriend anymore.

Shit. *Shit.*

That . . . He hadn't meant to break up with him. Not really.

Fuck.

After all, Gigi was *his*. Okay, Brock constantly warred between wanting to fuck Gigi's brains out and wanting to *shake* them out, but that was just part of loving him. Yeah, he could be reactive, loud, and seriously self-involved, but the flipside of that was this self-awareness, intelligence, and sharp sense of humour. Sure, he was high-maintenance, but it fed into his perfectionism, his work ethic, and made him the performer he was. The femmy bitchiness that got Brock so hot also meant some serious inner strength on Gigi's part, because Brock knew exactly what that had cost him as a teen, and he knew Gigi had earned every single moment of being himself.

The thing was, everything in life was a trade-off. No way did Brock expect anyone to be perfect, because that was literally impossible. Enjoying all the good things about Gi meant handling all the not-so-great things about him, and Brock was okay with that. He really was. Because he knew the negative stuff fed into the good parts, and helped make Gigi so amazing and worth the wall climbing. And the negative stuff wasn't even that negative. Not really, in the grand scope of things.

And Brock had told him he as good as hated him.

He didn't.

Shit, he *didn't*.

But he also didn't see how he could repair this.

"I'll think about it," he said.

"Great." Naomi patted his shoulder, then stood with a small groan and several clicks. "Oh my God. My knees aren't getting any younger, that's for sure."

Brock stood too, suddenly at a loss now that he wasn't so sure he wanted to leave Gigi behind. He followed Naomi downstairs, then slipped his shoes and coat on so he could go outside to think. He walked around the block, his return trip showing Ed sitting on the front steps with a cigarette.

Ed waved at him. "'Sup, my man!"

Brock waved back uncertainly. He hadn't spoken much with Ed since coming here, so he wasn't sure exactly why Ed seemed to be waiting for him.

Ed stood up and went over to Brock, his cigarette trailing smoke behind him. He gestured with it. "Don't tell Aunt Naomi, okay? She and my dad would totally freak if they knew I smoked."

"It's not the greatest habit."

Ed shrugged. "I know. Cravings are a bitch. But the smoke is a sweet mistress." He took a drag, then flicked his ash on the grass. "Listen. I know you're having the worst weekend ever, what with that fight, and you and my cousin having some—" he made air quotes "—'issues,' but I was hoping you'd stick around for tonight. I hear you rock at pool, and I'm totally shotgunning you for my team."

"Pool?"

"Yeah, at Warner's." Ed grinned. "It's gonna be us, Alan, his buddies, and maybe Uncle John and my dad standing around drinking whiskey and playing pool. Freaking sweet, man."

And suddenly, more than wanting to go back to Toronto, more than wanting to get his head together and figure this fucking weekend out, and way more than talking to Gigi, Brock wanted a drink and to shoot some damn pool.

Which was how he found himself at Warner's three hours later, after a meal out that had seen him and Gigi seated at opposite ends of the table, the full bachelor party between them. They'd arrived in separate cars and had immediately gravitated apart, deliberately avoiding each other. Same thing happened arriving here at the bar— they were at opposite ends of the table while the guys sat drinking between them. Not that Brock was ready to talk to him, not yet, and it looked like Gigi wasn't exactly raring to get into it either.

It was weirdly reminiscent of high school—Gigi, at a distance, yet within sight and so, *so* obvious, his presence like a winking glint in the edge of Brock's eye. It wasn't just the pink button-down with white stars all over it, which, yeah, was eye-catching and possibly the gayest clothing item this town had ever seen, but also Gigi's dyed-red hair, and the way his whole body moved when he spoke. Just so expressive.

Brock glanced at himself. Jeans and a flannel shirt. Same as most of the guys here. Only, he suspected Alan's friends had paid more for theirs, and *he* wasn't wearing bow ties or suspenders or big glasses like some of them were. And his jeans weren't rolled at the cuffs. Despite all the extra hipster shit, he still fit in more than Gigi did.

But these guys seemed like a good bunch. He hadn't had a chance to talk to them much until dinner—the hike had been mostly him, John, and Alan's dad swapping hockey and work stories—but they were chatty and full of jokes. He didn't know if one of the Rosenbergs had mentioned him and Gigi sounding off, but they seemed pretty okay about talking with both of them individually.

Not that he'd have expected them to do anything else. Because this was the twenty-first century, and Canada, and if these guys were aware of any problems, they were too polite to draw public attention to them.

Besides, they were clearly more focused on Alan's upcoming nuptials and giving shit to Keith.

Keith finally broke, and smacked the table with one hand. "Guys, can't we just let it go? It's a bunch of fucked-up coordinates, not the end of the goddamn world."

A chorus of insults raged back:

"Tell that to my blisters, man."

"You're such a fucking douche bag, Keith."

"Two hours, dude! *Two*! My Converse are ruined."

"Suck my dick, Keith."

Brock couldn't help glancing at Gigi, who was taking everything in with a small smile.

The best man, Julian, gestured for silence. "Everyone, shut up. Keith, you're buying the next round." Keith groaned as the guys around him cheered and patted his back. "But first! A toast and an ode to our brother-in-arms, Alan Wong!"

First Julian, then Alan launched into speeches about their friendships and love and marriage, then everyone started sharing anecdotes about Alan's apparently reluctant transition into adulthood. Brock's attention wandered during the speeches, and he glanced around the bar. It was mostly as he remembered it: dark wood and metal furnishings, plenty of tap beer and decent whiskey, pool tables on one side, darts on the other, and board games piled on a shelf. They were one of several groups in here, but he didn't recognize anyone else.

Brock had visited Warner's a lot with friends in his last year in town, when he was only a year underage and could persuade the bartenders to sneak him some beer. So his pulse jumped when he recognized one of the bartenders there tonight—Val, the one who'd always been cool with not checking ID when he'd bought beer. She spotted him and waved. Julian was finishing a story about Alan's last day of work at the Toronto firm where they'd met, so Brock ducked away and approached the bar.

Val was fortysomething now, still tattooed and chill. Without batting an eye, she said, "Hey there, stranger. ID."

He managed to crack a smile. "Seriously, Val?"

"Nah." She leaned against the bar. "Brock Stubbs. Look at you, all grown up." She gestured at his face. "And getting into accidents. Least, I hope it was an accident."

"Let's say it was."

She grinned. "I didn't think I'd ever see you back here again. You in town for long?"

"Nope. Just for the wedding." Maybe. He still hadn't decided if he wanted to take off tomorrow.

She looked behind him. "Oh, the Rosenberg wedding? Nice. Didn't know you were close to them."

Behind him, Gigi had started telling the story of Alan meeting his family for the first time. Alan was trying to stop him, but was restrained by Keith and Julian. Gigi was the centre of attention as he reenacted Alan stammering a poorly phrased compliment to Naomi.

Brock shrugged. "Things happen. How have you been?"

"Good, good." She gestured at the bar. "I'm managing this place now."

"Congrats. That's awesome."

She smiled. "It has its perks. So what can I get you?"

"And I was like, 'Oh *honey*, I know my sister is all in love with you or whatever, but that is my *mother* you're talking to,'" Gigi said, to a round of groans. From the sounds of it, his camp was at Friday-night-in-the-Village levels.

Shit. Brock hated it when Gigi amped it up in places like this. Not that he'd ever say anything, because there was nothing wrong with him being like that (and Gigi had totally read him the "it's not okay to ask anyone to Tone It Down" act way back at the beginning of them dating), but he dreaded to think of the attention he'd get here.

"Bourbon," Brock said. "Double. Straight."

Val raised her eyebrows, then turned away to pour the drink. Someone banged into him from behind, and he twisted to find Julian there. "Man," he said happily, "your boyfriend's a total legend."

"Good to know," Brock said. "Buy you a drink?"

Julian held up his hands. "Whhhoooaaa, sorry, don't swing that way!"

Brock had jumped and started stammering out a response when Julian grinned and clapped his shoulder. "Just messing with you. And shut up with the buying talk, it's Keith's round." He turned and yelled at Keith, who rolled his eyes and reached for his wallet.

Val placed the whiskey in front of Brock. "Anything else?"

Brock smiled at her. "I think these guys are going to ask for a big order."

"And I'm paying," Keith grumbled, appearing next to him. "I'll have a Lug-Tread and everyone else is getting pitchers of your cheapest beer."

Val nodded and began grabbing empty pitchers.

Julian slung one arm over Keith's shoulder. "Man, you *hate* us right now if you're buying us Molson."

"Damn straight."

"Oh my *God*, sweetie," Brock heard Gigi say, "do I *look* like someone who follows hockey? Or any sport?"

He sank the whiskey and promised himself he wasn't going to talk to him. Nope. Not at all. Easier. Safer.

It worked for a while. Many pitchers, shots, stories, and games later, Brock had retreated to the pool table with Ed, Keith, and Alan's cousin Luc. Alan had lost a drinking game and was wearing antlers while losing another drinking game. Gigi was playing pool against one of Alan's friends on the table next to Brock's, and Brock was desperately trying to ignore him.

It was hard though. Every move he made seemed to emphasize just how close-fitting his ridiculous shirt was, or how his jeans stretched over his ass when he bent over to take a shot, or that he was more LaMore than Rosenberg tonight. Brock wasn't sure if he was doing it intentionally or not.

Either way, Brock really wanted to fuck him. It was confusing because Brock was sure they were supposed to be angry at each other right now. When had that changed? *Had* it changed? Could he be this furious with someone and still want to fuck him?

Maybe it would be better to just not think too much about it and dodge Gigi when they rounded their tables at the same time. Focus on his game, which he and Ed were winning.

Finally, something he was good at.

Brock was in the middle of discussing the upcoming hockey season with Luc, so he didn't notice the man until Luc got distracted and didn't answer him. He felt rather than saw the guys around him go still, and he turned around.

Standing before the pool tables was Josh Rogers.

Older, heavier, more bald, but undeniably him.

And he was staring straight at Gigi.

Gigi stood under the pool table lights, cue caught in his fingertips, hip jutting out defensively, and eyes glittering dangerously. He stared straight back at Josh with chin uplifted.

Magnificent.

Then Brock's thoughts scattered as Josh stepped forward aggressively.

"I'll be damned," Josh said. "Look who it is. I just walk in here, and it's like nowhere's safe for normal people anymore."

"What a surprise to find you still here," Gigi said in a tone that implied it was no surprise at all.

"I didn't recognize you without your man boobs, Rosenberg."

Gigi arched an eyebrow. "And I didn't recognize you without your hair."

Keith took three steps and threw an arm over Gigi's shoulders. "Hey, homeboy. Hey. This shit-stain giving you grief?"

"Nope." Gigi smiled evilly. "Not anymore."

"Who're you? His boyfriend?" Josh asked.

"Nah, man." Keith took a swig from his microbrew. "Just his buddy wondering what the problem is."

"My problem is that I didn't realize this was suddenly a fag bar."

Same old Josh. For fuck's sake. How had Brock pretended to be friends with this guy for so long? Sure, after high school Brock had dropped him like he'd dropped everyone else in Maney, but before that, he'd counted Josh as one of his friends. They'd fumbled through homework together, drunk together, and played soccer and hockey together. Brock had always cringed when Josh had gone after Gigi—cringed, then thanked anyone who was listening that Josh didn't know *he* was gay.

That ended now. Even though *another* showdown with a homophobe wasn't exactly how Brock had hoped this day would progress. It was great that he'd drunk enough to not feel scared, just pissed off. After all, if he was going to go out with a bang, he might as well include his old friend in the collateral. And if Brock survived this one too, he was going to order three fingers of the most expensive bourbon on the shelf, sleep it off, then drive home first thing in the morning, regrets about Gigi be damned.

"I wouldn't say two gays make it a gay bar," Brock said.

Josh looked over at him, and his eyes went wide. "Brock? Brock Stubbs? The *fuck*, man?" A pause. "What happened to your face?"

Brock put down his cue and stepped forward so he was standing slightly in front of Gigi.

"Oh *damn*," Ed gasped. "You're in for it now, shit-stain. You're, like, round two today for this guy."

"Shut up," Josh snapped. His eyes stayed on Brock's, and his expression was a strange mix of confusion and shock. "The fuck is this? You don't call, you don't write, then you show up in town with this faggot?" He gestured at Gigi, then frowned as the penny dropped. "Seriously? You two? What the *fuck*?"

"Yeah. Seriously. Us two."

"So, uh, who *is* this asshat?" Ed asked behind Brock.

"He used to go to high school with us," Gigi replied.

"Wasn't that like ten years ago?"

"Almost."

"What the hell do you want?" Brock asked.

Josh's fists clenched, and his eyes flickered beyond Brock, at Keith, Ed, and Luc. When his gaze returned to Brock, Josh's jaw tightened. "Outside, Stubbs."

"Brock." Gigi's voice held a warning in it.

He'd already dealt with worse that day. Brock nodded, and both he and Josh made for the front door. He heard people following and hoped there wouldn't be too big of a crowd. Having one did make this seem less scary. Even so, Brock still had a twinge of fear when Josh spun to face him in the parking lot.

"So you're a fucking fag now?" Josh spat. "Or are you just fucking one?"

"It's none of your business."

Josh sneered at him. "I guess that's right, seeing as we haven't spoken since you left."

Josh looked furious but still slightly confused. Brock remembered that expression from when they were kids—Josh had always been the kind of guy who lashed out instead of asking questions whenever he didn't understand something. Always aggressive and forward, but not very forward-thinking.

Come to think of it, that was sort of familiar.

"Guess I figured you wouldn't want to be friends once I came out," Brock said.

"No shit, Stubbs." Josh crowded him, getting in his face. Boozy breath hit Brock's nostrils. "So you better not be lying to me right now."

"I'm gay. I always have been. I never told you because you and your brother were fucking assholes to Gi—Toby, and I didn't need that shit too."

Josh reared back, something like guilt crossing his face. "That right?" He retreated a few steps, then narrowed his eyes. "So that time in school . . . ?"

"That was me. All me."

Josh shook his head. "Jesus effing Christ. Are you shitting me? I stood *up* for you. I can't believe that." He pointed a thick finger at Brock. "You lying piece of shit. You're worse than Rosenberg, you know that? At least he was always honest about being a goddamn queer. Fuck, I feel sick just looking at you."

Brock's stomach sank. God. When was today allowed to be over? "Then don't look. What's it matter anyway? I don't live here anymore."

"It matters because you're a traitorous piece of shit." Josh was shouting now, face red and spittle flying. "You think you can come back here with fucking Rosenberg, drink in my bar, and be all faggoty in public? Now? Here?" He flung his hands at the bar, where Brock could clearly see people watching through the windows at them. "It's disgusting. I don't wanna see that. Nobody here wants to see that."

"Tough." Brock kept an eye on Josh's fists. Even though the guy had always been less inclined than his brother to actually hit people, he could still be hard to take down if he was pushed far enough. "Like I said, you don't have to look. And this is our town too. We might not live here anymore, but we came from here, and we *will* come back if we want to."

"Not if I have something to say about it."

God. He was so sick of this. So sick of angry, hotheaded, self-righteous piss-heads like this yelling bullshit at him. Rage seared through him, white-hot and uncontrollable, and before he knew it, he was roaring. "What're you gonna do, huh?" Brock was aware he was advancing on Josh, but he didn't care. "You gonna call the police? 'Help, there are some fags in my bar and I don't like it'? You fucking *child*. You ignorant redneck piece of *shit*. Grow a pair and find something *important* to shout about. Fucking get out of here before I actually give you a reason to call for help."

Josh actually took two steps back, his face paling. "Look—"

"No! Fuck off! Just fuck off and leave us alone! Who the *hell* asked you for your opinion anyway?" Brock got in his face, itching, fucking *itching* to tear Josh's hick head from his hick shoulders. "Give me a reason," he snarled.

Josh's eyes were wide. "Nah. We're good. I'm going. I'm going." Josh had his hands up, was backing away. "See?"

Not good enough. Not quick enough. Brock was ready to pound that pasty, clueless face and recessive hairline into the goddamn pavement. Everything in him was ready—his legs, arms, hands, fingers *burned* to do it. Not just hit him and smash his head into the sidewalk, but make him bleed, tear him apart, shred muscle from bone. He reached forward—but there was something heavy holding his arm. He tried to shake it off, but it wouldn't go away. He couldn't go anywhere.

But it was okay. Josh kept walking.

"You better fucking leave!" Brock yelled. "Get out of here!"

Josh backed up to his car, got in, and drove away, flipping Brock off through the car window.

Brock was about ready to run after him, car or not, when the person gripping his arm tugged at it.

Oh, they were talking to him too.

He turned to see Gigi standing there, both hands on his arm, face stricken. "Gi?"

Gigi exhaled in relief. "Oh thank sweet baby Jesus, you're okay."

Brock jerked his arm away from Gigi. "Of course I'm fucking okay."

"Breathe, babe."

"I'm breathing!"

Gigi's eyes shone. "That was crazy. I have *never* seen you like that. I want to fuck you so bad right now."

Adrenaline was still pounding through Brock, making him twitch with unexpended energy. Sex sounded *amazing*. The idea of sweeping Gigi up against the wall of the bar and wrecking him had him hard. And Gi was up for it, if the dark smile on his face was any indicator.

"Brock Stubbs. You motherfucking stud."

They turned to see Marjorie Pine standing in the parking lot, staring at them. Brock then noticed the bachelor party clapping and whooping at him in the front door of the bar. The reality of what he'd just done hit him like a ton of bricks. He'd almost gotten in a fight.

Another one.

And he'd *wanted* to. He'd wanted to literally tear the guy's face off and had felt so able to, it was scary.

Is this what his dad felt like?

Oh God, he was going to fall down.

Marjorie pulled out her phone. "Aditya is going to *flip* when he hears this."

"Marjorie?" Gigi gasped. "Is that you?"

She looked at him, then did a double take. "*Toby*? Oh my God!"

"Girl, what the hell are you doing here?"

"Brock invited me!"

Brock turned away and stumbled back to the bar. He needed to sit down, and the guys seemed only too happy to lead him to their table and present him with more beer and water than he could ever need. Val even came over and plunked another straight bourbon in front of him.

He didn't want alcohol. He didn't want anything. All that was left of the rush of feelings was a sad hollowness. What the hell had happened there? It was like some switch had been flipped in his head, and he'd been roaring like . . .

Like his dad.

He clenched his fists. He was *nothing* like his dad. He *wasn't*.

Oh God, his fists trembled on the tabletop. He unclenched them. His hands kept shaking. Fuck.

"Man, you were, like, the fucking *man*," Alan was saying to him.

Brock shook his head. "No."

"Yeah, you totally were, man. *Totally*. Like, whoa. Just yelled at him and he ran away like a little bitch." Alan clapped his shoulder. "Dude. *Dude*. Way to go."

"So that guy was the brother of the dude who broke Toby's arm in high school?" Ed asked him.

Brock looked up at Ed. He was so serious Brock barely recognized him. Brock nodded.

Ed clapped his hands. "Okay. So, you're officially The Dude, and that guy has a date with my fist the next time I see him."

"Awesome. I need to go home."

Immediately, hands pressed on his shoulders and voices told him not to, that he had to stay, that he needed more to drink, and people put the whiskey into his hand. His still-shaky hand.

"There you are." He turned. Marjorie and Gigi stood beside the table. She beamed at him. "How about that catch-up drink?"

Brock couldn't handle this right now. He needed space. Air. Quiet.

"Excuse me a sec," he said, standing. He walked outside, glass in hand, went to the edge of the parking lot, and sat down on the raised curb of a parking bay. The night expanded around him, dark and a little too cool. The air carried a particular crisp smell of dead leaves and smoky wood and cold earth, bringing the past back in a rush. He shivered without his coat and sipped the whiskey in his hand.

Was he really as bad as his dad? He didn't think so. After all, he hadn't actually hit the guy. He'd been ready to, but he hadn't. Gigi had kept him from going totally apeshit and running after Josh when he'd flipped Brock off.

God, Josh Rogers. That asshole. It wasn't like he hadn't had something like that coming—he and his brother deserved all kinds of karmic retribution for the shit they'd pulled—but that exchange wasn't sitting right.

So much rage. That was . . . Had that really been Brock? He'd been angry before, but never to the point of actual willingness to hurt someone else. And it wasn't like that was the first time he'd had homophobic remarks thrown at him, so he knew he could react better than that. With less anger, less violence.

Okay, maybe he wasn't so much like his dad. His dad wouldn't be sitting here thinking like this, right? Brock didn't *think* he did that. Who fucking knew.

Besides, there had been other times, hadn't there? Travel had seen some dodgy moments, like with pickpockets and shitty parts of town. He'd once run away from guys attempting to rob him, and he had squared up to unreasonable drunks in bars. Those had been moments where he'd felt the same rush of heat and adrenaline, the same itch to *do* something.

But not quite so furious. Most of those times, he'd been scared. Here he hadn't been. So today was different.

It had to be this place. This place, his parents, all this stupid messy shit with Gigi . . . all of it was getting to him. He needed to leave. Not now—too drunk and tired and pissed off—but in the morning. He needed *home*, in Toronto, where his friends didn't know him as a closeted liar and son of an abusive whacko, and where this dark, fucked-up anger never surfaced. Where no one judged him anywhere near as much as he seemed to be judged here.

And once he was back there, he was going to get some professional fucking help with this shit, because he never wanted to find himself here again.

He sat for some time, slowly sipping the whiskey and breathing in the night air. A few people came to the bar, a few left, but no one approached him. After a while, he felt like he could maybe go in and be sociable for a little longer, if he hadn't made people feel awkward or weird. He hoped not. He hoped the guys were so smashed by now that they'd brush over it, and that Gigi wouldn't try to talk to him.

Brock was kind of done with today. He was done being nice. He was done being okay. He was just done.

CHAPTER EiGHT

Last summer

Gigi counted in his head as Mark's feet flew through the first of his solos. The jock was nailing it for the first time, *finally*. Mark executed three spins, tapping his foot on the beat with each spin, then finished with his arms spread wide. Gigi grinned and clapped.

"Fuck yeah!" Mark punched the air in victory, then came over for a double high five. Gigi indulged him for once and returned the high five. "Watch me own this shit!"

"Now do it again," Gigi said.

Mark's grin went flat. "Whaaat?"

So easy. Teasing Mark was turning into the highlight of Gigi's week. Practice number four and the hetebro was finally getting the routine down. He no longer squirmed whenever Gigi partnered him, and he actually seemed to enjoy being dipped. He sometimes even went quiet with concentration. Gigi had to admit it: he was impressed.

Granted, the least Mark could do was fucking concentrate after Gigi completely redid the choreography to be less Beyoncé-in-heels and more twenty-first-century vaudeville channelling a hefty dose of Rat Pack suaveness. This routine was so not what Gigi had imagined when he'd signed up for this competition, but it *was* turning out to be a lot of fun.

"Nah," Gigi said. "Take five."

Mark's beam returned in full force. "Sweet." He immediately sunk half his water bottle and dug into his bag for his phone.

Katie and Brock were due to film this session any moment now, which was super inconvenient because Gigi wasn't talking to Brock. It took a lot of energy and creativity to ignore someone in the same room, and it was proving really difficult, because if Gigi was being honest, he kind of wanted nothing more than to talk to him. And be touched by him. A lot. Especially on his dick.

But that was off the table now because Gi was a total freaking head case. *Goddamn it.*

Gigi spun a few times to let off excess energy, then went to his own bag for his water bottle. In between gulps, he stared at himself in the mirror, then struck a pose. Lean, muscular, strong, and fucking fabulous. The awkward, eager, shy little hometown Toby had died a natural death after a year of intimate acquaintance with the Toronto gay scene, and in his place had risen a sharp, talented, fucking gorgeous *queen*. He liked fucking and being fucked and dancing on stage, sometimes in heels and silk, and singing to an audience with good taste. Bears ate him for breakfast, and he loved it. He hadn't had a candy bar in six years. This was his life now. There was absolutely no *glimmer* of that hot mess of a teenager lingering on him.

At least, he *thought* there wasn't. Brock was making a serious mess of his insides right now and it was making him . . . feel things he hadn't felt since being a teen. Brock Stubbs, who was no longer in the closet. Brock Stubbs, who lugged cameras around with those sinful arms, whose mouth had learned some tricks since high school, and who took him out to dinner in public. Brock Stubbs, who was still hot and still interested and *still* made Gigi's stomach whirl like a butter churn.

The blowjob. It was all that blowjob's fault. Well, that and Brock fucking Stubbs being so delicious. Gigi couldn't believe how good the other evening had been.

It had started, of all places, with Brock on his knees on the sidewalk outside QS Dance. Gigi had been saying something about how he wasn't convinced Brock was on the level because of their history, when Brock had just dropped in front of him.

"I am one hundred percent gay," he'd yelled, keeping his eyes firmly on Gigi. "Gay as a rainbow. Gay as a handbag full of rainbows. Gay as a man bag covered in unicorns and full of rainbows and glitter. I am gay and I always have been and I always will be."

Oh.

Dear.

God.

"D'you think he lost a bet?" someone'd muttered as they walked around them.

"And I," Brock had continued, "have had a crush on you since grade ten."

Gigi's traitorous chest had swelled. So had his dick. Hail God and all the gay angels, not only was Brock very obviously out now, but he'd developed *game*.

"I fucked up bad because I *was* fucked up," Brock had added. "I'm asking you for a second chance—for friendship, for whatever you're willing to give me. I'm begging you."

Gigi's hand flew up to cover his eyes, and he had to remember to breathe. He loved it when they begged. He loved it that Brock was doing this for *him*.

A queen knew when to surrender.

So he cleared his throat, which had gotten all closed and lumpy for some reason, and told him to get up. Once he did, Gigi said, "Dinner."

The *Huh?* was clear on Brock's face, and Gigi allowed himself a small laugh. "You're buying me dinner," he explained. Brock opened his mouth to answer, and Gigi held up a hand, because he wasn't done yet. "This is *not* a date. This is not forgiveness, or friendship, or a promise of forgiveness or friendship, or anything to do with fucking, or a promise of fucking anything at all. Got it? It's dinner."

"I would love to buy you dinner," Brock said, a grin threatening to split his face.

After that crazy public declaration of being out, they had indeed gone to dinner, and talked, like properly talked. Brock had been full of stories from his years of travelling and years at university, talking about faraway places and people with an energy that hadn't been there in high school.

The guy had grown into himself, and not just physically. He seemed so much more relaxed and easy with himself. Being out of the closet did that, but Gigi didn't think it was just his acceptance of his sexuality. Despite that the new openness, Brock was still the guy

Gigi remembered. The shy glances, the blushes, the jokes, the innate sweetness. All still there.

So naturally Gigi had wanted him for dessert. Halfway through dinner, he'd been wondering if he could suck him off under the table without anyone noticing, then kicked himself for even considering it. Then they were walking and Brock was saying thank you for dinner and he'd looked so yummy in his goddamn shirt that before Gigi had known it, he'd pressed the guy into the nearest doorway and kissed him.

Brock had kissed him back. Hard.

Hands had groped under clothing. Brock's lips had moved to Gigi's neck, stubble rasping. A question and Gigi had said, *"Yes, do it, God, yes,"* and the next thing he knew, his high school dreams had come to life. Brock's mouth on him, those brown eyes looking up into his, his fingers entwined in Brock's curls. Gigi'd felt like he was on fire, like every part of him was falling into that steady gaze, and it was absolutely fucking perfect.

And when it had been over and Gigi'd been panting, head pressed hard against the brick wall, Brock had kissed him again, tasting of come and beer and himself. Suddenly Gigi had been back behind the blackout curtain, kissing his high school crush like nothing bad had happened and six years had never passed. *Toby* was back.

So he'd flipped out, shoved past Brock, and run.

Worse than giving into lust when he knew he shouldn't have, worse than cutting and running without an explanation, worse than everything was how Gigi still, days later, felt like he was that seventeen-year-old boy again.

Even though he really, really wasn't. Not anymore. He *wasn't*.

It was unreal how *aware* of the guy Gigi was. After Brock's declaration of just how much his closet no longer existed, followed by (an amazing) dinner, that (epic) blowjob, and Gigi's (unbelievably stupid, crass, embarrassing) meltdown and departure, Gigi had been unable to meet the guy's eyes. Instead, he had upped the waspy camp and ignored him, preferring to focus entirely on Mark. Practically cooing at the poor dude, all *Marky Mark* and *hon* and *sweet thang*, bitching with Katie, swinging himself around the practice room as though he had a horde of horny twinks shadowing him. Occasionally even *he* thought he was laying it on a bit thick, but he couldn't seem to stop himself.

Of course, this had to happen in the middle of a goddamn competition. *Of course*, Brock was filming him. Talk about ridiculous coincidences. It was like he was stuck in some fucking bad rom com. The analogy worked because Tyler, Gigi's best friend who'd been languishing at ease for a year, was also suddenly too busy making eyes at *his* dance partner, Evie, to be interested in helping Gigi out with this stupid dilemma of past lust brought to fruition.

"Talk to him." That had been Tyler's advice.

Yeah fucking right.

Mark was texting furiously, and Gigi wanted to rip his phone off him. The guy spent all his free time on it, mostly texting or calling his girlfriend, Frannie (otherwise known as *baby*). Gigi was going to have to start a no-phone-during-practice rule. The madness had to stop. The guy wasn't using his break properly to, like *have a break*. He was all tense and uptight—

Gigi frowned. Wait a minute. The jock *did* look upset.

Mark tossed his phone into the bag with a heavy sigh. "Gi, dude, can I, like, ask you a personal question?"

Oooh. That sounded juicy. What possible problems could a handsome hetero jock like Mark have? "I'd be honoured, sugarplum."

"So, you're gay." When Gigi didn't immediately respond, Mark gestured. "Right?"

Gigi indicated his shirt: *HERE FOR BEEF*.

"Right. And you're out to your family?"

Gigi frowned. "Yeah." *Oh God. He's gay. He's going to tell me he's gay. Or bi. No way. No fu—*

"How did they react?" He was fidgeting with his water bottle. "Were they, like, cool with it?"

"Hell yes." He'd officially told his mom, dad, and Sophie over dinner one night when he was twelve. Granted it was old news by then, but he'd still said the words *I like boys and there's this one boy I like and he's really cute*, and none of them had blinked an eyelid. "They were totally fine with it. I've crushed on boys since I was a kid."

"Hey, man, that's great." Mark finally looked up, his face genuinely happy. It clouded over again quickly. "But you know guys who've come out and their families weren't so hot about it, right?"

"Yup." It was a common story. Hell, kids were filming the not-so-hot-coming-out scenes and sticking them on YouTube these days. What a time to be alive. "Marky Mark, where's this coming from?"

Back to the water bottle. "I know I said in the interview that I'm doing this dance thing because it seemed fun, and Frannie said I should go for it, and because my brother is gay so it's all like personal and stuff, but there's this whole, like, layer to that you know? Like, my parents kicked him out when he told them."

Gigi's chest hollowed. Oh *hell*. "How old is he?"

"Sixteen."

Gigi remembered being sixteen. Sixteen was when he'd first noticed Bro— *Nope, not going there.* It was when he'd first listened to the *Rent* soundtrack. His whole life had been dance, music, school, avoiding being beaten up at school, and trying to find Tom of Finland pictures online.

If he'd been kicked out of home at sixteen, he'd have been chewed alive.

"I'm sorry, Mark."

Mark shook his head. "Nah, man, it's cool. I mean," he added hastily, "it is what it is, and it fucking *sucks*, but it's not your problem. And it's like under control and stuff. He's staying with me for now, but the dorm isn't so down with it, and social workers have been talking to my parents and to him and stuff."

"He's staying with you?"

Mark stared at him as though Gigi was an idiot. "Uh, yeah? He's my baby bro. Of course he's staying with me. If I was done with university and had a job and shit, I'd take him in and get him through school and stuff, but I'm, like, not. Which sucks, you know? I offered to give it up and work and support him, but the social workers said it would be better for my parents to take him back."

Gigi cleared his throat, which had been blocked by some nameless emotion he didn't deign to examine very closely right now. "Child abandonment doesn't sit well with the government, no."

Mark glared at his phone. "No shit. I just got a text from Cal saying my folks *are* going to take him back and put him through school, but with a whole list of bullshit rules. No friends over after school, no parties, no posters of guys, restricted internet use, no boyfriends. And no support after high school. Man, I am *pissed.*" He tossed the water bottle down. "Cal's life is fucked. My parents don't get it, and they're going to mess him up, and there's nothing I can fucking do about it."

"He'll be okay." Gigi somehow found himself in front of Mark, patting his shoulder. "Getting through school will be tough, for sure. But he won't be homeless. He won't have to hustle for food or shelter. That happens to a lot of queer teens."

Mark glanced up at him, misery on his dumb jock face. Gigi had to change that.

"Plus, he has a macho big brother looking out for him."

Mark's mouth quirked.

"Lots of kids don't even have that much. You're a good guy." To Gigi's eternal surprise, he actually meant that. "I think it'll make a lot of difference knowing you're in his corner."

"Fuck yeah, I got his back." Mark pointed at himself proudly. "*I'll* make sure he gets to university one way or another. Or whatever he wants to do and stuff. But, like, this is my question, man. He's so down about it all, you know? I've never seen him this down about anything. And he sometimes says stuff like he's being a burden to me and that I'm only helping him out because no one else in our family will. So, dude, I was wondering, if you were in that situation and your straight older brother did a dance competition like this with a dude, would that, like, convince you your bro was seriously on the level?"

Gigi wanted to laugh in his face but managed to restrain himself. "I think he'll appreciate it, and he'll get it. But I have a question for you, Marky Mark."

The guy leaned forward, hanging on every word.

"Have you told him you're looking out for him because you're his brother and you love him?"

Mark's eyes went wide. "Dude. That's, like, obvious. Do you think I need to actually say that?"

Gigi nodded. "Yeah."

"It'll help?"

"Oh yeah."

"But the dancing thing is cool too, right?"

Gigi couldn't help smiling. "Honey, it's fucking excellent." He waggled a finger. "Or it *would* be if someone would get it right all the way through."

Mark groaned. "Man, you are *killing me* here."

"I think that's the point," Katie said from the door. Gigi and Mark jumped, but Gigi resisted the urge to look around. How the hell did she and Brock sneak in like that?

CHAPTER NINE

Gigi woke up, the sense of being interrupted lingering in a sleepy haze. Dregs of some dream involving Mark and Brock and a battle and Jason Momoa sifted weirdly in his head, and he blinked up at the ceiling to help clear it. His room was quiet, and downstairs activity was muted through the floorboards.

Something had woken him up. Maybe a door closing? Or a phone ringing? Not his alarm, which he'd failed to set again after last night.

Whooaaa, yes, okay, last night. Time to think about last fucking night. A night of nights. Gigi was going to have material for his show for *years*. The bachelor party had been kind of tame in the end—just lots of pool and drinking, which was pretty much what Mark had said it would be. And bellowing. Disappointingly tame, except for that small intermission where Brock had stepped up and owned Josh Rogers's ass.

Holy.

Fucking.

Shit.

Gigi had never seen Brock like that. Never. So fucking *fierce*. But in this crazy, manly, rough, primal way. His gentle giant had turned into this roaring muscular fury, and Gigi had been scared *and* turned on. Mostly turned on. Massively so. Like, *ughn*. Who wouldn't love their guy sending their school bully to the curb?

The memory of the intense way Brock had looked at him afterwards sent shivers down Gigi's spine. If Marjorie and the entire bar hadn't been watching them, Gigi had no doubts they'd have been fucking in seconds.

Kind of a shame they hadn't. After all, they'd barely touched each other this weekend. That almost *never* happened, even when they'd fought before.

Though Gigi had to admit, a tiny part of him had been kind of worried. Tiny. *Miniscule.* But big enough to step in and hold Brock back when he looked ready to pound Josh into the tarmac, even when Josh was backing off. Because Brock was normally not that guy, not *at all.* It was one of the things Gigi loved about him.

Shit. Forcing him to be here this weekend had been an awful idea.

After the fight-that-almost-was, Brock hadn't wanted to talk much—he'd just gone all quiet and moody, and after sitting outside for a while, had come back in, played some pool, then requested a lift home without even talking to him or Marjorie.

And *she'd* been a surprise too. Two blasts from the past in one evening. It had been great to catch up with her, actually. She'd talked about her life in Edmonton, and how she'd had a bad time in high school too, then they'd rehashed the shit they'd given each other back in the drama group. Turned out she'd known about him and Brock at the time, but hadn't said anything. Surprise of surprises, Brock had bumped into her earlier that day and invited her out, after telling her they were together, and she'd been really happy to see them.

Huh. Who knew people could be crazy nice when there weren't rumours flying around about their sex lives?

It meant something, the fact that she'd known about them at the time. Like, her knowing and not really caring, even though they'd kind of hated each other, meant a lot. It was like his and Brock's thing behind the curtains had been more sweet than secret and bad. Even though it hadn't even been *bad,* not until the end.

Plus no one else had given him shit this weekend. Literally no one. He'd gotten a few Looks from people, especially in the bar, but no one had actually said anything. That was an improvement on his adolescence. And when Josh had appeared, no one had joined him. Okay, Gigi'd had a team of guys around him, like, immediately, which helped, but it seemed important that no one had backed Josh up. When Brock had diverted him outside, the rest of the guys had been ready to pile on if things got ugly. Like, the *support.* People had *been* there. And afterwards, the people in the bar had said a few disparaging things about Josh that confirmed to Gigi he was better left behind.

Maybe he'd overblown just *how* bad this place was. Like, he'd assumed the intense, petty, everyday shittiness of school extended out into the town, but maybe it hadn't. Or it had, but over time things had improved, and people had stopped caring, especially about someone who no longer lived here.

Ah. Well. So he'd overblown the expectation of constant queer-bashing. But it was better to be pleasantly surprised by a lack of it than to be underprepared for it, right? And it was good that people had moved on. Seemed that he wasn't the only one who'd changed since he left.

The number of voices and steps going on downstairs meant there was probably chaos happening.

Oh, right. His sister was getting married today. Time to move.

He sat up and gasped.

Brock's bag was gone. Brock had been asleep by the time Gigi had come home, but now he and his stuff were gone and that wasn't okay.

His skin prickled. Gigi tore out of bed and ran down the stairs, almost colliding with his dad, who was helping Ed with his tie.

"Morning, Toby," Dad said.

"Nice shorts," Ed said.

"Where's Brock?" Gigi asked.

Dad finished the tie. "In the kitchen, I think."

Gigi practically skidded through the door into the kitchen. Sophie sipped coffee there in her wedding dress—which was a frankly stunning mermaid cut of ivory edged with carmine. *Wow.* She looked beautiful. Gigi couldn't have made a better dress himself.

There was a problem though: no one else was there, not even Grandma.

Fuck.

"Hey, bro," she said.

"Have you seen Brock?"

"Nah. He's probably getting ready like everyone else." She glanced pointedly at his boxers. "I know you have clothes."

Gigi paused. "How are you all made up and dressed so quickly?"

She shrugged. "Got up early to serve tea to the new in-laws. It's a Chinese thing. I'm just waiting for everyone else now." She put down her coffee cup. "Hey, did Josh Rogers *really* gate-crash the—"

"Gotta go." He ran through the hallway to the front door and checked for the rental car. It was still there. *Ohthankgod.*

Gigi stalked through the various rooms downstairs, dodging kids and adults putting on clothes, and found his boyfriend sitting on the couch at the far side of the rec room, braiding Gigi's littlest cousin's hair.

Brock wasn't wearing a suit like the other guys. He wore a sweater and jeans, and there were dark circles under his eyes and stubble on his face. The bruises had turned a nasty purple, and one eye was completely encircled. Gigi ached. His guy looked so tired and crumpled, yet still incredible.

Plus, the sight of him with Rosie, who was five and the flower girl, was so freaking cute. And somewhat darkly weird, given the contrast between bruised face and little girl. She patted the tulle folds of her dress as Brock gently folded and wove her hair into a French braid. She said something to him, and he chuckled quietly, his smile sending small shockwaves through Gigi. Holy mother of God. Adorable. *So* adorable. Gigi finally got the whole hot-dad thing. Look at that shit. His proverbial ovaries were totally exploding.

Brock caught sight of him and the smile dropped. "Gi."

Oh jeez, since when did seeing him make Brock sad? "Babe. We have to talk."

Brock nodded. "Sure. Give me a sec."

Rosie giggled. "Toby's in his *underwear*."

"That's because he doesn't know how to get dressed," Brock said to her.

Her eyes went wide. "Oh my gosh. *I* know how to get dressed, and I'm *five*."

Who was going around teaching five-year-olds how to give shade? "Don't listen to him," Gigi told her. "I am the best dresser."

"But the wedding is starting soon!"

Brock nodded. "It's in an hour, Gi. You seriously need to put some clothes on."

Gigi crossed his arms. "Can I ask why *you're* not dressed, honey?"

Brock rolled his eyes and tied off Rosie's hair. "All done."

"Thank you, Brock!" She jumped up and gave him a hug, then ran away, making her dress floof around her.

Damn. Gigi needed a tulle skirt. Well, *LaMore* needed a tulle skirt. Huh, there was a thought—his queen hadn't come out as much as he'd expected her to this weekend.

Brock rose to his feet. "Upstairs."

Gigi led them upstairs, mind churning quickly over what the lack of bag and suit meant. Brock didn't plan on going to the wedding. Why? What was going through his head?

It wasn't like Gigi hadn't wanted to talk to him yesterday after that stupid fight. But it had been hard to pin Brock down. Gigi had given him some space during dinner, and then at the bar Brock had totally ignored him, then Josh had happened, and Brock had definitely shrugged him off right after that and gone all moody, and Gigi just hadn't known what to do then, so *argh*. Letting him have space seemed the best thing, but now he was wondering if that had been a good idea. Brock had gone straight home afterwards and now he seemed to be going *home* home.

Gigi really didn't want that to happen.

In his bedroom, Gigi shut the door behind them and gazed at Brock nervously.

Brock stared back, his eyes roving over Gigi. He was suddenly very aware that he was only wearing boxers, that his chest and legs were exposed, and that Brock was looking at him with that expression that Gigi absolutely *loved*, the one that said Brock wanted to eat him up like ice cream.

Brock blinked and looked away. "Put your suit on."

Oh no. None of that. Gigi went up to him and put his hands on Brock's shoulders. Brock went still, then stepped back. Gigi let his hands drop. "And where's *your* suit?" He could hear the disappointment in his voice.

"In the car."

Oh *no*. "Brock, don't leave."

"I don't want to be in this town anymore." Brock suddenly looked incredibly sad, then he turned away, his face contorting into a scowl.

Gigi took a deep breath. "I want you to stay."

Brock threw his arms up. "Seriously? Still? Why? *How*? Aren't you pissed off about last night?"

"Uh, no? You totally owned Josh Rogers."

Brock's eyes went wide. "Did you *see* me? I lost it."

"Yeah, but not totally." Gigi let himself grin. "It was kind of hot."

Brock shook his head. "No. It's not a good thing, Gi. I'm not that guy."

"What guy? The guy who shows assholes where to go? Because you're totally that guy."

He grimaced. "The kind of guy who goes for other people. Fights them."

"You're right. You're not that guy."

"But I *was*."

Gigi was super confused. "No, you weren't. He started shit and provoked you into yelling at him. You didn't actually fight him."

Brock shook his head. "I was ready to, though. I *wanted* to. That's the scary part."

Yeaaahh . . . Still didn't get it. "I wanted to fight him too. It's kind of human to want to fight someone who's pissing you off, you know? It's, like, a legit reaction."

"No, it's not!" Brock dragged his hands through his hair. "Oh my God. Are you being this clueless on purpose?"

Clueless? Excuse me? Gigi put his hands on his hips. "No. Are you being this incoherent on purpose?"

Brock snorted, then stared at Gigi's chest. Without a word, he turned around and knelt down to dig into Gigi's bag.

The hell?

"What are you doing?"

"Getting you a shirt."

"Oh my fucking God, Brock, can you just fucking *talk* to me?"

Brock pulled out several shirts, including the one Gigi had planned on wearing to the wedding. "I'm trying, but you're not listening."

"I think my listening skills are fine, actually."

He was turning the bag inside out. Gigi made a frustrated noise and took his intended shirt out of Brock's hands. He slid it on.

"Okay, so I didn't beat him up, but I was angry enough to want to do it, and I'm still angry now." Brock tossed the rest of the shirts back in the bag. "I want to go and not feel like this anymore. Getting out of this town will help."

Okay, Gigi could vaguely get that. "I know this weekend has sucked, baby. Leaving here will totally help. I know. But, like, the wedding is literally less than an hour from now, and the weekend is almost over. Don't you think having fun at the wedding would make all this worth it?"

Brock scowled. "No. I don't. And at what point did this weekend suck for *you* anyway?"

Gigi paused in buttoning up his shirt. "Excuse me? Did you just say what I think you did?"

"Yeah."

"Did you miss the part where you got hit in the face? By your *dad*? Whose assholery, by the way, you neglected to ever mention? And where Josh got nasty? And the part where you told me I'm so fucking high-maintenance that you're done with me?" Gigi was almost yelling now. "Because all of that fucking *hurt*, sugarplum, and I didn't expect any of it."

Brock sighed. "I didn't mean that. What I said about you."

"I think you meant some of it."

Brock glared at him. "Even if I did, it's not something I want to change about you. And I wasn't the only one dishing out some hurt, *honey*."

"Oh please. I don't mean half the shit I say *normally*, let alone when I'm angry." Gigi finished buttoning his shirt. It was slightly creased, but he thought the suit would cover it. "Okay. You're right, I said shit too, but it was a fight. Those happen. We've fought before, you know?"

"This was different."

Gigi couldn't disagree with that. "Yeah." He went to where he'd hung his trousers and jacket and began pulling the trousers on. "It felt super fucking personal."

"It *was* super fucking personal."

"I'm sorry." Gigi zipped them up and tucked the shirt into the waist. "I get that this weekend has not been pleasant for you. But here's the thing, boyfriend: you fought back. You *owned* this weekend. You kicked its ass."

Brock shook his head. "That's not the point. That's not what I wanted from this weekend. And I don't think that's even what you wanted. You don't get it."

Oh for fuck's sake, what now? "*What* don't I get?"

"Brock?" Dad called. "Can you come here?"

They froze. Gigi glanced at Brock, who looked as surprised as Gigi felt. Like, everyone in the house had to have been hearing their conversation through the walls, so why would his dad interrupt them?

"Now, please." That sounded serious.

They went downstairs together, Gigi buttoning up his cuffs. He could hear muted chatter from the living and rec rooms as his family got ready. His dad, though, stood by the front door. Standing next to him was a man Gigi had only seen before from afar: Brock's dad. Instantly recognizable as an older, creased, and less-happy version of Brock, with bruises on one side of his face.

Huh. Brock really *hadn't* been kidding about that chair.

He wore the basic uniform of everyone over the age of forty in Maney: a light cap, a heavy-duty jacket over baggy jeans, hiking boots, and an aw-shucks-buddy expression. If Gigi didn't know better, he'd've said he was your average, friendly neighbour stopping by for some coffee and a yarn.

Brock froze beside Gigi on the stairs, and Gigi instinctively stopped with him.

Brock's dad smiled. "Hi, Brock."

"What are you doing here?" Brock asked.

"Just wanted to have a chat." His dad's gaze flickered over Gigi, and his lip curled. Gigi felt his face heat up.

"Outside," Brock said. "Now."

"You sure? John has a nice place here." Brock's dad looked around, craning his neck to see into the rec room. A few people glanced back curiously, but no one moved. Trust Gigi's family to be too focused on buttons and hair styles to care about what was happening in the entrance hall. "Wouldn't you feel more comfortable inside?"

Gigi's dad cleared his throat. "Pete, we're, ah, we're kind of short on time here . . ."

"What's going on? Who's this?" Sophie stepped forward from the kitchen, looking at them all curiously.

Pete beamed. "This is your daughter, John? Congratulations, miss. Your fiancé's a lucky man."

She frowned at Brock's dad, but said, "Thank you."

Brock made a strange noise in his throat. "We talk outside or not at all."

He couldn't. Gigi grabbed his hand and glared at him. *You cannot. You absolutely must not, you hear me?*

Telepathy clearly wasn't one of Brock's strengths; he didn't even look at Gigi.

Pete held up his hands. "Okay, okay! Sheesh." He grinned at Gigi's dad. "Kids, eh?"

Dad's mouth had gone into a hard line. "Wouldn't be without them."

Pete nodded at Sophie and stepped through the front door.

Gigi immediately grabbed Brock's arm. "You're not going anywhere near him."

"Don't tell me what to do," Brock hissed.

"Don't do stupid things, and then I won't have to tell you what to do!"

"Sorry to interrupt, boys, but he said he wasn't going to move until he spoke to Brock." Dad looked worried.

Sophie was peering through the front door. "Is that his car parked in front of our driveway?"

He'd blocked them in?

Gigi let go of Brock and went down the rest of the stairs so he could look through the front door and past the figure of Pete Stubbs, who stood by the steps up to the door.

On the driveway were three cars: the Rosenbergs' Jeep, Gigi and Brock's rental, and a limousine rented for the wedding. Parked directly in front of the driveway, blocking the other cars, was a huge tank of a truck, like a Jeep on freaking steroids. Yup, he'd blocked them in.

"Is he trespassing?" Sophie asked in a whisper. "Because we can call the police if he is."

"He's not," Dad said, voice low. "He's on the road. But it's a parking violation—we could definitely get the police in for that."

"Calling the police will take time." Brock's voice had gone raspy. He'd come up behind Gigi to take a look too. "You'll be late for your wedding. He's got friends there anyway."

"That's news to me," Dad said.

Brock's dad paced by the front steps. Gigi got bad vibes just *looking* at him.

Gigi spun to Brock. "Don't go out there."

Brock was staring at his dad, his face pale. His throat worked. "I think it'll be okay if you're all watching."

"No!"

"I can speak to him," Dad said, and Gigi could've hugged him.

"No. It's fine." Brock took a deep breath. "I don't think he'll try anything."

He couldn't know that. "Don't you dare go down there."

Brock glared at him. "I know what I'm talking about and you don't. I'll be fine. And stay here, or I swear to God I will actually break up with you." Then he went out the front door and down the steps to his father.

What the *fuck* was he thinking? Gigi took a step to go after him, but his dad and sister grabbed his arms and stopped him.

"Let me go!"

"I don't want *two* guys with messed-up faces at my wedding," Sophie hissed at him.

"You're not going to get either of us if you don't let me help him."

"Think, Toby." His dad's voice was urgent. "How are you going to help him? What are you going to do?"

The thing was, he had no idea. Ugh, this brought his old self back out, the inept, avoidant, scared Toby, which was awful because that wasn't who he needed to be right now. It reminded him of how he'd had to deal with shit like this back then. But his bullies had never followed him home. He'd usually managed to run away or hide, and the few times he'd fought back, he'd barely landed a punch. Jesus. What had he been thinking of doing—singing at the guy? He might be able to execute a high kick, maybe, but that was about as physical as he got. Toby had no clue how to fight, and he could've wept at how fucking helpless that made him feel.

But he couldn't just stand back and let Brock go to his dad like it was nothing. Brock was *Toby's*. His dad had hurt him. Hadn't Toby seen the scars already? What other shit had this asshole put Brock through? What if he took a swing at Brock *right now*? In front of all of them? What if he had a weapon hidden on him?

Toby didn't know what to do except watch and listen, and maybe record the interaction—but his fucking phone was *upstairs*. *Fuck*.

Brock stood a few feet away from his dad. "What are you doing?"

"Making sure I have your attention. We need to have a little chat."

"About what? Everything was said yesterday."

They were strange mirror images of each other, shoulders back and glaring at each other. Brock was taller than his dad, which was a good thing, right? Or maybe not. *Shit*. Toby knew a lower centre of gravity was better for dancing—probably for fighting too. *Omigod omigod*.

Fuck it. Even if Toby couldn't fight, he'd be in there if Brock's dad so much as burped on him.

"You need another chair to the face, Dad?" Brock asked. "Because I can arrange that for you."

Brock's father smiled, a greasy, victorious thing that made Toby's skin crawl. "No need for threats." He did take a step back though. "All I want is a calm, rational discussion between adults." He gestured at Toby and his family. "I'm sure we're taking up very precious time for these nice people. Come home, and we'll take things from there. Let that pretty girl get to the church on time, as they say."

Suddenly Toby couldn't see much likeness between them at all. Sophie was muttering darkly under her breath.

"I know what you're doing." Brock didn't sound scared at all. Toby felt a rush of pride. "If you think pulling me out of the wedding will ruin the Rosenbergs' day, or change anything between us, you're totally wrong. I wasn't going anyway. So fine. Have it your way."

Oh, fuck this shit. "Brock, no!"

Brock and his dad turned to look at him.

Toby knew he was shaking, but he refused to look away or acknowledge the warning noises from his family. He pointed at Mr. Stubbs, making sure he was staring him straight in the eye. "If you touch him, I'll end you!"

Mr. Stubbs sneered, then turned around and walked to his oversized, totally compensatory car.

"It's okay, Gi!" Brock said before following him.

Toby watched in numbed shock as his boyfriend got into the steroid Jeep and was driven away.

It wasn't okay. It really fucking wasn't. What would happen now? More chairs? Knives? *Guns*? No way. Nope. This wasn't something Brock should have to do. Why was he doing this? Didn't he know there were other ways they could kick Mr. Stubbs out of the freaking driveway? Being late to a wedding wasn't the end of the world.

Worse, he was totally cutting Toby out, like he had *all freaking weekend*. Didn't he trust him and his family to help out?

Well.

Actually.

Maybe not.

Maybe if he'd grown up in the kind of family that gave scars like the ones Toby had been wondering over for the past year, he wasn't going to be open about difficult things, or to expect other people to help him.

Okay. So, yes, Brock had been stupid and hadn't told Toby about his family issues or why he didn't want to come back here or about all his hang-ups over their past. The thing was, Toby hadn't exactly made it easy for him. What was it Brock had said about feeling judged all the time and second chances? Ugh.

Also, this weekend had actually been pretty okay for Toby, all things considered. He was standing there on his family porch, with his family around him (and probably watching everything through the windows and door behind him), his face was completely unmarked by anyone's fists, and he'd only had to deal with one major asshole.

But who did Brock have around him?

Because Toby had a suspicion his family had been nicer to Brock than he had this weekend, and the shame of that made him want to cry. Shit.

Yeah, this weekend had been sucky. But not for Toby—for Brock. It had just gotten a ton worse, and who was it who'd said they were in this together? Who was it who'd said things would be better if they were together?

Time to fucking *be* together.

And time to get his man back where he belonged.

Deciding that felt good, like he'd snapped back into reality.

Someone was speaking to him.

He blinked. His dad and Sophie were staring at him. "What?"

"Are you okay?" Sophie asked. "I thought you were going into shock."

"I'm not going into shock. I'm going after him."

He made for the rental, but his dad stopped him. "Toby, stop. You don't have shoes on."

Ah. Great point. He turned around and made for the stairs. Okay, shoes. Shoes and car keys. And his phone.

His dad blocked him *again*. "I'm sure Brock will be fine."

"No, he won't."

"If Pete Stubbs knows we're looking out for him, he won't hurt him."

Gigi threw his arms up. "You don't know that, Dad!"

His dad gazed at him with a worry that made him look years older. "Toby. Son. You think I want *you* to go into their house? Uninvited? After what they did to Brock yesterday?"

"No. But I have to do this, and you're not stopping me. I'm going to get him, and we'll be at the wedding. He's family too, now."

His dad sighed and dragged one hand through his hair. "Do you need me as backup?"

Oh man, his dad was the best. "No."

"At least take your phone and record everything."

"I have a hockey stick you could borrow," Sophie said.

Omigod, best sister ever. He didn't want her wedding wrecked by their drama, not really, but there was no helping this. "It's okay, Sophie. I'm sorry, but we might be late. You can start without us."

She gave him a fond but exasperated look. "I think you have time if you hustle. And I mean it about that hockey stick."

He kissed her cheek, then ran up the stairs. He finished pulling on his wedding outfit, grabbed his cell, then hunted for the car keys and found them in Brock's coat, which still hung from the hook in the hallway. Then he got into the car, backed out, and drove to the Stubbses' place as though he had an army of pissed-off drag queens running after him. There was certainly one inside him who was sharpening her nails at the thought of ripping Mr. Stubbs's face off for hurting Brock. He tried to focus on that, rather than on the fear bubbling underneath the furious queen.

When he pulled up outside the Stubbses' house, he didn't give himself time to think about what he was going to do or say. He'd wing it, like he winged everything, or LaMore would step back in if needed. Gigi strode up to the front door and banged on it with his fist.

Brock wasn't sure why he'd felt okay about coming back, but his dad had been . . . different. Nervous. Not quite meeting his eye. Had barely said a word or looked at him at all once they got in the car, actually.

Crazy what a chair to the face could do.

That said, Brock was on edge the entire trip to the house. The worst thing was the uncertainty. Like, what the hell could his dad have to say to him? Hadn't he got what he wanted? But Pete was acting weird—showing up at the Rosenbergs' place was *not* something he'd've done back in the day—and seeing as Pete wasn't yelling at him, Brock was kind of curious about what his dad wanted. Beyond attempting to interrupt the wedding, which . . . nah. Not on Brock's watch.

Not that he cared much about going to it himself, but he didn't want it wrecked. Getting his dad out of the Rosenbergs' way was a big plus for the inconvenience of having to come back here.

Inconvenience. Ha. But what the hell could his dad do to him now? Seriously? Things were different now. Brock wasn't even sure how to explain it. Pete's silence didn't feel like any of the silences Brock could remember. He wasn't in trouble. It was like . . . Was his dad trying to get things back to the way they'd been? If so, tough. Things couldn't ever be that way again. If Pete tried to get physical, Brock would get physical back, and if he wanted to yell at him, then Brock could simply walk away. There was nothing his dad had on him to keep him there.

Whatever was going on here, Pete definitely wanted something.

So, Brock had geared himself up to expect pretty much anything as he and Pete arrived at the house: shouting, more fighting, or maybe his mom in a bad state—something like that.

He hadn't expected paperwork.

Once they'd gone in, Pete had directed him to the table and then said some crap about the family taking him back if he dropped the being-gay thing—which hadn't worked. Obviously.

So then he'd shoved a copy of his will in front of Brock and said that this would be the consequences of his actions. It was difficult reading legalese while keeping an eye on his dad—who so far hadn't touched him at all—but Brock suspected he was getting to the interesting part where his father bequeathed his estate.

God, the sooner he made his point and got out of here, the better.

Okay. *Distribution of property* blah, blah. Brock's name wasn't listed at all as a beneficiary. All his dad's estate, which included a house, several investments, a side business, some expensive junk he owned, was down to go to Brock's mom, cousin, or his dad's friends.

"You were going to receive the house and some of the funds," his dad said smugly. "They're worth over two hundred K each, you know that?"

Brock was so fucking *tired*.

He slapped the paper down. "Cool." He stood.

Pete stood too, but didn't move towards him. "I haven't signed it yet. You can still make this good, Brock. This cannot be taken back, do you understand? You will receive nothing from me or your mother. You will never receive *anything* from us. You won't be acknowledged by us or anyone else in our family. You'll be alone for the rest of your life."

Fucking bring it on. "Go to hell."

Brock turned and started towards the door.

"You're making a big mistake, son. Huge. No coming back from this one."

He'd heard that before. Brock just stepped up the pace. *Don't turn around. That's what he wants you to do. Just walk. Don't—*

Pete's chair screeched backward, and Brock flinched.

Thump-thump-thump.

Someone was at the front door.

Brock paused, then cast a glance back at his father. Pete was closer than he'd expected, definitely heading for him. There was a flashlight in his hand, one of the heavy-duty ones that needed a large battery and a strong grip but was compact enough to be hidden under a table or down the back of a shirt.

They froze, staring at each other.

"The fuck you planning to do with that?" Brock asked him softly.

Pete blinked in surprise, then scowled. But he didn't move.

The banging stopped as the front door was opened. "Who are you?" Brock heard his mom ask.

"Hi-eeee Mrs. Stubbs! I'm Toby Rosenberg, and I'm here to pick up my boyfriend!"

Brock felt his blood chill. Gigi? Here? *Ohshitnononononononono*—

"Hey, you can't just—"

"This is a *charming* place you have here, Mrs. Stubbs. Very, um, atmospheric." Gigi walked into the living room where Brock was still frozen. Gigi wore a black suit, white shirt, and a red bow tie that matched his dyed-red hair. Red sparkled in his earlobes. He'd shown up here in his *wedding clothes*. And he looked so damn handsome, Brock wasn't sure whether to cry or laugh.

Gigi took in the scene, and if he was taken aback or scared at all, he didn't show it. In fact, he grinned. "*There* you are." He held out his hand. "You done here, babe?"

Brock had been done years ago.

"Who the fuck is this?" Pete growled behind Brock.

"Now, Mr. Stubbs"—and Gigi actually put one hand on his hip—"that's not very nice. But you have a point. We weren't introduced. I'm Toby, and I'm here to pick up my boyfriend. Who happens to be your son. Your *very* gay son."

Brock kept one eye on his dad and took a few steps towards Gigi.

"I warned you about consequences, Brock." His dad moved after him.

Gigi cleared his throat. "I wouldn't, you know. There are chairs all over this place." Glancing at him, Brock realized he'd whipped out his phone and was filming them. "Granted, I'm not as big and rugged as my baby, but I can definitely swing a chair. And what in the hell are you carrying? Is that a *flashlight*? You do realize it's broad freaking daylight? I know we're in the ass crack of the Canadian wilderness but it's not that dark here." He scanned the room. "Though, this place is kind of gloomy. What gives? Your curtains aren't nice enough to be kept closed all day."

Pete made the strangest noise. Brock would've bet all his savings that no one had ever spoken to him like that before.

Gigi chattered on, phone held blithely up. "Like, honestly, Mr. Stubbs, is that the best you got? A freaking flashlight? I've crapped out bigger things than that. Hell, I've *fucked* bigger things than that. What were you gonna do, make shadow puppets? Swing it around near him? I promise, he's seen bigger."

Holy shit. LaMore was coming through, and she wasn't taking any prisoners. Not that Brock would want her to.

Safe under the watchful lens of his boyfriend's phone—and the steely glint in his eyes—he walked up to Gigi and took his outstretched hand. Gigi's hand was clammy, but clenched his with all the strength of fear and dancer-toned muscle.

"Brock. Not one more step. Last chance, boy." Pete still hadn't moved though.

Brock met Gigi's eyes and smiled, warmth welling through him. Gi had come after him. Stupid on his part, but Brock had to admit, it felt so good to have someone on his side in this place.

He turned, making sure he stared his old man right in the eye. "You take one step after us, and I will kill you." It was a promise. "Drop it."

Pete sagged slightly, then set the flashlight down.

"Well," Gigi exclaimed, "this has been *lovely*, but frankly, we have better places to be." He tugged Brock's hand and dragged him to the front door, phone aloft the entire way. Brock's mom waited by the door, her mouth in a hard, sad line. She stepped forward, so Brock slowed, forcing Gigi to stop in the doorway.

"Mom," Brock began, but she shook her head.

"Go with your—" her eyes flickered uncertainly at Gigi "—friend. And I prepared this in case you decided to leave." She reached over to a side table and picked up a shoebox. "Things of yours." She handed it to him. "Bye, sweetie."

What the . . . Was that *it*?

Brock took the shoebox in one hand as Gigi tugged on the other. "Byeee, Mrs. Stubbs! Nice to meet you!"

And Brock was pulled out of his parents' dark house and down to the rental car by his crazy, handsome, and insanely brave boyfriend.

Gigi threw open the passenger door and pointed at it. "In."

Like anyone was arguing. Brock climbed in and shut the door as Gigi sprinted around to the other side and got in. The phone was tossed onto the dash, and Gigi started the car.

"I cannot believe you followed me," Brock said.

"Believe it." Gigi did the barest of mirror checks before pulling out and screeching away. Brock caught the phone when it slid off the dash. "I'm like two seconds away from hyperventilating, boyfriend, so be prepared." He took a deep, long breath, then exhaled. Another one. Then, "Did I just walk into your house like that? *Did I just do that*?"

Brock put down the shoebox and reached over to touch Gigi's shoulder. "You totally did."

"Oh my fucking God. Oh my *God*. I'm a trespasser. A criminal." Gigi screwed up his face. "Sort of. Was it me or was he ready to freaking deck you?"

"Probably."

Gigi began breathing even louder. "Oh Jesus. Oh my God. No freaking way."

"I'd've gotten away or hurt him first."

Gigi glanced at him. "I believe you, baby. 'I will kill you.' Damn."

Brock couldn't stop grinning. He couldn't believe he'd said that. *Him*. To his *dad*.

"Fuck. Me. *Fuck me*. That was what, three minutes? Longest three fucking minutes of my life. I thought I was going to pee myself when I saw his face. Holy shit." Gigi dragged a hand over his face and into his hair. "God. *God*."

"Nah. Just you." Brock wanted to pull him over, shove his clothes off, and fuck him into the car seat. Was this how Gigi had felt last night? Like he was so overwhelmed with just how amazing his boyfriend was?

Still taking deep breaths, Gigi glanced over at him, and a wicked smile curled his lips.

Brock leaned in. "You came to get me."

"Yup."

"Even though I told you I was leaving and was being a total disappointment."

Gigi turned back to the road, his smile fading. "You're not a disappointment. Don't ever think that."

Oh please. "Have you been around this weekend? I don't know if you noticed, but I yelled some nasty shit at you yesterday. I've basically been the crappiest boyfriend ever this weekend."

"I don't see that. You had a bad weekend, yeah." Gigi made a face. "Pretty much the worst weekend."

Brock snorted.

"And you said some stuff that I think you needed to say." Gigi reached over, and Brock took his hand. "Like, I know I'm high-maintenance and stuff. It's okay to tell me when I'm being a total bitch drama queen. I'll still love you."

"I said I didn't mean that. I love how you're high-maintenance. And I adore your queen. I love everything about you." Brock hesitated. "Even if you drive me crazy sometimes."

Gigi beamed at him. "And I love everything about you, boyfriend."

Brock's heart jumped a little in his chest. "Even during this weekend?"

His hand was squeezed. "I think especially during this weekend. I saw some new sides to you." An arched eyebrow. "I liked what I saw."

Brock had a ton of stuff to say to that, including that he liked what he'd seen of Gi this weekend too—especially just now. But there was something more urgent to do than talk. "Pull over."

Gigi arched an eyebrow. "Why?"

Brock let go of Gigi's hand to squeeze his leg. "Pull. Over."

Gigi gasped, then scanned the road feverishly.

Brock turned all his attention to Gigi's fly. He gently unzipped it and pushed his hand against the rapidly hardening bulge in Gigi's pants. Gigi swore and steered a corner. Brock stroked through the material, making sure to rub his thumb against the head of Gigi's cock. Pre-come had well and truly soaked through his boxers by the time Gigi brought the car to a stop and parked it.

Gigi slapped Brock's hand away, unbuckled his seat belt, then climbed over the gearstick to straddle Brock's lap. Brock steadied him, then Gigi clasped Brock's face, avoiding the bruises, and kissed him fiercely.

"I missed you," Gigi breathed.

A lump rose in Brock's throat. "Me too." He drew Gigi closer, then the seat fell away under him. He jerked back with a start, Gigi on top of him.

"There we go," Gigi said, adjusting himself so that their crotches lined up.

He'd levered the seat back. *Fuck*, Brock loved him. Brock reached forward and pulled Gigi's pants down, then his boxers, enough so Gigi's dick sprang free. He wrapped a hand around it and stroked, causing Gigi to arch and hiss. His cock was leaking like a dripping faucet, and the familiar smell of Gigi enveloped him.

"Oh *God*," Gigi moaned, hands pressing against Brock's chest.

Brock brought him down for another kiss as he kept slowly stroking Gigi's cock. Gigi made a mewling sound when Brock flickered his tongue along Gigi's lips, his hands bunching Brock's sweater. Brock thumbed the underside of Gigi's cock, where he was especially sensitive, and more pre-come ran down his length. Gigi broke away from the kiss with a groan.

"Fuck, don't stop." Gigi's hand scrabbled down to Brock's jeans. "And don't you dare stain my suit."

Brock laughed, his strokes slowing in his delight. God, what a gift this was, being here like this, with his guy.

Gigi shoved Brock's shirt up, undid his jeans, and pulled Brock's cock out, sending shivers through Brock as Gigi wrapped his hand around it and brought it up to meet his own. He spat in his palm and began to stroke their cocks together, the extra slickness making the grind better. Brock groaned and pulled him down so he could kiss him some more.

He'd missed this. The taste of Gigi, the scent of his skin and come, the feel of their bodies against each other, the tingles that shot up and down his spine whenever Gigi touched him—all of it was so familiar, yet always slightly different each time.

Gigi's hand picked up the pace, turning frenetic. His mouth went lax on Brock's, and Brock took advantage of his free hands to hold Gigi close and go to town on his neck, prompting groans.

It didn't last much longer than that. Gigi came with a breathy gasp, pouring onto Brock's stomach, and Brock finished himself off a few seconds later as Gigi slumped back against the glove compartment, keeping his pants well away from their combined spunk. His mouth was bruised and puffy, his hair in disarray, his bow tie slightly askew, and his shirt rumpled.

Perfect.

"Oh my God," Gigi panted. "It's Syracuse all over again."

Brock carefully pulled off his sweater, which had caught a few drops, and cast around for something to wipe up. Eventually, he found leftover napkins from one of their snacks on the trip up and began dabbing at his stomach and cock, then cleaned off Gigi. Once he was satisfied there was nothing left to stain Gigi's precious suit, he pulled Gigi on top of him and held him close. It had been too long since he'd felt Gigi's familiar warmth against him.

"We need to do that again," Gigi said in his ear.

"Uh-huh."

"And maybe without all the shouting next time."

"Got it. I'm sorry about this weekend."

Gigi reared up to look Brock in the face. "No, *I'm* sorry about this weekend." He frowned. "You and I have a lot of stuff to talk about, and we're starting right now."

Brock blinked. "Now? About what?"

Gigi lightly slapped his shoulder. "About your parents!"

Ah. Right. His parents. Brock felt the easy, happy mood slip. "You've seen them. What more could you want to know?"

"Plenty. Here's what we're doing, boyfriend: I'm asking you questions and you're answering them *honestly*. Don't think about what I want to hear, okay? Just tell me the truth. I mean it."

Brock thought he could handle that. "Okay."

Gigi sat back slightly and tugged at Brock's shirt, then deliberately fingered the scars along one side. "These happen because of your parents?"

Oh man. Brock hadn't expected him to bring those up—but then again, he'd never explained them. Not really. And knowing Gi still wanted him after this weekend, despite all the shit he'd seen, made him think maybe he'd also be okay with this. "Some of them. Others were me."

Gigi's thumb rubbed against Brock's skin, a distant sensation but still soothing. "You? For how long?"

"Years." He'd first started when he was twelve and had figured out how cathartic and purifying pain could feel when it was self-inflicted.

"While we had our thing?"

Brock grimaced. "Yes. But not as much."

Gigi stopped rubbing Brock's scars and moved his hand up onto Brock's chest, warm and solid against his skin. "And when did you stop?"

"Indonesia. No privacy to do it, and after a while, I stopped needing to."

"Done it since?"

Brock shifted; Gigi was all muscle and pretty heavy. "Nope."

Gigi nodded, apparently satisfied. "And you couldn't tell me all this before *why*?"

Wasn't *that* just the million-dollar question. Brock sighed and dropped his head back, avoiding Gigi's gaze. "Look, I . . . The scars are all bound up with my parents and the shit they put me through. I don't like thinking about it. I don't like rehashing it. It's behind me, and I want it to stay there."

"But they hurt you. That kind of stuff doesn't get left behind just because you decided it does, you know? It stays with you, baby."

The edges of Brock's eyes suddenly prickled. Ugh. Was that true? Probably. He should've mentioned all of this to Gigi sooner. He really should have. Other people shared things, didn't they? Like, Gi shared pretty much everything he thought with everyone, including his family. Brock had never had that before.

Damn it. He didn't want to start crying now, in front of Gi. "I guess it did stay with me."

"It's okay, hon." A small pause. "Did you think I couldn't handle your parents?"

Oh come on. How was that a fair question? "Of course you can." But seeing as he was being honest here, he should probably elaborate. "To a certain extent. I didn't want them to hurt you. And you've already been through enough shit. I saw it happen. You got it all through school, you got it from Rogers and his goons, you got it from the freaking drama group. You got it from *me*. You still get it, from assholes at your shows and when we go out. So why would I add to that, right? I didn't want you to deal with any more bullshit like that."

Gigi's expression turned grim. "You don't get to decide that. I'm going to get shit for who I am all my life, and I can handle it. You know what makes it easier for me? Sharing it with you and knowing you have my back. You handle my shit all the freaking time." He leaned in close. "I can deal with your shit too. I've got you. Me, my parents, my entire family, our friends: we all have your back. Understand? We're here for *you*. We want to help you. We love you. *I'm* here for you too. I got your back. Always. I haven't been good at that before now, and I'm sorry. But I'm yours, and I got you."

Brock thought he might need a tissue. Damn it, he'd already used the napkins.

"One more thing." Gigi held his chin so they looked at each other. "You're such a quiet guy. Like, you just show up and do your work and pay attention to me and outside of that, you do your thing. And I love how you totally aren't fazed by anything life throws at you. Your dad looked ready to brain you, and I was totally about to shit myself, but you were fucking stone cold."

"I was definitely about to shit myself." His voice had gone thick.

"My *point*"—Gigi shot him a meaningful *shut up* glance—"is that you aren't fazed by me and my brand of crazy either. You, like, balance me. Ground me. And it's so easy for me to forget that you might be dealing with other stuff, because you just *handle* it. If I wasn't around, you'd be fine on your own. You don't ask for much, but you give and give and give. Babe, you don't always have to deal or be fine. You can ask me for stuff. You can ask me for anything, and I'll give it to you. You're not on some second-chance checklist, and you don't have to prove anything. You're *it* for me, and you always were. This weekend doesn't change any of that."

Blood pounded in Brock's ears, and his chest felt tight. His face was warm. This was ... this was ...

Oh no. A lump rose in Brock's throat, and the prickling in his eyes turned fierce. Tears tipped over and began trickling down his cheeks. He swiftly covered his eyes.

Gigi made a small alarmed noise and stroked the side of Brock's face. "Are you okay? Look at me."

Brock shook his head. He couldn't. This was way too much. He needed to pull himself together, but he couldn't do that if he was crying and oh God too much, way too much.

Gigi kissed his knuckles, then settled against him and languidly stroked Brock's hair.

It was a nice feeling compared to the hot, wet mess that was currently Brock's face. He let the tears run out, taking big, deep breaths and wiping at his face until they'd mostly stopped. His bruises throbbed, his eyes ached, and his nose ran. *So attractive.* He didn't need a napkin, he needed an entire freaking box of tissues.

Gi didn't stop stroking his hair, but after a moment, he said, "I guess this stuff is pretty intense, huh?"

Brock gave in and used his shirt to wipe his face. "Just a bit." His voice sounded clogged. *Ugh.*

"You better?"

Brock nodded, then risked looking at his boyfriend again. Concern was written over Gigi's face, which got Brock's chest all tight once more. He didn't want the crying to start back up, so Brock kissed him instead. "I'm okay. Thank you."

"You think maybe you could tell me what you're actually thinking from now on? Because I'm not going to get mad about that."

"Um. I don't think that's something you'll be able to stick to."

Gigi made a *pfft* noise. "Oh my God, *okay.*" His fingers stopped trailing through Brock's hair, and he leaned forward so their foreheads met. "But seriously, I'm not going to flip my shit or break up with you because of whatever's in your head. You gonna try this honesty thing we're doing right now?"

Brock had never felt so freaking exposed. "I can try."

"Good."

Somehow he no longer wanted to cry, but he still felt way too raw. Kind of hollow and achy, but in a feelings way. He closed his eyes, putting one hand into Gi's hair to keep him there. It was stiff from product, but that was normal. Familiar.

"Don't mess up my hair." He could hear a smile in Gigi's voice, and he managed to give a small one too.

"I love messing up your hair."

"I know."

Brock opened his eyes and took a deep breath. "I'm sorry. For not telling you about this."

"How about for freaking me out too?" But he was smiling.

"That too." Something settled deep inside Brock. "Are *we* okay?"

The smile faded and Gigi was quiet for a few moments. "Here's the thing—and I was thinking about this on the way over to get you—you've changed, but not really? Like, I got used to the way you were when we first met, and I thought that's who you were. Then you graduated and you got your job and you work office hours, and soon you weren't that guy anymore. You were, what, tired or something? And over the last few days, I saw this whole other side to you, and it's fucking hot. Maybe I'm messed up, but it is. I realized it's not that *you* changed, but my understanding of you that did. So I think we're okay, but I have to be with you as you are. And you have to be open and honest about things."

"Okay. That's good." That actually sounded pretty awesome. But he really needed to unload about his job. "Look, I have to work, and sometimes that means I don't have the time or energy to do all the things we used to do. But I am still the guy you're dating, and I don't know about your idea of me, but I'll try to make more time for us. I don't want my job to make you feel bad." This felt like a way safer topic, and it was crazy how much easier this was to talk about than all those feelings earlier. "But I need to put in the hours to save up enough money, you know?"

Gigi looked up at him. "Money?"

"Yeah."

Gigi frowned in confusion. "What for?"

Wasn't it obvious? Oh. Maybe not. This probably fell under that whole openness thing. Brock felt his face warm. "Uh, us? So we can take a trip somewhere exciting? Or maybe a house, if that's something you want to get. Or we could move somewhere else for a while. Anything."

Gigi's eyes went wide. "Oh."

"I guess that's a thing we need to talk about."

"Oh my *God*." Gigi put his face against Brock's shoulder. "Why the hell didn't you say so earlier? This explains so much! See, this is exactly why you need to tell me things. I can live with extra work stuff if it's for *us*. Jesus."

That . . . meant a lot. That meant everything. They really were on the same level, weren't they? If this was what talking shit out was like, Brock was on board. Even the crying wasn't so bad, especially since Gi didn't seem to care, and Brock felt way better now. His whole body was lighter, somehow, and everything seemed easier. All the weird, angry vibes between them were gone, and they were back to just being each other, together and happy.

And if it worked for him and Gigi, it had to work for him and his past. If he had issues that would affect him and his relationship like this—and he was certain he did—Brock owed it to himself to talk those out too. He would look into counseling when he got back to Toronto and gauge his options.

Everything was suddenly just *better*.

Brock put his arms around Gigi and hugged him tightly. Oh man, his familiar hard body and distinctive Gi smell. Brock *had* missed this.

He'd also missed the way Gigi squawked breathlessly and how he always hugged back.

"I think we'll be okay too," Brock said to him.

"Damn right we will. But I have a requirement." Gigi leaned back and gave Brock a very serious look. "We're having sex in my room tonight."

Brock laughed. "Seriously?"

"Yeah."

"The walls are super thin though. What is your family going to think?"

"So be quiet— Oh my *God*." Gigi sat up abruptly. "The wedding!" He spun around to look at the dashboard clock. "Five minutes. We have five minutes. Fuck. Fuck. Fuck."

"Really?" He still wanted to go?

Gigi opened the door and clambered off Brock, who had to rejigger the lever to get the seat back upright. By the time he'd done that, Gigi had returned to his door and given him his bag. Brock blinked at it. "What is this?"

"You're coming to the wedding, right?" Gigi's face was flushed.

Brock stared down at the bag. His outfit was in there. And he knew if he really didn't want to, Gigi wouldn't make him go.

However, they were here together. And this *was* Gigi's sister. And Gigi was right—even if he felt like shit, it would be okay because Gi had his back.

Plus—and maybe it was down to clearing the air—but he finally thought the wedding sounded kind of fun. "I guess. But what about these bruises? I don't want to show up looking like this."

Gigi waved dismissively. "I brought foundation that'll cover those."

"You did?"

"Uh, yeah? How do you think my skin has been so flawless around my family's cooking? Get in the back and change. I'll drive." Gigi rounded the car and launched into the driver's seat. "We're showing up late and smelling of sex. God, she's going to kill me. And you. But mostly me. I think my family likes you more than they like me. *Omigod* we're so *late.*"

In the end, they were only ten minutes late, and people barely even noticed because most of the bachelor party were also late on account of severe hangovers. Alan, to his credit, wasn't one of them, but even so, Sophie was visibly annoyed. She managed to smile and wave at them when they came in, so Brock assumed they were forgiven for being late.

Once everyone was there, the wedding went off without a hitch. Well, without *many* hitches. Brock noticed Grandma falling asleep during the couple's lengthy vows, then it turned out the official photographer was just a friend who had been instructed to take "authentic candid pictures," and the family mothers decided this was an outrage and that there needed to be at least a few formal family portraits (which Brock was dragged into, making him extra glad he'd let Gigi put makeup on him). *Then* an entire roast lamb *and* roast pig turned up during the wedding reception, which caused Sophie to yell about disrespecting veganism and prompted a few red faces. Brock had no idea what the hell was going on, but it was food, so whatever. Despite no one owning up to ordering them, everyone tore them to pieces—while also savouring the vegan spread. Which was actually really tasty, though Brock suspected saying that to the older generations of both families would get him an annoyed lecture about millennials.

Really, by the time the party got under way, Brock was glad he'd decided to stay. It was way more fun than driving home in a sulk, especially once he'd started dancing and found himself spinning with Gigi in the middle of the dance floor.

"This is fun!" he shouted over the music.

Gigi beamed. "I knew it would be!" He glanced around and wrinkled his nose. "Oh my God, the décor though." Sophie and Alan had chosen red flowers, white runners across otherwise plain oak tables, vintage settings, and a mix of lanterns and fairy lights in mason jars for lighting. "Rustic chic was over like two years ago."

"You don't say." Brock thought everything looked pretty cool, actually, but he had no clue about wedding decorations. Had never thought about it.

Gigi got the far-off expression on his face that said he was daydreaming. "I do. Our wedding isn't going to be anything like this. I have *taste* for one thing."

Their wedding? Was he talking about . . .?

"It's gonna be way nicer than this," Gigi rattled on. "Like, with lights on the tables. And not in *jars* for fuck's sake. Drinks would be served in proper glasses, not jars. No jars at all. And no tempeh. *None.* Or kombucha. The strong colour would be an *accent*, not a main feature. And we'll be somewhere that's not nature."

Oh my God. He *was* talking about them. "So you wouldn't want to get married here?" Brock asked, somehow managing to keep a straight face.

"No! Hell no. Would *you*?" Gigi's outrage was priceless.

Brock grinned. "Nope. Gi, is this a proposal?"

Gigi actually stopped dancing and gaped at him, then whacked his shoulder. "No! No, it's not! I'm not that tacky! You think I'd propose to you at my *sister's wedding*?" He scoffed. "Like I'd propose to you *at all*. That's not how this works. *I* don't propose to anyone. *You* propose to *me*."

Brock was laughing too hard to dance.

Gigi made a frustrated noise and pulled Brock's arms back around him. "Stop laughing at me."

"I'm not laughing at you."

"You totally are."

Brock drew him in closer. "You're right, I am." He felt slightly breathless, though he wasn't sure if that was entirely from laughing. "So I'm proposing to you?"

Gigi was almost as red as his hair. "Yes. But not *now*. Oh my God, we've only been dating for like a year. There's a time frame for this stuff."

"Got it."

Gigi burrowed in close, resting his head (or possibly hiding his face) against Brock's neck. "And it has to be a surprise. And romantic."

"I think the surprise is kind of ruined now."

"No, it's not! This is a *discussion*, Brock. There's a difference."

Brock started laughing again.

Gigi pulled him tighter. "Shut up."

Brock squeezed him as hard as he could. "I love you."

"I love you too."

They drifted in slow circles for a while, Brock's head turning over the fact that Gigi could see them married. *Them*. Somewhere deep in him, his sixteen-year-old self was cheering. In the now, his happiness was completely filling him up, pressing uncomfortably against his skin like his body was too small to contain all this joy.

Brock hadn't even thought that far ahead. Not to marriage. Or anything beyond that like—his brain began to fizzle around the edges—kids. Holy shit. No. He hadn't thought about any of that yet. Fuck, he couldn't; it had all seemed way too far away and intangible.

Like it wasn't really meant for him. But somehow it was? Or it could be? Everything suddenly seemed a lot more possible.

And actually, he *had* been thinking about his future with Gigi, hadn't he? Not something huge like marriage, but something a little less scary and absolute. Still big.

He cleared his throat. "Gi. You said there's a time frame for this kind of stuff."

Gigi pulled back enough to look at him. "Uh-huh."

"How do you feel about moving in together?"

EPILOGUE

Brock was exceptionally glad it was the weekend because it had been one long, long week. Work wasn't as nuts as it had been in the lead-up to the holiday season, but it was still crazy trying to get as much done as possible before the break. Plus, his order of a certain pair of rings had finally shown up, and he'd stopped by the store to collect them right after work. Not that he was actually going to use them anytime soon—he just liked having them on hand. Ready for when he and Gigi were. It had only been a few months since that mess of a weekend in Maney, and Brock wasn't sure he was totally recovered from *that*, let alone ready to plan a proposal and do it. But he liked being ready.

As he walked through the snowy streets to the apartment he now shared with Gigi, he considered good hiding places for the rings. Anywhere in the kitchen was a bad idea; Gigi watched what he ate like a hawk and knew the contents of everything in the kitchen. Ditto with the bathroom, but for other reasons. The living room was a slightly better idea: plenty of boxes full of random crap Brock had collected on his travels and games and DVDs and just stuff. Problem there was they were still unpacking, and Gigi could definitely be counted on to have a cleaning spree one afternoon and finish the boxes in the living room.

Bedroom, then. In some of Brock's old T-shirts, the ones Gigi hated? No, because he kept threatening to throw them out. Maybe some of LaMore's out-of-date outfits, though that seemed risky too. Or Brock could pack a box of clothing and put it in the wardrobe?

Argh, no doubt Gigi would go looking through that too. Endlessly curious. Or nosy, depending on who was asked.

Just as he reached the apartment building, he had it. The shoebox.

They'd rediscovered it in the car on the way home from Maney. Brock had chucked it down when they'd had sex in the car, and both of them had forgotten about it in the ensuing madness of getting to the wedding on time. So when Brock's foot had knocked against it the following morning as they drove out of Maney, he'd been surprised, then slightly apprehensive.

"Open it," Gigi had said, focused on the road.

"Here?"

"Yeah." His mouth twisted. "If we have to throw it out, I think the middle of the goddamn forest is the best place."

Brock sighed. "Littering's wrong." He pulled off the lid.

What met him were report cards. All of his school report cards. Tucked in with them were some school certificates, a few drawings, some sports medals, and medical records. He listed each thing as he pulled them out, and Gigi's jaw tightened with every word.

As Brock worked through the box, he found a stack of photos under the school things. All him, from when he'd been a baby to when he'd reached about ten.

Gigi looked over when Brock mentioned them. "Baby pics? Omigod, I wanna see! Let me see those!"

"You're driving."

Gigi tsked. "I guess."

"Later." Brock paused. "There aren't many of them."

"Really? Didn't they take lots?"

"I don't trust your definition of 'lots.' But no, I don't think so." He couldn't remember a camera coming out for any vacations or important occasions. All the pictures he held now were . . . well, were from when things had been better. "I guess they did for a while."

"And now they gave them back to you?" Gigi shook his head. "Babe. Babe. I'm going to take so many selfies of you and me from now on."

"You take a million selfies of us as it is."

Gigi shifted in his seat. "Is there anything else?"

Not really. A few small toys that tugged at early memories, a paperback he'd left in his room before going to Indonesia (only to come back from abroad and find they'd cleared everything out so his room could be a guest room), an ancient Game Boy—and right at the bottom, a rusty razor blade.

He went slightly numb as he picked it up. Wow. His parents had gone over his room with a fine-tooth comb if they'd found his stash of these. He'd left a few in a hiding place under the bed, along with antiseptic and bandages for afterwards.

Gigi glanced across. "What is . . . Fuck! Throw it out!"

Brock blinked and looked over at him. "What?"

"That *thing*. Stop touching it. Throw it out! Now!"

"But we're in the middle of the highway! It's dangerous."

Gigi's eyes blazed at him. "Not as dangerous as I will be if you don't throw it away *right the fuck now*."

Brock dropped it back in the box. "I'll get rid of it properly when we stop somewhere."

Gigi seemed to be struggling to breathe. "Put the box in the back."

"Gi, seriously—"

"Do it!"

So Brock closed the box and put it in the backseat. And once he faced forward again, Gigi reached across and took his hand. "I'm never letting you shave again."

Brock rolled his eyes. "Gi, I told you, I'm done with those. I'm fine."

"I don't care! I don't want to see you touching one, *ever*."

Brock rubbed his thumb against Gigi's skin. "It's okay."

"Did your *mother*"—Gigi was practically spitting now—"seriously, *seriously* put a fucking *razor blade* in a fucking box full of your childhood shit as a fucking *good-bye present*? Or did I make that up?"

He sighed. "She did."

"Then it is *not okay*, Brock."

Brock pressed Gigi's hand between both of his. "It's not a surprise to me."

"It should be! I can't believe this!" Gigi glared at him with suspiciously shiny eyes. "Your parents are dead to me. *Dead*."

Whoa. Hey there, melodrama. Brock tried to reassure Gigi that he really was fine, that this was kinda typical of his shitty family, but Gigi hadn't calmed down until they'd stopped at a gas station and Brock had thrown it out (safely taped in cardboard, of course). Brock had dug through the box to make sure there weren't any more, then handed the baby pics to Gigi to help him relax.

Brock had kept the box because he didn't see the point in throwing it out. Yes, it was painful to see it and to be reminded of how he'd gotten it, but the stuff in there was fascinating to him. He liked seeing his old report cards and pictures and remembering some of the good times he'd had in Maney. There *had* been some. And this was proof that, on some level, his parents had cared about him. They'd cared enough to track his progress through childhood, to document and observe it, then keep those things as mementos. He would never be able to replace this stuff.

So he kept the box.

And Gigi had refused to touch it since.

Therefore: perfect hiding spot. Maybe he could add a few more things to it—ticket stubs from his travels through Southeast Asia and Europe, pictures from university, and so on—to mark other major points in his life. In that sense, the shoebox really was a perfect hiding spot.

When Brock got home to their apartment, he took off his winter gear, then headed straight to their bedroom and the corner of the wardrobe where he'd stashed the shoebox. He crouched down and opened it. Gigi had taken the pics out, but the school stuff was still in there, and there was plenty of space for a small ring box to nestle inside.

He paused, then pried open the ring box to look at them just one more time. Bright silver nestled within dark velvet, catching the light as Brock angled them. They were pretty basic—no huge fancy rocks or engravings or anything. But they were titanium and had this really nice matte finish that Brock thought looked kind of awesome in a subtle way. His friend Katie had helped him pick them out, and she said they were classy—so if Gi hated them, it was totally her fault.

Brock didn't think Gi would hate them though.

After all, they meant this big life decision Brock and Gi had made to each other, to *be* with each other. Brock had never bought into this marriage stuff before, but honestly? This shit was so cool. Knowing Gigi was totally on board with spending their lives together was the best feeling ever. Why *wouldn't* they want to show that off?

He snapped the box shut and tucked it under his school reports. Just as he put the lid back on the shoebox, he heard the front door open and close.

A pause, then Gigi called, "Honey, I'm hooome!"

Brock quickly shoved the box back into its corner spot and stood up. He left the bedroom and found Gigi unwrapping his scarf, coat on, cheeks still red from the outdoors, dance bag at his feet.

Right, he'd had a dance thing tonight. Brock hadn't been able to make it due to work and because he'd planned to pick up the rings.

"Hey," he said.

Gigi smiled. "I saw your boots. You're home early."

"I managed to leave earlier than expected. Sorry I missed the performance."

A shrug. "It wasn't the best. Hardly anyone was there. Stupid snow."

He looked super cute with red cheeks and his favourite reindeer toque. *Argh, adorable.* Brock stepped forward and pulled him into a hug. He still smelled all wintery, that crisp, cold scent that came from being outside in Canada's worst season, but underneath was his familiar scent. He'd sweated while dancing. *Mmm.*

He must've been hugging hard, because Gigi squawked, but in a pleased way. "Happy to see you too." He bussed Brock's cheek, then wriggled out of the hug. "I have to shower before Tyler and Evie get here. You get the wine?"

Brock froze. Oh. Shit. He'd completely forgotten about that. Tyler, Evie, takeout, movies, and wine. Which he was supposed to have picked up on his way home.

Gigi pulled off his toque and fixed him with a knowing look. "I freaking knew it." He bent down to his dance bag, opened it, and pulled out two bottles of red.

Oh man. "You got it anyway?"

There was a resigned but fond expression on Gigi's face. "I know what battles to pick. How much do you love me right now?"

A few months ago, this would've resulted in a fight. But right now, Brock was just blown away. Gi realized Brock would forget the stupid LCBO run and did it for him anyway. How well did Gi know him? Embarrassingly (but also awesomely) well, clearly. "I love you *so* much right now. But I'm sorry I forgot."

Gigi rolled his eyes. "Just get food ordered. I'm freaking starving."

Ah, fuck it. He reached forward. "I have something you could eat."

Gigi snorted. "Oh my *God.* Lame. *So* lame."

Then Brock shut him up by kissing him fiercely and sliding his hands down Gigi's body until he melted and kissed back. Gigi didn't *touch* back because his hands were busy, which left Brock free to grab his ass firmly and pull him flush from mouth to knee. *Oh.* There was a hardness against Brock's hip that felt promising. Brock rocked his hips as he ground them together, and Gigi made one of his small gasping noises that Brock loved so much.

Gigi ended the kiss and gazed at Brock with dark eyes. "I like where you're going with this, boyfriend."

"Oh yeah? Do we—"

"*But* we don't have time before our friends get here, and I would like to be *clean*, not filthier than I already am." He winked and pressed the bottles against Brock's chest.

Brock grabbed them instinctively.

"I'm going to *shower*. Behave." Another quick kiss, then Gigi walked away.

Leaving his dance stuff on the floor and Brock to get their night organized.

Brock picked his battles too. He put the wine on their coffee table with glasses. He ordered the food. He dumped the dance gear into the laundry. Then he tidied so Tyler and Evie didn't accidentally find anything that would test the limits of their friendship. The thing was, Brock didn't even mind. These small things were amazing and wonderful.

Like, this was it. This was all he'd ever wanted. A man he adored, and who loved him, good friends around them, a job he could do that paid well, and nothing but possibilities for the future. *Good* possibilities. It was simple, but that was who he was. And life might be simple and sexy and sometimes difficult—because he was Brock and Gigi was Gigi, and they were never not going to clash over things—but overall it was so, so sweet. If Brock could travel back in time to his teenage self, at his lowest points, he'd give him a hug and say that yes, everything *would* be all right. He'd get out. He'd *come* out. He'd get the boy. And all would be well.

Explore more of the *Toronto Connections* at:
riptidepublishing.com/titles/universe/toronto-connections

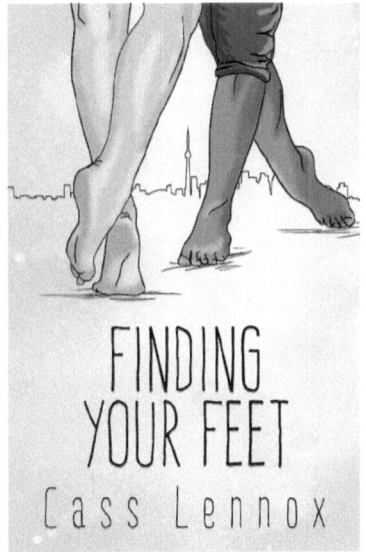

Dear Reader,

Thank you for reading Cass Lennox's *Growing Pains*!

We know your time is precious and you have many, many entertainment options, so it means a lot that you've chosen to spend your time reading. We really hope you enjoyed it.

We'd be honored if you'd consider posting a review—good or bad—on sites like **Amazon, Barnes & Noble, Kobo, Goodreads, Twitter, Facebook, Tumblr,** and your blog or website. We'd also be honored if you told your friends and family about this book. Word of mouth is a book's lifeblood!

For more information on upcoming releases, author interviews, blog tours, contests, giveaways, and more, please sign up for our weekly, spam-free newsletter and visit us around the web:

Newsletter: tinyurl.com/RiptideSignup
Twitter: twitter.com/RiptideBooks
Facebook: facebook.com/RiptidePublishing
Goodreads: tinyurl.com/RiptideOnGoodreads
Tumblr: riptidepublishing.tumblr.com

Thank you so much for Reading the Rainbow!

RiptidePublishing.com

ACKNOWLEDGEMENTS

As always, a huge thank-you to my editor, Chris Muldoon, for getting the best out of my writing.

Thanks to my housemates for listening and for advice; my Canadian friends for being amazing (and patient and understanding and good-humoured); and A.B. and P.K. for getting me out of the house.

Despite the fictional events in this book, I don't advocate confronting abusers. Once you're out, stay away. If you or someone you know might be affected by the issues raised in this book, please check out the links below for resources, advice, and help. For emergencies, call your country's emergency number.

Tips to cover your tracks when looking up resources online:
www.nationaldomesticviolencehelpline.org.uk/site-services/cover-your-tracks.aspx
www.awhl.org/security

Canada
   Assaulted Women's Helpline (www.awhl.org)
   1-866-863-0511
   TTY: 1-866-863-7868

   LGBT Youth Line (www.youthline.ca)
   1-800-268-9688

   2 Spirit (www.2spirits.com/2SpiritLinks.html)

More resources
Shelters in Canada: www.sheltersafe.ca
Other hotlines: www.dawncanada.net/issues/issues/we-can-tell-
and-we-will-tell-2/crisis-hotlines
LGBT+ info sheet on abuse and list of LGBT-specific
resources: www.rainbowhealthontario.ca/wp-content/uploads/
woocommerce_uploads/2014/09/LMLMN-gay.pdf

USA

The National Domestic Violence Hotline (www.thehotline.org)
Specific LGBT+ page: www.thehotline.org/is-this-abuse/lgbt-
abuse
1-800-799-7233
TTY 1-800-787-3224

The Trevor Project (www.thetrevorproject.org)
LGBTQ+ teen crisis line: 866-488-7386

More resources
Information and LA resources: lalgbtcenter.org/health-services/
mental-health/intimate-partner-domestic-violence
Other hotlines: www.feminist.org/911/crisis.html
Shelters: www.domesticshelters.org/

UK

National Domestic Violence Helpline
(www.nationaldomesticviolencehelpline.org.uk)
0808 2000 247

Galop (www.galop.org.uk)
National LGBT+ domestic violence helpline
0300 999 5428
help@galop.org.uk

Men's Advice Line (www.mensadviceline.org.uk)
More resources: www.mensadviceline.org.uk/pages/gay-and-bi-
male-victims-of-domestic-violence.html
0808 801 0327

More resources
Advice: england.shelter.org.uk/get_advice/domestic_abuse
Information: www.stonewall.org.uk/help-advice/criminal-law/
domestic-violence
Women's Aid: www.womensaid.org.uk

Australia
**National Sexual Assault, Family & Domestic Violence
Counselling Line** (www.1800respect.org.au)
1800 RESPECT (1800 737 732)

Lifeline (www.lifeline.org.au)
131 114

Kids Helpline for those between 5-25 (kidshelpline.com.au)
1800 551 800

More resources
LGBT+ support: www.anothercloset.com.au/finding-help-1
List of resources, including helplines and men-specific help:
www.humanservices.gov.au/customer/subjects/family-and-
domestic-violence
State specific helplines: au.reachout.com/domestic-violence-
support

New Zealand
Are You Ok government helpline (areyouok.org.nz)
0800 456 450

Women's Refuge (womensrefuge.org.nz/get-help/help-for-
women)
0800 REFUGE (0800 733843)

OUTLine (www.outline.org.nz)
(LGBT+ specific)
0800 OUTLINE (0800 6885463)

More resources
Comprehensive lists of other organisations and helplines:
youmeus.co.nz/organisations-that-can-help
www.kahukura.co.nz/organisations

ALSO BY CASS LENNOX

ABOUT THE AUTHOR

Cass Lennox is a permanent expat who has lived in more countries than she cares to admit to and suffers from a chronic case of wanderlust as a result. She started writing stories at the tender age of eleven, but would be the first to say that the early years are best left forgotten and unread. A great believer in happy endings, she arrived at queer romance via fantasy, science fiction, literary fiction, and manga, and she can't believe it took her that long. She likes diverse characters who have gooey happy ever afters, and brownies. She's currently sequestered in a valley in southeast England.

Blog: casslennox.wordpress.com
Facebook: facebook.com/Cass-Lennox-1704635609768647
Twitter: twitter.com/CassLennox

Enjoy more stories like
Growing Pains
at RiptidePublishing.com!

Earn Bonus Bucks!

Earn 1 Bonus Buck for each dollar you spend. Find out how at
RiptidePublishing.com/news/bonus-bucks.

Win Free Ebooks for a Year!

Pre-order coming soon titles directly through our site and you'll
receive one entry into a drawing for a chance to win free books for
a year! Get the details at RiptidePublishing.com/contests.